TROUBLE
IN THE
HEARTLAND

TROUBLE IN THE HEARTLAND

Crime Fiction Inspired by the Songs of Bruce Springsteen

Edited by Joe Clifford

GUTTER BOOKS

www.gutterbooks.com

www.zelmerpulp.com

Trouble in the Heartland: Crime Fiction Inspired by the
Songs of Bruce Springsteen

Copyright © 2014 by Gutter Books LLC
All stories copyright © their respective authors

Produced in association with Zelmer Pulp

Cover design by Chuck Regan

ISBN-13: 978-1939751027

Visit www.gutterbooks.com for other titles and
submission guidelines.

Printed in the USA

CONTENTS

Introduction by Joe Clifford   xi

State Trooper
Dennis Lehane   3

Prove It All Night
Jordan Harper   16

Candy's Room
Chris Leek   22

Hungry Heart
Hillary Davidson   25

I'm on Fire
James R. Tuck   32

Dancing in the Dark
Lynne Barrett   38

Thunder Road
James Grady   46

Dry Lightning
Dyer Wilk   53

Local Hero
Tom Pitts   59

Glory Days
CS DeWildt   65

Queen of the Supermarket
Chuck Wendig   72

CONTENTS

Something in the Night
Mike Creeden   75

Rosalita
Rob Pierce   83

The Ghost of Jim Toad
David James Keaton   84

What Love Can Do
Peter Farris   91

Mansion on the Hill
Chris F. Holm   96

Highway Patrolman
Ryan Sayles   99

Wreck on the Highway
Brian Panowich   107

My Hometown
Matthew Louis   110

Death to my Hometown
Christopher Irvin   117

Nebraska
Paul J. Garth   122

Pictures on the Edge of Town
A collection of images by Mark Krajnak   129

The Iceman
Les Edgerton   135

We Take Care of Our Own
Todd Robinson   138

CONTENTS

My Best Was Never Good Enough
Keith Rawson   148

Streets of Fire
Isaac Kirkman   154

Spare Parts
John McFetridge   160

Does This Bus Stop at 82nd Street?
Ezra Letra   164

It's Hard to Be a Saint in the City
Jen Conley   169

Atlantic City
Benoit Lelièvre   177

Because the Night
Richard Thomas   183

Darkness on the Edge of Town
Lela Scott MacNeil   185

Radio Nowhere
Chuck Regan   191

The Promised Land
Court Merrigan   196

Open All Night
Eric Beetner   205

Meeting Across The River
Steve Weddle   214

Wrecking Ball
Chris Rhatigan   218

CONTENTS

Born to Run
Lincoln Crisler   225

Straight Time
Gareth Spark   231

This Little Light of Mine
Jamez Chang   236

Last to Die
Richard Brewer   240

About the Authors   247

Thanks to Mona Okada at Grubman Indursky Shire & Meiselas, P.C., and to Jasmin Guerra at the Bob Woodruff Foundation.

Thanks to Nigel Renton for his proofreading.

And special thanks to "Big" Jim Petersen for his tireless follow-ups, correspondence, and editorial assistance.

Introduction

Like that Incident on 57th Street, this love affair began innocently enough. We were hanging around the office (Facebook) one summer morning. Zelmer Pulp's Chris Leek just had his flash fiction piece "Candy's Room" published at *Shotgun Honey*. Being a Springsteen fanatic, I read the story on title alone. That it was so terrific, a bonus. I made a casual remark that we should do an entire anthology based on Bruce Springsteen songs. And like a head-on collision smashin' in your guts, man, *Trouble in the Heartland* was born.

Once we announced formal plans for our project (which we decided would benefit the very Boss-like cause of assisting veterans), we were inundated with requests from the noir community to pitch in. It caught me by surprise. An East Coast boy from a blue-collar town, I've been a fan for years, but I had no idea so many other crime writers loved the Boss as much as I did. Makes sense, though. Bruce, like the best pulp fiction, champions losers and loners on lost highways, those seeking last shots at redemption. The very heart of hardboiled, every cynic a wounded romantic. Sure, they come up short most of the time. But when you think about it, a broken heart ain't *that* high a price to pay for a shot at glory. And, hell, at least it proves we were here.

For me, getting the chance to edit an anthology inspired by the work of Bruce Springsteen brings it all home. When you ask a writer about his biggest literary influences, he's probably going to cite other authors. And I have plenty of those, too. But if you put that proverbial gun (knife or wallet) to the head and make me choose one, I'm picking the Boss. His depiction of small-town life and big-city dreams helped form my literary tastes as much as Salinger and Kerouac, Chandler and Vonnegut, and it came at a crucial time in my life. Springsteen's narratives gave a sixteen-year-old wide-eyed misfit reasons to believe he had better days ahead.

For *Trouble in the Heartland*, each writer selected a Springsteen title and used it as a launching point to create his or her original vision, moving this collection beyond merely homage. The results are often dark, but dark does not exist without contrast. These selections you're about to read, like the best of Springsteen, are buoyed by the possibility of a richer life, and it's that specter that keeps us all moving down those Rattlesnake Speedways, searching for our own place to belong.

Not that everyone in these stories is a hero or a saint, or even a tragic figure. Many don't deserve our sympathies at all. Often it's bad people doing rotten things for the worst possible reasons. But you never can say who's who till you walk that mile. Some of these people you're about to meet are downright hard to root for, and many get what they've got coming. But there are plenty of spare parts worth saving, too.

Several of the contributors in this anthology have novels out. Some have had their work optioned and turned into award-winning, internationally acclaimed films; others are just embarking on careers. But the tie that binds all these terrific authors together is an intimate glimpse into the criminal heart, and an ability to elicit hope in those moments where it is least likely to be found.

The track listing reads like a Greatest Hits package. From Dennis Lehane to James Grady, Hilary Davidson to Chuck Wendig, Steve Weddle, Todd Robinson, Chris F. Holm, James R. Tuck, Jordan Harper, David James Keaton, Les Edgerton, Lynne Barrett, and the rest of the A-list, top-tier talent too numerous to mention, you'd have a tough time finding a more impressive roster of who's who in modern pulp fiction.

So pack your bags, kick that screen door open, and climb inside. *Trouble in the Heartland*, like that two-lane highway, is about to transport you somewhere magical.

Lights out tonight!

Joe Clifford

TROUBLE
IN THE
HEARTLAND

State Trooper

Dennis Lehane

The state trooper emerged from the dark of the road near Linden, New Jersey. He'd been parked along the shoulder when Dale passed, white cruiser backlit by the glow from the refineries along a stretch of the turnpike Dale had always found otherworldly, those refineries lighting up the dark like alien outposts on a dead planet. Dale checked his speed, saw that it was two miles above the limit, perfectly respectable, neither too under nor too over, both of which invited suspicion. Nope, just humming along at sixty-seven in a sixty-five zone. Not a damn thing suspicious about the car; Dale had checked when he picked it up in the Bronx forty-five minutes ago. Checked the taillights, brake lights, headlights. Checked that the inspection sticker on the rear license plate hadn't expired. Checked that the tires weren't bald and the wipers worked. Everything about the car looked legit.

It wasn't, of course, but it sure as shit looked it. A dark gray Honda Accord, early 2000s vintage, it had been sitting outside a Jamaican chicken joint on the corner of 175th and Clay Avenue. The chicken joint was closed for the night and a few of the streetlights were out but the Accord sat just where J'Marcus had said it would be. The key waited in a magnetized hide-a-key box stuck inside a wheel well. Dale got in, drove away. Nothing to it. Now all he had to do was drive it a hundred ten miles, cross the Delaware, and drop it in Philly behind the last Polish bakery in God's Pocket.

But here was Johnny Law slipping in behind him in the center lane. The trooper hung back a couple car lengths, and it was too dark to tell whether he was keying his mic and putting it to his lips, calling Dispatch to run the plates. Or maybe he wasn't doing anything of the sort. Maybe he was just pulling onto the road because he had him some jones for the Roy Rogers about forty, fifty miles south. Maybe he had a date. Maybe his shift was over. Hell, maybe "he" was a "she." And maybe, whatever gender, there was no reason at all to look twice at a ten-year-old Honda the gray of a pigeon. Then again, the way Dale's luck had been running lately— or most of his life, depending on which way you looked at it, glass-half-empty or glass-never-fucking-was—maybe he'd caught the one state trooper in the entire Garden State who had a thing against gray Hondas that drove two miles above the speed limit at three in the morning on a damp Tuesday night.

To keep the veins frosty, he turned on the radio. All he found on FM was hip hop and Latin music, both of which made his blood jump, so he switched over to AM and got Jesus freaks and talk radio. The Jesus freaks were all talking about judgment and end times and he sure didn't need to be ruminating on that shit but the talk shows were worse because they all trucked in nothing, pure nothing, with a steadily increasing fury. You all deserve yourselves, Dale thought as he went to roll down the window and flick his Kool into the wind. But then he remembered the cherry top behind him and found the ashtray.

He pressed *Seek* on the radio, went to the next station.

"These maggots," the guy was saying so harshly Dale could see the spit hitting his microphone, "these parasites, they, they, they suck off this country and they breed other parasites and maggots and none of them work and, you know, they're demanding we teach

Ebonics in our school. Ebonics! Look it up. A woman in Brown-ville, Texas, I'm gonna guess her name was Shaniqua or D'Qwanza because I know it wasn't Ruth, she went to the board of education there—again you can look this up—and she told those good people her boy needed to be taught his native—hear me, folks, I said, nay-tive—tongue. And the, um, our Trayvon in Chief, what's his name there, Barack Hussein Osama, I mean, excuse me all to hell, Barack Hussein *Oh-Bama*, he's okay with it. They want to put this in our schools, and they don't even pay taxes. They don't even believe in this country. Hell, they barely vote. Unless, it's you know, for Trayvon in the White House and OJ out the door. And we give them welfare and we give them jobs, but that's not enough. Now they want to *double* the minimum wage! For flipping burgers! For saying, 'Would you like to Super Size that?' into a microphone. 'Cept they ain't axing you like dat, is dey? They asking you all, 'Ya'll want mad portions up in this here, be-atch?' And if you mention that to the wrong people—the media, say—you're a racist. But, folks, I'm not a racist. I'm just someone who loves the English language. I'm just a man who wants the English language to stay the language of kings, not the language of a bunch of do-rag-lovin' homies can't tell the difference between crystal and Cristal. Know what I'm saying, yo?"

Dale could feel a weight press down on his head, a broom sweep through his soul. This voice had listeners, maybe lots of them, maybe millions. And they lapped it up. Made them feel strong, or at least less afraid.

Less afraid of what?

Of the dark. Of the cold.

Dale glanced in his rearview again and didn't like what he saw. No cars in between him and the trooper anymore, but the statie hanging back the same distance, maybe fifty yards, sixty at the most. Letting Dale know he was there.

Letting him know he wasn't going anywhere, either.

Dale pressed *Seek* again.

"—and, and how come the Chinese come here and learn the language but Paco can't? Last time I checked, Mandarin and Japanese are a lot harder to learn than Mexican or, I mean, you know what I mean, than Spanish. But our Latin friends can't seem to master our mother tongue the way the Asians can. Could it be lack of intelligence or lack of initiative? Because the Asians, I'll tell ya right now, folks, they get 'er done. That is for certain. They. Get. 'Er. Done. They believe in hard work and math. No, seriously. That's it, that's the list—hard work and math. They're not whining. They're *grateful* to be here. And they—"

Dale hit *Seek*.

The state trooper wasn't in his rearview.

He stared at the empty space behind him, at the vortex of asphalt and white lines, evenly spaced, and black sky yellowed at its base by the lights of Trenton. There weren't any exits here. No turn-offs that Dale could remember. And the statie had vanished in the time it took Dale to glance at the radio and hit *Seek*. Unless the ETs had gotten to him, sucked him up into their ship for anal probes and night tremors . . .

Dale flicked his eyes to the left, saw nothing. Glanced to the right, and there the man was, cruising alongside him. He looked straight ahead but Dale knew that in the split-second before Dale had turned his head, the statie had been looking right at him.

Seek.

". . . well the Bible is very clear on this—"

Seek.

"—but it *is* racism. Yes, it is. If you attack his music, the truth he speaks from the streets, then you are, in essence, saying a black man, a proud African American man, should be muzzled. You are! It's sending the Negro buck out the house cuz you don't like the way he looking at the white women. And lemme tell you something else, because it's important you hear it—"

The cruiser swooped in front of Dale and then crossed all the way into the passing lane. A smooth, effortless move. Just a public servant changing lanes. But pulling in front of Dale to do it. Dropping back now, easing off the gas pedal. Playing with Dale now, no question about it. Dale looked at the speedometer: 67.

You,

he wanted to tell the statie,

do not

want to fuck

with me.

Forgot you ever saw me. Forget you're seeing me now. Pull over at the next service area, have a smoke. Hell, have a drink. Call your wife or your girlfriend. Live.

Because if you pull me over, all that future you take for granted could end. Ain't no Wednesday for you to wake up to if this turns into Final Tuesday.

And you don't want that. You want to save up for your vacation, maybe go to the shore, get some sun on your face and baked into your shoulders, bitch about the jellyfish, have a beer before 4, grill out, tell the missus how pretty she looks in that sundress.

You got parents probably, maybe a brother or two, a sister. Got a woman waiting for you in a warm bed. Got bills, shows recorded on the DVR, poker night in two weeks. Maybe you got kids, got a promotion on the way, got a new restaurant out past the mall you've been meaning to try. You got a future.

Only thing that I got's been bothering me my whole life.

Well, that, and a gun.

I'm the thing that doesn't play ball. I'm the broken toy. I don't pay taxes or go to church or own a power tool. Never mowed a lawn or applied for a mortgage. I don't plan for retirement. I don't worry how I'm going to raise my kids in a terrible world, because I won't raise any kids, even the ones I might already have. I own next to nothing. I am next to nothing. And the only moral code I live by is this:

I will never go back to prison.

Dale looked in his rearview and saw the circular lights of a Jag he'd passed a while back. In the passing lane, a hundred yards back, the high square beams of a tractor-trailer flared.

But the statie was gone. Not behind Dale, not to his right or left. Dale double-checked each sideview. Nope. The guy was gone. Must have dropped back and slid over to the shoulder again, was lying in wait for a pack of teenagers in Mom's Grand Cherokee, everyone jacked up on Stellas and Molly, pedal to the floor, looking for just the right slick surface or the right tight turn to prove to everybody what everybody'd always known—that they were fuckheads who were gonna die young and die stupid.

Dale lit another Kool and heard his own sigh of relief in the exhale. If the trooper had pulled him over, there were so many ways it could have gone wrong and just about no ways it could have gone right.

Dale was a two-time felon. Had, in fact, walked out of one of Christie's halfway houses—if that's what you could call a three hundred-bed facility surrounded by barbed wire—that peppered North Jersey these days, as common as lice on a tomcat.

Dale knew soon as he'd done it—shit, maybe even before—that it was as stupid a move as he'd made in a lifetime full of stupid. But he hadn't liked the look he'd seen in Verda's eyes the last few visits. It was a sad look, sympathetic even, Dale unable to identify it fully until he realized it was pity. Broke out of Community Education Centers' Harbor Facility by not breaking anything really, just walked the fuck out, caught a ride half a mile away from a guy, it turned out, had happened to walk out of the same facility nine months before. Name was Nickel, and he asked Dale if he wanted to make some real money. Dale said he'd definitely think about it and wrote down the number of the man's burner. Nickel was a little high, which made him a little sentimental and he said he'd had woman troubles before too, plenty, more times than he wished to admit; he drove Dale all the way to Verda's house in Camden.

Dale had grown up in Camden, so he felt a little more comfy there than most, but he still knew what an act of courage it took to drive in there, particularly for a Long Branch nigger like Nickel. Nickel acted all cool while they drove the cracked streets, the weeds taller than the car, the vacant houses sliding sideways like someone had tilted the entire earth, forgot to tilt it back. But Nickel kept his eyes on the dipping sun too, moved his gaze steadily left to right, right to left, left to right. When he dropped Dale off, he kept the engine running.

"You be all right?" he asked, and it was clear as all hell he was hoping the answer was going to be a quick yes.

"Absolutely," Dale said. "I'm from here."

"I know motherfuckers from Somalia," Nickel said. "That don't mean they go *back*."

Dale smiled. "You ain't heard? 'Round here, we got us a higher murder rate than Mogadishu."

He thanked Nickel and patted the top of his ride and walked up the canted walkway to Verda's stoop. Last one standing on this side of the street. Three left on the other side. Rest of it just rubble, ash, or on its way. Jobs had left here so long ago people talked about them the way they talked about elves and angels, fucking Santa and shit. Then, not too long ago, state just threw in the towel on the whole city. Closed up the clinics and the afterschool programs and the shelters. Cut the police force in half. Police who were left on the payroll banged-in half the time or spent their days with the nose of their patrol cars pointed at the river, hats pulled down over their eyes. Shit, Dale's brother Leon said to him on a visit to Harbor, can't even compare it to the Wild West cuz at least them cowpoke niggers had a sheriff or two.

It was Leon who answered the door at Verda's and Dale saw it all at once, saw it in his eyes, even before Verda showed up in the hallway behind him wearing only an old white shirt of Dale's, one from when he'd been a waiter at that fish place in Asbury ten years ago, back when he still believed he was living, not just drowning slow.

"Aw, shit," Verda said, "you don't call?"

"Where's Antonio?"

"Like you care, Dale. Like you fucking care."

"You ain't gonna make trouble now, are you?" Leon said, the guilt in his voice, all over his face, coming off his pores.

"Just want to see Antonio."

"Don't even know he's yours," Verda said.

"Let me see him and I'll go." He held out his hands. "No fight."

She'd been amping herself up for battle but his words pinched it off in her. Her eyes—damp brown beauties as wide as the Hudson—softened and she went into the back long enough for Leon and Dale to make some awkward small talk about the Knicks and the Eagles, and then Antonio was standing on the other side of the screen in the *Transformers* T-shirt Dale had given him and the Lees with the rolled-up cuffs that had been passed down to him from Joaquin, the half-brother 'Tonio couldn't even remember anymore, which was just as well.

'Tonio was five but looked seven or eight. Was going to be a big beast of a boy. Around these parts that put him slinging by ten or eleven, officially inducted into the Kings or the 7th Ave Caps by twelve.

Right now, though, for a minute or two more, he was a little boy.

Leon pushed open the screen and stepped back so Dale could crouch down by his son.

"You miss me?"

Antonio shrugged.

"Come on now, boy. You miss your old man?"

"I don't know."

"Come on now."

"He say he don't know," Verda said. "Leave him be."

Boy kept looking at his bare feet.

"Can you look at me?"

Antonio looked up, met Dale's eyes for just a moment before his glance skipped away.

"I gotta go," Dale told him. "Won't be around for a while."

"Yeah. Okay."

"Your Uncle Leon'll watch out for you."

"Yeah. Okay."

"You listen to him. Him and your Mama."

The boy said nothing.

Dale could feel he was losing the boy to the sound of the TV in the back of the house. He felt wild suddenly, his throat drying up.

"Hey," he said, "you remember that time we played in the snow piles?"

"Oh, Jesus," Verda said. "Here we go."

"Hey," Dale said a little sharper than he intended, "you loved me once. Used to hold me so tight my bones up and got bruised."

"Enough," she said, letting some hard air out of her small body as she reached for their son, "enough."

"'Member that time in the snow?" Dale said, quick as he could. "You up on my shoulders? We tried to climb that drift? It was right down there, end of the street. And I fell."

A small smile appeared on Antonio's downcast face. "You lost your shoe."

"I lost *one* of them."

Antonio chuckled. He met his father's face one last time. "That was funny."

"Yeah, it was."

And then he ran off into the back of the house where Dale could hear that TV going.

"We good?" Leon wanted to know. "Or I got to sleep with iron under the pillow and one eye open?"

Dale looked at Verda for the answer.

Those gorgeous fucking eyes of hers were damp. Not popping with hate, not flaring with anger. Just tired with sadness. She waved at the street. "When you in there? Can't protect me from all this."

"I'm out," he said.

"You'll go back."

He couldn't think of an argument for that.

"It's your way," she said.

"What's yours?"

"Surviving," his brother said and Verda nodded. "Got me a job, man. Ain't forty, ain't no bennies, but it's steady and I string me a couple more things together, I get us across that bridge." He chin-gestured toward Philly. "Next time you come 'round, we won't be here."

And they weren't.

♦♦♦

Nickel led Dale to J'Marcus, and J'Marcus supplied Dale with the shit he needed to get his head up and keep it there, keep him hovering one half-inch above the ground, just enough not to touch the world or let it touch him. Dale dreamed some nights that he was a clock someone had forgotten to wind. He could feel himself wearing down, could feel the hands starting to stick. Couldn't say he was living for anything but the living. Breathing only because it's what you did, not because you thought the next breath was going to be any better.

Didn't much matter the *whys*, did it? Sooner or later, all you were left with were the acts themselves. And in Dale's case that was a long string of bad decisions piled on top of worse ones.

He stopped at a service area, deserted this time of night. Walked past the locked-up sunglass display cases, the grated Burger King and grated Cinnabon, the vending machines. Went into the bathroom, did his business, washed his hands, and went into the gas station mart for a bottle of water and a couple bags of Combos. He was paying at the cash register, the only person in the place besides the round little Muslim woman behind the register, when the state trooper walked through the door.

He was young, just as Dale had feared. Young with something to prove. Young, thinking he had nothing to lose. When the truth was the opposite. He looked at Dale with cold cornflower eyes and jerked his thumb at the parking lot. "Those your wheels?"

"Which?" Dale said.

"The ones right behind me."

Dale looked past the kid, saw a red Toyota Yaris. He shook his head.

"Not yours?"

"No, sir."

"It's mine," the little Muslim said. "Is there a problem, Officer?'

"No, Ma'am," the trooper said, smiling at Dale.

And Dale got it several steps too late—his was the only *other* car along that side of the building. He was parked twenty yards back by the main entrance to the plaza, but he'd just identified himself as the driver of the same Honda the trooper had been following for the last forty minutes.

Dale gave the trooper a polite nod and walked to the door. The trooper opened it so Dale could pass, but then leaned into him. "That wouldn't be marijuana I smell on you, would it?"

"Menthol," Dale said.

The trooper searched Dale's eyes and Dale, who never used on a job, looked right back. The trooper's eyes were adrenalized. He didn't know how he knew Dale was wrong, anymore than he could explain how he'd known the Honda was wrong, but he knew it. And now, with the menthol smell coming off Dale's clothes, he could always claim probable cause for pulling Dale over.

Dale gave the trooper a tight smile and moved past him.

"You have a good night now."

"You too, Officer."

The man had worn a wedding band on his left hand. The name over his right breast pocket had been *Whitman, L.*

Laurence? Lloyd? Not too many other options. Llewyn?

Whatever lay stashed in the Honda's trunk was due at the Polack's at 5. Not 5:15. Not 5:30. Definitely not 6. Those Philly Polacks didn't play neither. Wouldn't think nothing of capping a nigger who showed up late if under no other assumption than the one that said he'd been talking to someone—anyone—when he should've just been driving, plain simple.

Dale got in the Honda and turned the key because to sit around waiting for the cop to pull out of the plaza ahead of him would have been inviting the trooper to arrest him right there in the lot. Give the boy time to call in reinforcements.

Once back on the turnpike, Dale thought about stepping on the gas, going balls-out in the hopes he could put distance between him and the trooper before the overeager fuck finished taking his dump or his piss or whatever he was using as an excuse to make the hunt a little more interesting.

But a 2003 Honda had no shot against a souped-up-cop-engine Crown Vic. And that was before you took into consideration the weight of whatever was in the trunk. Trooper Whitman could take a shit, pour himself a coffee, flirt with the little Muslim cashier, and exchange a few texts with his wife before sauntering out to his unit, easing himself behind the wheel, and fixing his crotch just so before he keyed the ignition. And he'd still catch up to Dale in the time it took to decide to do so.

The suspicion of a narcotic in Dale's system, though, that was all Whitman needed for justification. And now he had it. *"Your honor, I smelled cannabis on the defendant. I then observed him getting behind the wheel of the vehicle in question and driving off."*

This wasn't a case of *if* anymore, only *when.*

Dale removed the .38 snub from the glove box and tucked it in between the seat and the console.

He turned the radio back on:

". . . and I don't know what happened to us. I honestly don't, my friends. It's like a ship sailed from our shores and took everything I grew up believing in with it. We used to be somebody, didn't we? Didn't we?"

The lights appeared in his rearview then, strobing through the car, pouring down the back window like soapsuds tainted by blood.

Dale remembered that day he'd lost his shoe in the snow with Antonio. They'd gone back for it three days later, when a warm spell hit and the snow melted, but somebody had already gotten to it first.

"Who steals one shoe?" Dale had said aloud. "I mean, what's the point?"

Even now, for the life of him, he had no answer.

He pulled to the shoulder. Trooper Whitman pulled his cruiser in tight behind him.

Dale rolled down his window with his left hand, wrapped the fingers of his right around the grip of the .38.

She's young, he thought.

Sleeping in your bed right now, she's young. She'll get over you.

Prove It All Night

Jordan Harper

No future, no past.

Just that animal *now*. All the fears and doubts and memories are gone and there's nothing left but me and the single moment that flows around me.

I don't find it in some ashram or on a therapist's couch. It's here in this gun and this car, and through that glass door. It's inside the gas station. It's pouring like tears from the terrified eyes of the clerk. It's inside that cash register. It's under the counter as the scared man's hands go out of view. It's in that moment when maybe it's the money he's going for or maybe it's a shotgun to sillystring my guts on the chip rack behind me. I tell you that moment lasts forever and blinks by like it's nothing.

It's money. He fills a plastic bag with it, hands shaking.

My ears fill with blood so that the muzak turns itself down and all I can hear is my heartbeat and the click of the hammer as I thumb it back to show the man I mean business. I hear the jagged hiss of his breath and he's right here in the moment with me. He's not thinking of next month's rent or the way he thought life would be when he was back in high school. No. He is here with me, and only me. I tell him to throw in a carton of Camel Wides.

And in front of the liquor store comes a honk, Mark telling me the clock is running. Time passes after all, so move along, little lady. I scoop up the cash and the cartons of Camels and I run to the car. Mark's got the passenger side door waiting open for me, such a gentleman, and I slide in and the back tires spit gravel until they sink their teeth into the asphalt beneath and we rocket out onto the road.

Mark likes that loud deep metal as his getaway music, so that's what pours through the speakers as we head down the road. The wind whips his hair—it grows like the rainforest, and I can't keep my hands out of it—and that devil's smile splits his face and I know now how he looks so animal and alive. He's found the magic elixir. Armed robbery.

I crash back into myself like one of those old-timey trick divers who'd jump off a roof into a kiddie pool. Time isn't timeless anymore, the world isn't infinite. It's 1994 and we're someplace in the middle of Missouri, on some curvy old road that used to be Route 66.

"How'd we do?" he asks me.

I show him fistfuls of money and dump the carton of smokes in the backseat. There's four other cartons there. They're sort of like the scalps we've been taking all night. But that fifth one was the first one for me, the first one with the gun in my hands.

"Oh my God," I say. I can feel the strings of my flesh all individual rubbing against each other inside me.

"I told'ja," he says.

"I want to do another one," I say.

◆◆◆

My mom pierced my ears when I was four years old. She took an ice cube from the freezer and cracked it in two with her molar. She made a sandwich with my left lobe as the meat. She held the ice there until the lobe froze into numbness and a dull ache. Then she took a sewing needle in her right hand and the heel of a potato in the other. She held the potato behind my ear. She pushed the needle through my frozen lobe and into the potato backstop. And I screamed. The needle found the center of the lobe where the nerves weren't dead and pain pushed through the cold.

The day I meet Mark I am seventeen and as full of nothing but cold ache and numbness. And Mark—twenty-one and on parole, with a car bought on credit from a foolish man—is the needle through the heart of me.

"Where are you going?" he asks me.

"You tell me," I say.

And he smiles. Sometimes it really is that easy.

◆◆◆

We drive for days. We drive across the state. We eat at Made-Rites and Steak 'n Shakes. We fuck in the front seat and sleep in the back. We buy cassettes in small-town record stores and gas stations. We listen to heavy metal, doo-wop, gangsta rap. We crank it all up loud. We blow the speakers three days in. We blow the money in four.

Mark won't let me fret. He points out people driving next to us. He tells me that most of them—most everybody—is screaming almost all of the time.

"They're just screaming real quiet," he says. "It's true, you know. Look around at the faces on the bus. Look at the guy taking your order and pushing the plastic tray, the plastic wrapped burger with plastic cheese, look at the face he's wearing under the smile. You listen and tell me he's not screaming.

"It's part of the human condition," Mark says. "Humans went and built their own cages, and they didn't fucking build a door. We are the result of unnaturalness. You ever see a dog chew up his own leg? I mean chew it until it bleeds, just out of plain worry?"

I nod.

"No animal out in the wild ever chewed its own leg into hamburger for no reason. No, it's only cages, real or in the mind, that makes an animal chew at itself."

He takes my hand in his—the touch causes my heart to double-time—and turns it so I can see my own fingers. The nail tips arc out just over the tips of my fingers. They aren't chewed ragged the way I've kept them since I was ten years old.

"You stopped chewing at your leg. You feeling free?"

I answer without words. My hand in the crotch of his jeans finds him half hard already. I feel his devil's smile on my own face as I fish his cock out into the night air.

"Drive straight," I say. "Drive slow. You crash into something or slam on the brakes, I won't be responsible for my reactions." I click my teeth so he gets the picture. And then I swallow him all the way down. He drives straight, but not slow. The wind whips and roars around us as he pushes his foot down on the gas and his hand down on my head. I can feel what I'm doing to him in the throbbing hardness in my mouth and the jerks of his stomach muscles. As his hips buck and he shoots down my throat I realized both his hands hold my head, not the wheel, and the car roars pilotless down the road as I drink him in.

We start our spree an hour later.

♦♦♦

One two three four five gas stations and liquor stores before four a.m.

After I take down my first one, I want breakfast. But he wants one more first. "One more and we steer the ship to Florida," he says. "I heard the coffee in Miami is stronger than the coke. I say let's have them both and give it the old Pepsi challenge."

We find a gas station that meets our needs. Close to a highway junction, empty of customers, in good enough repair to suggest the robbery will be worth our time. We park in front of it, a few spots down from the door so the clerk won't be able to see our car.

"Can I go again?" I ask, taking the revolver from the glove-box.

"Fortune favors the bold," he says back. Then he steals a kiss and the pistol from my hand. "But you're not yet bold enough."

He yanks the ski mask down. He heads into the gas station and I shift over to the driver's seat just as the cop car pulls in next to me. The world turns down the volume again. There's two of them. The cop sitting shotgun gets out carrying a plastic mug with a logo of the gas station on it, like he always comes here for refills. My hand inches up to the horn, to give two short blasts like we planned, to let Mark know to come out shooting.

But I don't do it.

My hand drifts over to the gearshift and I put the car in reverse. That's about the moment Mark comes out the door of the gas station with a bag full of cash in one hand and the pistol in the other. He sees the cop and the cop sees him and the plastic cup drops out of view as the cop goes for his gun and Mark pulls the trigger and then the cop drops from sight as well. The other cop crawls out his door and takes cover behind his car and draws down. And Mark looks to me for a split second and his eyes say everything: put it in drive. Slam on the gas. Smoosh this motherfucker like the mosquito he is. And we'll ride this moment on out 'til it ends, and maybe we'll die but we'll live every moment until we do. And I understand it all in that split second.

But I don't do it.

I turn the wheel the other way. I pull out towards the highway. I can still see his eyes in the rearview as the cop comes up shooting and Mark fires back, six times, putting that cop down on the gravel. When I read about it in the papers later, the coroner says Mark must have pulled the trigger those last few times on animal instinct, 'cause the cop's first and only shot went through Mark's skull and cleaned his brainpan straight out.

I drive and drive and although once I hear sirens that make me freeze like a rabbit in the desert they fade away after a while and I keep driving. I leave the car up in North St. Louis with the keys sitting on the driver's seat. I leave everything but enough money to get me home.

◆◆◆

After that there's not much to tell you. My life went the way it was supposed to go. I work in an office. I married a good-enough man with a job and scared eyes. We never went bust and we never went boom. Yesterday I watched my mother, hollowed-out, with tubes jammed in her and thousand-dollar pills that could keep her on this side of the shadow for another week. On the ride home my husband and I held hands and I told him don't you ever let that be me. And he lied to me and told me he wouldn't and I lied to him and told him the same.

Sometimes I hear Mark laugh, and some days in the car the right song will come on the satellite radio and I'll feel him beside me, tingling like a phantom limb. But I know he's not there. And I know that when you die there's not even darkness, and I know Mark and me won't meet on some cloud or in some pit of fire. And I guess that's a good thing. I couldn't take those eyes seeing what's become of me, those eyes looking down at my hands and my chewed-up, ragged nails.

Candy's Room
Chris Leek

Candy told me she had never seen the ocean. She told me a lot of things that night.

Her father was a truck driver from Wisconsin; his sideline was knocking over drug stores with a ski mask and a snub-nosed .38. Her mother was a hooker who used to turn $20 tricks on Fremont before it cleaned up. As for Candy, she was a waitress at the Showboat. She worked the graveyard shift for minimum wage and lousy tips.

I didn't have to ask her twice to come back to San Diego with me.

♦♦♦

We met in the lounge bar at the Showboat, Candy, catching a smoke before starting her shift upstairs, and me, drinking my last $50 instead of dropping it at the tables. Candy was twenty-two, petite, and in a harsh way, beautiful. I was none of those and the wrong side of forty. But so what? We were good together and I don't just mean in the sack, although I guess that was part of it.

We got talking over a vodka and lime and fifteen minutes later she had blown off her shift and we were out on the Strip. The rest of the night was a blur. Cocktails, blackjack, and Candy's dark eyes.

I woke up the next morning with $2,000 plus change and Candy curled up naked in my arms. Someday I may have a better night, but I doubt it. I traced my finger along the curve of Candy's shoulder and down her spine to the eagle inked at the top of her ass, its wings spread wide across her tanned skin.

Dusty rays of morning sunlight slanted through the blinds and played on the cracks in the mirror, making her busted motel room sparkle like Christmas morning. I spent the best days of my life in that room. Just me, Candy, a pint of tequila and the oldies playing on KQOL. Looking back now I realize it could never last; bright things are made to burn quick. But if I could trade all my tomorrows to have just one of those days back again, I'd do it in a heartbeat.

♦♦♦

I saw cherry tops spinning lazily in the parking lot as I pulled up in my Cutlass. Two metro cruisers and an ambulance were drawn up in front of the motel. Yellow crime scene tape, like you see on CNN, was stretched across the door to Candy's room. Before I knew what to think, I was out of the car and screaming her name, pushing my way through the small crowd of gawkers, until I was tackled by a big Mexican cop called Chavez. Over his shoulder I saw the paramedics carrying out a body bag.

"Easy buddy," he said, "she's gone."

My whole world was in that bag and I don't mind admitting I cried for Candy.

I still do.

♦♦♦

Chavez drove out to my place at Imperial Beach about a week or so later. He didn't have to do that, but he was good people. He wanted to tell me in person, they had caught the son of a bitch who raped and murdered Candy. Seems he was run down coming out of a liquor store in Henderson. The cops had found Candy's credit card in his pocket and made the connection. DNA did the rest. He had priors, all small-time stuff. Chavez said he was just another lowlife piece of shit. A nobody.

He would always be somebody to me.

Chavez told me he was pretty beat up. A witness said the hit-and-run driver had slammed it in reverse and backed up over him. It would be a miracle if he ever walked again.

I told Chavez, I hoped it hurt.

We sat on the back porch, pulling on bottles of Corona, not really saying much, just staring out at the ocean. Candy would have liked it here. Chavez must have seen my Cutlass out front with its stoved-in grille and cracked windshield, but he never said a word.

Hungry Heart
Hilary Davidson

Tommy flirted with the waitress for three weeks before she finally invited him back to her place. Her name was Liz and she worked at a diner outside Hellertown, PA, where Tommy was crashing for the summer. They'd been playing a little cat-and-mouse game since he'd first clapped eyes on her. Liz rebuffed his overtures a couple of times, but gently, on account of her kid. When he strolled into the diner that Thursday evening, he was half-worried her brat would foul up their plans for the night. But then he saw Liz's wide mouth curve into a sly smile, and he knew he'd be going home with her.

She sauntered up to his table. Liz was a brunette with a thick mane of hair that cascaded around her shoulders and full breasts that threatened to pop out of her polyester uniform. He figured her for a knockout when she was younger, but youth had worn thin and she'd gone a little hard around the eyes. Not that he minded; he wasn't looking for a girlfriend, just a great screw.

"Feeling lucky, punk?" Her voice was a low growl.

"Hell, yeah."

"Jake's got an *Iron Man* marathon at his friend's house."

She said it like he should care about what her kid was doing. He didn't, but he grinned. "Great. What time do you get off?"

"Less than an hour."

"I guess I'll wait for you here." He'd already showered at the country club where he worked, and it wasn't like he wanted to go back to his motel room. The roaches didn't seem to mind his company, but he didn't care for theirs.

"All dressed up." Liz smoothed the edge of his collar. "Now you got someplace to go."

Tommy smiled at that. He was wearing what he thought of as his work uniform. He'd lucked into a job at the Silver Creek Country Club, and even though he didn't know the first thing about golf, he had a talent for flattering the self-important. More importantly, he was a quiet purveyor of all the quasi-legal and downright illegal pharmaceuticals such gentlemen required as a balm for their inflated egos and saggy cocks. All of them had families they secretly hated—wives growing flabby, or else working out like maniacs so they could screw the pool boy—teenage kids who gave them no end of heartache, elderly parents who wouldn't shut up and die already. Tommy regarded them with a peculiar kind of horror. He'd been one of those losers once. He was lucky he'd gotten out alive.

"I'll get you some coffee," she offered.

As she moved off, his phone buzzed. It was a text from Carlos, a guy he'd known since forever. They'd lost touch when Tommy had spent a few years out in California. But life out west never matched the dream, and when Tommy returned to his old stomping grounds, he'd reached out. Carlos supplied good product, and Tommy's country club clients hoovered it down.

Can't make tomorrow, Carlos texted. *But I can drop by right now.*

Tommy glanced at his watch and groaned inwardly. Carlos could be such a pain in the balls. *How far away are you? I'm at a diner.* Tommy texted the address. He couldn't blow Carlos off. He'd get what he needed for the weekend and be done with it.

When Carlos walked in, they did their back-slapping bro-hug. "Sorry for the change of plans, man," Carlos said. "Marie's mom is sick, and I gotta—"

"Shit, that wife of yours has you locked down tighter than Fort Knox."

Carlos shrugged. "It's just one of those things."

Tommy snickered. "One of those things that says you're whipped."

"Yeah, well. You'd know how it goes if you'd stayed with your wife and kids."

"But I was smarter than that."

Liz dropped a menu on the table. "You want something to drink?" she asked Carlos.

"Coffee, please. No, wait." Carlos consulted his watch. "It's too late for caffeine. You have decaf?"

"No."

"Uh, just water, please."

Liz glanced at Tommy, as if to say *Thanks for bringing your deadbeat friends in, buddy,* before moving toward the water pitcher on the counter.

"You're not going to believe who I ran into," Carlos said.

"Who?"

"Ashley."

Tommy blinked at him, trying to remember an Ashley. There'd been so many girls over the years, he was sure there were a handful of Ashleys sprinkled in. "Ashley who?"

"You kidding me, man?" Carlos said. "Ashley, your daughter."

Tommy sat back and ran a hand through his hair. "Huh. She's got to be, what, fifteen or sixteen now?"

"Eighteen," Carlos corrected him.

"Whoa. Time flies."

"She looks a lot like your ex did at her age. A knockout, if you don't mind me saying so."

"Knock it off, man."

"What?"

"That's my kid you're talking about."

"Come on. You haven't seen her for a decade, Tommy. Kids grow up. You want to see a picture? It'll blow your mind, where I saw her."

"No, I don't," Tommy said quickly. "Look, I need to get out of here soon."

Carlos was clearly miffed, but they made their transaction, and he took off. Liz took her sweet time circling back to the table.

"You want to head out now?" Tommy asked.

There was a crease between Liz's eyes, like she was thinking hard. Too hard. "You didn't tell me you have a kid."

That caught Tommy by surprise. What business was it of hers if some of his DNA was out walking around?

"I don't. Not really."

"What does *that* mean?" Liz asked. "You either have a kid or you don't. It's not something you go halfway on."

"I broke up with their mom years ago. We're not in touch."

"*Their* mom?" Liz's tweezed eyebrows shot up. "There's more than one?"

Tommy didn't want to have this conversation. There was a boy and a girl and it had been forever since he'd tried to picture their faces. If he passed them on the street now, they'd be strangers. "Does it matter?"

Liz's eyes got flinty. "You know my scumbag ex walked out on me and Jake, right?"

"Okay . . ."

She stared him down. "Why would I want anything to do with a pig who did to his own family what my ex did to me?"

She turned on her cheap heels and clattered off. He watched the back of her head and felt like punching it. Some used-up slop-server was going to cop an attitude with him? Well, fuck her.

He hit the john, locking the door and laying out a line of coke. That made him feel better for all of sixty seconds. He had a love-hate relationship with coke. The high was so brief and it left him all jumped up and buzzing afterwards.

He walked out without a word. Forget that stupid waitress, he'd find better action. He didn't want to hit anywhere in Hellerstown, because he couldn't afford to run into any of the creeps from the country club. So he drove aimlessly for a while, wishing he was back on his bike instead of a car. His ex-wife had made him give it up after he got into an accident with a tree, and he still resented the hell out of her for it. He should've bought another bike after he ditched her, but after he walked out, he'd given up on the idea of owning things. He never wanted to be tied down to anything again. He'd had enough of that life. He'd tried living it for eight years, and he'd hated it. Every day, he felt like something was dragging him down, and he knew he'd feel like that until the release of the grave. Something had to give. Caught between a rock and a hard place, he ran.

He cruised into Allentown, parking outside a dive bar. Inside, he planted himself next to a twenty-something girl who reminded him of Jennifer Beals in *Flashdance*.

"You know who you look like?" he asked her.

She didn't turn around.

He repeated himself.

She acted like she didn't hear him.

Stuck-up bitch, he thought. He left and walked a couple blocks to a bar that had some college kids in it. Now, these girls were hot. But they gave him strange looks when he tried to talk to them. Stuck up, that's what they were. Some guy walked up to a chick he was about to hone in on, a friendly looking girl with big tits. "Hey, Ashley," the guy said.

That hit Tommy like a hammer. Ashley? He had a fleeting vision of his little girl dressed in a tutu. He forced the memory into a box at the back of his brain, blaming Carlos for letting it escape. That wimp let his wife boss him around. Soccer games, ballet recitals, family dinners and Disney World trips. Tommy never put up with that shit. He was his own man.

He did another line of coke. All was right with the world for a moment, until he noticed his heart pounding. Was he having a heart attack? It was like even his own body was turning against him. When he was younger, he'd been able to party night after night. Now, the rush lasted about as long as a sneeze.

He drove aimlessly for a while, tasting bitterness. The truth was, as much as he insisted on having his freedom, the loneliness was hard to take. It was Liz's fault, he decided. That lousy cock-tease had wrecked his night. Well, he'd teach her a lesson. He knew where she lived—a sloping house just off the 78 in the no-man's land between Allentown and Hellertown.

When he pulled up in front of her place, he noticed her car parked out front. Maybe she'd had enough time to cool her heels? A guy could hope. He brushed off the front of his shirt and knocked on the door.

Liz opened the wooden front door.

"Hey, babe," he said.

"I thought you might turn up." She left the storm door shut between them. "What d'you want?"

"That's no way to say hello."

"What part of *fuck off* don't you get?"

"You don't mean it."

"Beat it before I call the cops."

That was the last straw. "You bitch," he said, grabbing the handle of the storm door and wrenching it open. Liz tried to slam the heavier door, but Tommy rammed his shoulder against it. "You think you can invite me over and turn me away?" he demanded. "I don't—"

The gunshot filled his ears. His stomach was being squeezed in a vise and on fire at the same time. He reached forward to grab the gun away from Liz, but the pain forced him to stumble back, against the storm door. He fell to the ground.

"Don't worry, I'll call 911," Liz snarled. "Just as soon as you bleed out."

Images of his life started to swirl in front of Tommy's eyes, visions of a little girl dancing and a boy playing with LEGOs. Birthday parties and recitals and play dates. Then his wife's face floated past. He'd pushed it to the furthest reaches of his mind, but his ex was still in there, a ghost that would never die. He saw their tiny little wedding and the look on her face when she told him she was pregnant. He remembered what she'd looked like in high school, how he'd craved her like he'd never wanted anything before. He'd spent years running away from them, but these ghosts were soaked into the fiber of his being. He didn't exist without them.

Liz's harsh voice broke through his thoughts. She leaned forward, just a little, and her voice dropped to a hiss. "It's not like anyone's gonna miss you."

I'm on Fire

James R. Tuck

I ain't afraid of Lowell Fulson.

I know he's a big motherfucker, got fists on him like cinder-blocks. Hell, I've seen him pick up whole hogs and hang 'em to butcher. Damn things must weigh a quarter ton, but he picks 'em up like they're nothin'. He'll butcher five, six of 'em in a row, using the same wide-blade knife that starts razor-sharp but by the end is edgy and dull as cardboard.

Doesn't slow him down.

Most folks are scared of Lowell.

But he's got the heart of a farmer.

It's soft and yielding and even though it lets him butcher a hog six ways to Sunday, he ain't got no hate in it.

No avarice.

No murder.

I ain't scared of him at all.

Lowell wasn't home when I went to his place.

But that ain't why I went over there.

♦♦♦

The frame of the door flakes when I knock, white paint coming off in long, thin rectangles. I can smell the rust of the screen in the door and it makes my teeth hurt.

It smells like blood.

A fly buzzes my face, zipping across my cheek like a stray bullet. I'm just about to knock again when she comes to the door.

Little Helena.

She stands on the other side of the door, wearing a blue gingham dress she got three summers' worth of growing ago.

It ain't much longer than a shirt now.

She might be wearing shorts underneath, but it's mid-August, sweaty and humid, and she might not be. I can't tell.

Barefoot, she barely hits the center of my chest. Her hair's pinned on top of her head, long strands hanging down, stuck to her skin with a fine layer of perspiration. She looks at me sullen-eyed, lids half shut.

I keep my voice low. "Hey, little girl, is your daddy home?"

She doesn't answer for a long minute. I don't fidget as she looks at me under those long, black lashes and shaggy bangs. "He's gone to market with the new slaughter."

I know this.

She knows I know it too, but she doesn't call me on it. She's playing the same game I am, the same game I've played with girls all across this holler.

Cat and mouse.

I wonder which one she thinks she is.

My hand slides down, brushes the handle of the screen door. "I ran into him at Shautey's General last week. He told me to come by and pick up a book." Lowell is always trying to get folks to read, as if anybody wants to stick their nose in a book when they could be out livin'. "He must've forgot he'd be out of town when he offered." I open the door and step in.

"Daddy doesn't tend to forget much." She stands her ground, doesn't back up.

This is a new move in the game.

This close I can smell her. Sweet girl sweat in the bloom of womanhood. Eighteen summers and damn near ripe. I breathe deep and it lights my veins like a white gas flashfire deep in the coal mines, coming on sudden and hot and inescapable. It burns me through, drawing my skin tight.

I'm on fire.

I glance around. The house is clean, spotless even. I can still see the presence of Lowell's wife, Helena's mother, gone some eight years now. Lowell loved that woman and she still haunts the place, her taste painted across every wall in every room, her ghost stamped on Helena's features, darker skin and sultry eyes over high Lakota cheekbones. The only part of Lowell to make its mark is Helena's heavy brow and her bramble-thick, honey-blonde hair.

I listen closely. I don't hear anyone but us in the house.

I look down at her. "Did he go and leave you all alone?"

"I'm old enough to stay by myself."

Yes, she is.

I realize she's looking at me with those witchery eyes and it's been too long since I said anything.

"What book were you borrowing?"

Damn.

"Um . . ." I look at the bookshelf across the room. All the books are stacked two and three deep. It's too far away for me to read any of the words on the spines.

Helena takes a step back, making distance between us, and I see it in her eyes, in the line of her narrow shoulders.

She's on to me.

Inside my stomach the dark thing I've had as long as I've had breath curls on itself, stretching like some great cat inside my skin.

My mojo rises.

It's my bad seed, my other, my id, my compulsion, my demon riding me hard and the devil's breath stokes the furnace in my guts and I can't help it. I'll burn to cinders if I don't quench myself.

Helena.

I must've moved because she darts back, putting the couch between us.

Prey runs.

My blood boils like an overfull kettle.

Helena points at the door. "You need to leave. Get on out of here." Raising her arm lifts the hem of her skirt.

No shorts, just a long, sleek line of coltish leg.

I knew it.

I walk toward her. Each step the fire builds. It hangs heavy as I clench and unclench my fists.

"Don't be like that, little Helena. You got no idea the things I can do to you."

I see it. The switch. I watch a line of defiance settle into her shoulders. The fear is raw on her face but she ain't gonna run, not Little Helena, not any more.

Dark coffee eyes narrow. "If you touch me, I'll kill you."

I laugh and it feels good rolling out of my chest. It's black and evil, the edge of the darkness inside lapping out over my tongue.

She doesn't move as I get closer.

Silly girl.

My hand clamps on her thin arm. I'm so hot inside it should burn her, raise blisters on her smooth skin, but it doesn't. I jerk, twisting her to the left.

She doesn't scream. Doesn't start crying like the rest. Her eyes go dark and narrow and her mouth hard with clenched teeth.

"My daddy'll . . ."

I yank her close.

"Your daddy ain't here." She smells . . . intoxicating. Strawberries in her hair and the ozone crackle of fear across her skin.

It makes my eyelids stutter as I draw in a lungful of it.

"You're a dead man if you do this," she hisses.

The laughter rolls again.

"You're wrong, little girl. I ain't never been more alive."

She fights me all the way to the bedroom.

♦♦♦

I wake up, a freight train splitting the middle of my skull.

It's dark. I reach out for Helena.

She ain't there.

Just a warm wet spot where she should be. The sheets I'd used to tie her down are wadded up next to me, soaking wet.

Damn little hellcat. Must've slipped the knots while I was passed out.

She couldn't have gone far. I'll catch her. I'll make her pay for running off.

She thought she'd had it rough before.

I'll show her.

I try to sit up.

My head weighs a thousand pounds, pinning me to the sopping sheets. I try to turn, to roll off the mattress, and a lightning sharp jag of blinding agony cuts a valley through my skull.

What the hell was that?

I reach up, fingers sliding on the slick skin of my forehead, stopping at a thing, a hard thing jutting from above my eyebrows. It's warm. Thin as cardboard and about as sharp.

I know what it is before I see little Helena standing beside the bed looking down at me.

Lowell Fulson's butcher knife is sticking out of my head.

My mouth opens. I try to talk, but the thing in my brain that lets me talk is outta whack, not working, on the fritz, zitz, zzzzz.

Helena's face is a shadow, hair a honey-toned veil that hides her from my dimming sight. She's put her dress back on. It hangs loose around her chest, torn in my need.

Her voice is the voice of an angel.

The Angel of Death.

"You should of listened. You should of left me alone."

Her hands move and light sears my eyeballs. Hard. Like a slap from a two-by-four. It's a match, a simple wooden match with a sulfur head and rough stick body. Now I can see the fires of Hell in those dark, witchery eyes.

"I told you, you were a dead man."

From around me comes the smell, the silky, heady scent of raw gasoline.

Helena turns to the left, then the right, looking around the room. My eyes jitter to where hers go and I realize this is Lowell's room. The big bed. The pictures of her mama. I didn't know it was their room when I drug her in here. I didn't care.

She sighs. The match flame flickers with her breath.

"Daddy'll be sad, but it's time he let Mama go anyway." The match light is an orange kiss on her tanned face. "With the insurance money we'll finally get outta Butcher Holler. We'll move to Culvert City and start a new life."

She drops the match and walks away.

Dancing in the Dark

Lynne Barrett

When I'd had enough of partying and wanted to settle down, I picked Chuck Keogh. Ten years older than me, he'd been a Piskemahwin High fullback and a Marine before becoming a cop. Tall, strong, a guardian, a good guy for a fourth grade teacher to marry. Yet our first spring in the house, there he was, my new husband, lying on the couch after he'd barely lifted the shovel to plant an azalea, telling me he had a bad back. "It just goes out sometimes," he said. When I suggested yoga, he scoffed. He'd take some Doan's and be fine next day.

Over the next four years, his back acted up at odd times. Opening clams. Once, laughing. But mostly when I asked him to help me in the garden.

Then, last October, as Sandy bashed New Jersey, the brook overflowed down in Piskemahwin Falls and Chuck went to rescue an old lady stranded in her car. When Chuck yanked her door, he said later, he felt something in his lower back pop. The EMTs took him to the hospital.

His chief, Ted Weiss, found time that crazy evening to call and tell me Chuck would be undergoing tests and wanted me to know I should "follow the plan" and stay home.

With Piskemahwin thirty miles inland and our Dutch stone house on high ground, I wasn't worried. From the kitchen drawer, I got Chuck's Sig Sauer, which was "the plan" Chuck had trained me for, in case anyone was stupid enough to try to loot here. Through the sliding glass door in the TV room, I watched the wind dance down the garden's slopes and flats to the thick firs at the property line. When the power failed, I lit the hurricane lamps. Apple trees flung off their branches. Shingles peeled from the shed roof. And then, off to my right, a big gust caught our copper beech, still heavy with leaves, and it toppled, smashing into the high hedge bordering Crow Lane.

In the morning, I assessed the survivals and losses. I found the Victorian rose arbor tilting drunkenly but, somehow, still standing, while the big beech had taken down twenty feet of hedge and the old chain link fence it had grown up around. The tree had shaded a wide circle with its low sweeping branches. A pest, in its way: nothing could grow under it and its spiky fruit was hard to clean up. But it had seemed so certain, so secure. Now its ball of roots had pulled free, opening a raw hole where I breathed in rich, disturbed earth.

In spring, I rototilled the new plot, enclosed it in chicken wire, and laid out a vegetable garden. On a Friday afternoon after school ended in late June, I was there staking tomatoes. I could see Chuck inside in his rocker, talking to Ted Weiss. Ted had steadily helped, writing up Chuck's heroism in the line of duty and handling paperwork for his disability leave.

Since his injury, Chuck kept to the first floor, not wanting to take the steep stairs. He slept on a hospital bed in the living room. Chuck's lumbar disc herniation didn't fully account for the pain that radiated down through his butt and thighs, sometimes reaching his toes. They did a laminotomy in March to relieve nerve compression, but Chuck said it didn't help. The doctors mentioned chemical inflammation, something called tumor necrosis factor-alpha, pain that feeds on itself and produces more pain. Still, with anti-inflammatories, a program of exercise, and patience, Chuck was expected to heal. He was forty-three years old and they'd found nothing else wrong with him.

Ted came down the slate path towards me, leaned over the wire, and said, "You should get Chuck to help you, out here in the sun."

"He says it hurts just getting down the steps, Ted."

"Do you think it could be his imagination?" Ted went to high school with Chuck, but looked older, his fair hair thinning.

"He groans in his sleep," I said. I'd tried sleeping near him, on the couch.

"Fortunately," Ted said, "you look great, Lilah."

I just nodded at the compliment, surprised. It wasn't usual for Ted, married with two kids, to make such a personal remark.

He went out through the gap in the hedge to where he'd parked. Though I liked having this side opening for bringing in supplies, easier than the path around the garage, Chuck wanted it closed up. I'd planned a high-arched wooden gate, with tall fence topped by lattice on either side, but contractors were still unobtainable, booked solid for hurricane rebuilding.

I walked up to the house, feeling how very fit I was as I climbed the steps between the tall blooming delphiniums and Jupiter's beard, and went in through the sliding door.

Chuck was listening to police band radio and drinking Bushmills.

"Ted thinks a little gardening might suit you," I said.

"I just bet he does. And then Ted'll get it on video. Don't you know they surveille people on disability, trying to prove they're faking? I guarantee they will if I put in for retirement."

The rules said Chuck could retire in three years, with twenty years' service, at 70% of full-time pay. But with injury in the line of duty, he could take disability retirement now, get two thirds, and even have another job, as long as it didn't duplicate police work. He kept going over it: Was it worth going back, with the risks involved, for 3.3%? Would he ever be well enough to? Would they believe him if he wasn't?

He sat in the rocker padded with pillows, his square jaw aimed at me. "I've told you. We need a good privacy fence, now. Can't you find *somebody*?"

I got a number from a woman at Zumba whose sister knew someone. Three guys with a van showed up the Tuesday after Fourth of July. Danny, in his mid-twenties, did the talking. He'd been working down the shore, could've stayed, but wanted to be up here. He and his helpers took cash only, pay-as-you-go.

I described my plans, and Danny took measurements. Figuring where new posts would meet old chain link, he hung upside down from a branch above the hedge, his shirt falling away from his tanned stomach, a line of dark hair leading into his jeans.

I turned away, knelt in the dirt, and thinned lettuces.

He scrawled an estimate, I laid out cash for supplies, and, to my surprise, the men all returned the next day, stacking materials on the level patch below the shed, by the rose arbor. Danny gave me receipts.

The other two were tough-looking and stolid, but Danny, headphones on, moved in the heat like he enjoyed it. Each afternoon, he reported progress, collected an installment, and offered information about himself. He grew up near Philly. Aspired to be an entertainer. He sang, studied acting. Came here to be where he could take the train into New York for auditions.

"Look, Mrs. Keogh," Danny said on Friday. He held out his phone. "This is me and a band I was in."

I watched: third-rate Springsteen. But his body was alive. I looked at the description. "Danny Sorrento?"

"Stage name. What's your first name?"

"Lilah," I told him, knowing it was a mistake.

He said: "The old man's sick, huh? That's too bad."

"He's recuperating from an injury." For some reason, I didn't want to mention that Chuck was a cop.

Over the weekend, I chose flowering vines I'd train up the fence and got Chuck to do his exercises on my yoga mat.

They finished hanging the gate Monday afternoon in 95° heat, with their shirts off. The wood looked bright but was supposed to age to silver.

"So what do you do for fun, Lilah?" Danny asked, while the others loaded the van. "Do you ever go out to clubs?"

"Not lately."

"Hey, you're young," he said. "You should get out."

"I'm a teacher. Sometimes I take classes. And I have book group, garden club."

"Do you ever come outside and look at the stars, Lilah?"

"Sometimes," I said.

"Me too. Especially now, summer, a shame to let it go to waste, you know?"

With Chuck asleep in the living room, I walked into the dark garden.

I wasn't surprised to find Danny sitting behind the shed, drinking a beer. "What are you doing here?" I whispered.

"Waiting and hoping." He reached for my hand.

I didn't care about him, not a bit, but it was summer and I desired desire.

The shed screened us from the house. And Chuck wouldn't walk down here.

"Ah, you're hot," Danny sighed.

I wished he wouldn't talk. I inhaled roses and tarragon and dirt. The garden loved me. I was just loving it back.

Later, we lay on the grass. Creatures whirred above us. New Jersey's not a bunch of buildings and roads, I understood. It's this, the open spaces, wildness that doesn't give a damn.

"Tomorrow night?" he said.

"I'm busy."

"With what?"

"Tomorrow's my book group. This month it's at a friend's. I have to go."

"When will you get home?" he said.

"Late. After eleven. Look, I'm married."

"Okay, okay. But you know I'm ready, willing, and"— he bumped against me—"able."

I thought I'd feel calm after getting laid, but I was alert and irritable. At book group, I noticed how they judged the characters' bad decisions and didn't mention any of their own.

Home just after ten, I looked for Chuck in the living room, then found him sitting in the dark with the sliding door open and a glass in his hand. Not Bushmills. Milk. I kissed his cheek, and he said, "I did leg lifts. Didn't feel too bad. I think I can come back from this."

"That's excellent."

"Shshsh. You hear something?"

I listened. Insects. Birds. Nothing bigger. "Could be deer?"

"I'm glad that fence is done," Chuck said.

"Me too."

"The gate needs a padlock."

"I'll buy one tomorrow," I said. "I'm going to go get changed and be down to say goodnight."

Halfway up the stairs, I heard a shout and a crash. I ran.

I saw the rocker overturned and Chuck down by the chicken wire, grappling with someone. Danny. What the hell? He knew I was out. Had he come to hurt Chuck? Was he crazy?

I retreated to the kitchen, got Chuck's pistol, and went outside.

Danny stood over Chuck, holding something long I thought might be metal.

Chuck's hand gripped Danny's ankle.

I only knew I didn't want them to talk. I found the safety with my thumb, raised the gun, and shot Danny in the stomach.

He looked up, said, "Hey," and I shot him in the head, even as he fell.

Chuck shoved him aside and got to his feet. "Good girl."

Ted coordinated the investigation. Danny's workers, probably illegals, had vanished. There were warrants out for Danny in Monmouth and Atlantic counties. Turned out he went in for a bit of burglary after he finished jobs. Like a tip he helped himself to. I assume I was one of those, too. Or maybe I just interrupted his plans that first night.

He'd left the shed with my garden tools in my carryall. Then Chuck ran down and punched him. He hit Chuck's leg with my pruning shears. Chuck says that whack pulled the pain right out of his spine. He was about to get up and clobber Danny when I shot him, not that I didn't do the exact right thing. No doubt about it. Everyone agreed.

After Chuck returned to duty, assigned to deskwork but hoping to recover all the way, Ted came to see me. He admitted he'd been asked to check if Chuck was faking, so he'd done some watching from the spruces, but all he saw was Danny flirting with me, making him worry I might do something silly.

I feared he'd seen more—I still wonder—but all he said was, "You should only fool around with someone trustworthy."

And I have to admit, he was right.

On a late-August afternoon, my runner beans spill over wire teepees, the tomatoes are staked high, and sunflower heads peek over the shed. And I'm under the arbor, straddling Ted. He likes to do it on his back. His left knee locks up sometimes, he says.

Thunder Road

James Grady

Montana's big blue sky cupped the snowy prairie snaked by gray highways escaping from Shelby's four block Main Street where a red neon TAP ROOM sign glowed even though it was only seventeen minutes till 9 on a Tuesday morning. Undersheriff Lucas Rudd unzipped his black leather jacket. Entered that wood paneled tavern filled with whiffs of vanished beer, burnt coffee, and marijuana.

"Lawman in the house!" announced Gary, the bartender who wore a blue Hawaiian shirt and, like the great American author rocking the jukebox, was old enough to be Luc's father.

Gary stood behind the bar pretending to read what was left to call itself a daily newspaper from the big city 87 miles away, but *really*, he was trying not to hear *that conversation* between his daughter Ruby and Adam, the apprentice lawyer come to town hoping to be set up if/when fracking banished Main Street's white-washed windows.

Some ambush of inertia had trapped Ruby and Adam at the far end of the bar, huddled on stools as she whispered, *"You know how you feel!"*

"And you know we're still working out what that means!" argued Adam, his hand on her arm more to hold her there than help her along.

A shrunken man working a big knife slumped on a stool halfway down the bar. He wore a tattered high school letterman's jacket, two sweaters over a pajama top, sweat pants revealing hospital greens where stick ankles led to soggy sneakers. The open spring blade knife in the man's right hand was simultaneously sawing a watchband and hospital I.D. bracelet looped around his left wrist. The watch and I.D. fell to the bar where pill bottles, a shot of whiskey and a coffee cup waited near a cell phone and a stack of wooden coins signifying free drinks at this tavern. A joint in the man's lips sent stoner smoke meant to quell chemo's effects toward the ceiling between everyone here and heaven.

Six stools away, Ruby said *that*, Adam said *this*.

Stalking toward the man with the knife, Luc said, "I'm a peace officer, not a cop."

"Whatever you call yourself," said the man, "I know who you are."

"You called me, Mike." Luc lowered himself onto the barstool beside the man he'd known since fifth grade. "And my badge has gotta say, smoking's been illegal in bars for years. It's Gary's license if we let that keep burning."

"But you ain't gonna say shit about *what* I'm burning. I'm not gonna rot in any lockup."

"I don't know what you're burning, where you're going—or why you called me at home."

"I was hoping Valerie would answer."

Luc wished he'd left earlier that morning so he wouldn't have gotten Mike's call. Maybe he could have even missed another marital burn.

Mike stubbed out the joint on a free drink coin, said, "Do you think if not for you, Val might have married me? Loved me?"

Lucas smoldered from what he didn't know he'd signed on for when gravity fused him to his wife. He reached in front of the pale man beside him, closed the jackknife, put it in his own shirt pocket. "Well, she probably deserves better than me."

"*Deserve* only matters when you can make it work." Never married, barely kissed Mike nodded to the urn behind the bar. "Get yourself a cup of coffee, that's the way it works here in the morning. We serve ourselves."

"I didn't come here for coffee."

"What time is it?" Mike asked.

"You shouldn't have cut off your watch." Luc shrugged. "About ten to nine."

"You got time for coffee. Don't make me buzz up alone."

Luc swung off the stool, walked around the end of the bar where Adam and Ruby whispered hollow lines about their "situation" as Gary kept pretending to read the day's ration of official news, giving everyone in the bar the back of his blue Hawaiian shirt. Luc poured powder as white as snow into his black coffee and watched chemicals fake into cream. Went back to sit beside the sick man.

"You owe me three things," said cancer's prey.

Luc felt weight in the right pocket of his black leather jacket as Mike's left hand placed something there before floating up to the bar to cover Luc's right arm, like Adam holding Ruby, so he couldn't check what it was.

"That's *One*," said Mike. "*Two* is not looking until you wash up after *Three*."

"Why do I owe you anything?"

"Because you're not just a badge. You're a good man. Go for justice."

"That's a hard road to find. What's going on, Mike?"

"Drink some coffee."

They sipped from cups until the jukebox ran out of songs to play.

Ruby whispered to Adam, "*Sometimes I feel so alone when I'm with you.*"

Mike stared at his bar mirror reflection, said, "Being alone plus being nothing is bad pain. Believe me, I know about pain and having nothing better than that on your horizon of *deserve*."

"Sorry," said Luc.

Forget about your petty shit, thought Luc. *You're lucky not to be him.* Then he thought about Valerie: *The luck you got comes with the luck you get.*

"I'm over being sorry," said Mike. "I get that I couldn't have somebody like Val. Still, I always wanted to do something people would remember."

"Everybody does."

"I should have hit the road. Left this town."

"Everywhere is pretty much the same."

"Maybe. Maybe it's more about *how* than *where* you go. Me, I never left where I was and I kept books for Wesley Hardin for seventeen years."

"And all your volunteering kept the old folks home from being a hellhole."

"Ironic, huh? Never gonna get to use what I done." Mike shook his head. "But I learned how to add any score and make it the way I was told it should read.

"You're a lawman, Luc, I worked for a crook. You know that in your heart even if you can't prove it with your head. Landlord Wes loves people your badge can't protect. Minimum wage folks. Welfare Moms. Anyone who falls behind in rent so Wes can force a deal, say a new lease that's officially a hundred dollars less than you were paying—though now, you really pay fifty bucks above that list in a cash deal that never gets written down for a taxman to see. Wes's got twenty-one rentals. You know what he does nine o'clock every Tuesday like today? Takes a handful of hard-worked cash to the bank two doors down from here, stuffs it in a safety deposit box, cheats every citizen taxpayer while cheaping his 'staff,' who are contractors, so they got no health insurance. After Wes locks his box, the bank president takes him out and buys him a coffee. Talk about *deserve*."

Mike raised the whiskey glass to his lips.

"What do you want?" asked Luc as Ruby whispered the same thing to Adam.

"Number Three," Mike said, "as much coffee as you been drinking, I want you to go to the bathroom."

"What?"

"I don't want you pissing your pants when you decide *what's what*. That would be embarrassing. Humiliating. Don't forget to wash afterwards. That's Number Two."

Luc actually did need to piss. Washed his hands at the men's room sink. Couldn't dodge seeing himself in the mirror. Seeing his face. Seeing raven-haired, river-eyed Valerie telling him: "I love *you*, not every one of your dreams."

He reached in his jacket pocket and found five bullets.

Like from a revolver rigged for Russian roulette.

Luc charged out of the STALLIONS bathroom.

Adam and Rachel still huddled at the bar.

Gary still pretended to read the newspaper, bent over with the weight of what he couldn't hold onto and couldn't let go.

A cell phone, pill bottles, a coffee cup, a whiskey glass, drink tokens: they all waited on the bar in front of an empty stool.

Luc rushed past Ruby and Adam, his cop voice saying, "Where's Mike?"

Ruby sighed. "Out to Main Street."

As if he might die and never see them again, some big brother voice in Luc shot words at the *situation* lovers: "Pick your road and go!"

Ending up somewhere is better than staying nowhere, thought Luc, but he didn't have time to say those words as he slammed open the bar door in the same heartbeat alarm bells rattled that Main Street morning.

Montanans call the wind that rises out of the west to melt snow a Chinook. That warmth pushed Luc's face as his shoes hit the sidewalk and he ran to the curved driveway of the bank built above Main Street, the money cathedral's doors level with his eyes.

Those grand doors flew open as two figures burst outside, one pressed against the other's back, almost like they were lovers. Mike held a revolver into his ex-boss Wes Hardin's skull. The Chinook flapped Wes's tan cashmere topcoat that he seldom buttoned over his beach ball belly where now his hands clutched a long metal box like a small coffin that held his life.

Mike yelled: "Throw it!"

Wes tossed the metal box through the air over Main Street.

Out of the tumbling box came a blizzard of green paper bills instantly claimed by the Chinook. Green bills blew all over town, out to the snowy prairie, many of them forever lost—or never returned. Still, many of them were crime scene logged or turned in by honest souls to be painstakingly counted and noted in official reports by bank robbery busting FBI agents and bank auditors and taxmen.

"Stop this!" ordered Luc.

Mike grinned like a winner.

Then above clanging alarms and shouts inside the bank, the whistle of a freight train rumbling through town, Luc heard that triggered metallic *click!*

Wes must've heard it louder with the revolver's bore grinding his skull. He screamed. A dark stain colored the front of his brown slacks.

Mike pushed the business end of the revolver against his own tumored head.

Six rounds, it holds six rounds; I have five in my pocket.

Luc heard a second *click*.

The bore of Mike's revolver locked on Luc.

Clear threat adding up to *justified response*.

Just as he knew he'd never drive away from Valerie, Luc knew that Mike had calculated every trigger he could squeeze.

And that he trusted Luc to drive toward the safest, surest, swiftest justice.

The .45 automatic everyone in town knew Luc used to win last year's Big Sky Combat Shooter Gold Medal filled his hand as Luc zeroed the pale skin over Mike's third eye. Lightning flashed, reddened melting snow.

Dry Lightning

Dyer Wilk

Tonight we'll escape, you and me, baby.

We make love on your bed while the world is sleeping. Arms and legs wrapped tight, holding on. Could go all night, but we rest awhile, light up Luckies and listen to the radio, as a warm breeze blows through the open window.

Sweat's drying on our skin and the fires are still burning. Never wanted you more than I do right now. But it's getting late and we have to get going.

Tonight. It has to be tonight, baby.

Spent my last twenty gassing up the Camaro. I'm busted broke, but there'll be more money soon. A good job and a nice little place. A bigger bed. Another town.

Somewhere down the highway.

Close my eyes and I can see the Interstate, low green hills and open road all the way to the sunset. Hear the engine purr and the gears shifting, feel the wind on my face. And you beside me.

I roll over and look at you. Neon light's coming through the window, making you look the way you did that night at the club, when you danced to The Troggs and drove every man wild. Bumping and grinding. All curves and legs for miles.

Never thought I'd get so lucky, the way you smiled and invited me back to your place. Stepped inside and knew I was the luckiest man alive. But I still wondered, babe. All those pictures above your bed. Elvis and James Dean. Marilyn Monroe and JFK. That first time making love. That sadness behind your eyes.

Tried to ask and you told me not to worry. You said the past is the past and you can leave it all behind. Doesn't matter where you've been, just where you're going.

Now the pictures are gone and our bags are packed. Got a million reasons to leave and not one to stay. Always and forever, you said. It's us or nobody.

I stand up and dress, you still lying there. Eyes out the window, down into the street. See boarded-up storefronts and two wide lanes. The calluses on my hands remember better days.

You sit up and pull a sheet around yourself tight. Warm breeze is turning cold tonight.

Down in the street, a car drives past and turns at the corner. Rumble starts to fade, V8 echoes coming up to the window.

I turn around and tell you it's time to go.

You give me a nod and find me that smile.

You get dressed slowly, but I don't complain. If this town wasn't dead, I'd want us to stay.

Turn off the radio and slide on my boots. This is it, babe. We're cutting loose.

You're only halfway dressed when I hear the sound outside the door. Feet on the stairs.

A key in the lock.

The door swings wide, you still standing there in your bra.

Three men walk in like they belong, step right through the door. I'd shove them back out again, but I hesitate.

I've seen them before.

The short one, he used to stand behind the bar at the club. And the fat one, he used to work the door. But it's the man out front—in his nice clothes—that I worry about. Don't remember his name, but I know that he owned the place.

His eyes take me in and then look away. He's looking at you. He calls you by name.

Says he isn't surprised and didn't expect much better. Maybe someone taller and halfway tough. But it's time to come back to work now. You've had your fun. Enough is enough.

I step between you and him, and tell them to leave. To show them I mean it, I roll up my sleeves. The owner man just smiles and lets out a laugh. Says I'm not the first and I won't be the last.

I look at you, babe, and ask what he means. You tell me it's us or nobody, no in-betweens. You're done with them and you're done with dancing. You chose me. Tonight we're escaping.

I look at the men and ask if they heard. You and me are in love. No two ways about it.

But they keep on standing there and the owner man keeps smiling that smile.

He says he's been out to see your mother in Henrysville.

Don't think I've seen you get mad more than once since I met you, but you look at him like he's the devil. You say your mother's no fool and knows better than to talk to strange men who look like brutes, even snakes who hide their scales under three-piece suits.

The owner man laughs and his boys laugh with him. Oh, he says he knows. Mean old woman didn't want to open the door. But she welcomed him in when he told her the law might be coming for Sarah.

Something happens to you, babe. I'm not sure what's wrong. His words have stopped you dead. You're standing there frozen.

A moment later, you blink it away and shake your head hard. You come back at him fierce and call him a liar.

The owner man just pouts and says he thought that's how you'd feel. So he's got something here he wants to show you. Hand goes into his pocket, comes out with something small and square and white. He holds it out to you, not letting me see the other side.

You take it from him and take a step back. At first your face remains hard, then your expression goes flat. Your eyes go wide and then they get wet. Your hands start shaking, and I see it's a photograph.

The owner man speaks and his voice is soft. He says he's known you a long time. Maybe knows you better than you know yourself. Says he wonders what the courts would think, if they'd be okay with it. Chances are they wouldn't, he says. They'd find your mother unfit.

I feel anger, red hot, watching you cry those tears. What right has he got just barging in here?

But he doesn't even look at me. It's like I'm invisible. He holds out his hand and smiles that smile. Says if you come back with him now, he'll forget the whole thing. No courts. No law. He'll keep Sarah safe.

Well, I'm done putting up with him and his friends. I'm not gonna stand here and watch him hurt you, babe. Right now it ends.

I take a step toward him, raising my fists. He smiles and shakes his head, and the doorman does the rest.

Down on the floor, the pain's ripping up my guts. Try to stand up and fight, but it's just no good. Doorman's got a hammer for a hand, and the barman probably does too. The owner man looks at me with pity, and then he looks at you.

The world stands still as you stand there in tears. Your sadness is all too real, and so is my fear.

I see it all come apart, babe. You look at him and nod your head, trying not to look at me. You drop that picture and he covers you with his jacket, telling you it'll be all right. It's gonna be different now. He swears that it's true. Won't be like it was before. He'll take care of Sarah. He'll take care of you.

I can't believe it. His arm's on your shoulder now. You're heading for the door. You and him are walking out.

I start yelling, begging you to stop. Grab onto the bed, but I still can't get up.

The owner man turns back and looks at me again. Tells me not to take it so hard. Some days a man wins, he says. Tonight I lost.

I try one more time. I beg you to stay. I plead. I cry. But you still won't look at me.

I watch you walk away.

Your room goes quiet, baby. No sound except a car out on the street. I sit here and ask myself why. Thought it was you and me. Thought it was always and forever, and no in-betweens. Thought all these weeks together had meant something. Just two people trying to make their own way. Call it love or something else.

Call it fate.

The minutes pass and no reason comes. Just me and my pain in the neon light. Then I see it sitting there on the floor in front of me. Something small and square and white.

Reach out and pick it up, flip it over to see the other side. Two people sitting in a dining room somewhere. The owner man and a little girl who has your eyes.

♦♦♦

I'm driving now, baby. This highway don't ever seem to end. I'm heading to the horizon where the sun won't rise. Sometimes I think I see something there.

Just a flash. A flicker. A moment, and then it's gone.

I hear the sky thundering. But the rain don't ever come.

I've been through towns like the one I left behind. Seen the plywood on the windows and the out-of-business signs. Seen the bars and the clubs and the neon glowing bright, the curves and the smiles that I can buy for a special price.

I've been everywhere and seen everything, and it just ain't ever enough. These wheels are always turning. Don't know if they'll ever stop.

I smoke Luckies and listen to the radio, searching the highway as the headlights cut the dark. But this highway goes on forever, and I got a dead end road in the middle of my heart.

I think about you all the time, your smile on that first night. I think about what you said to me, how you can leave it all behind. I'm not saying you were wrong, but somehow I think, babe, that you've got nothing when you come into this world and you've got nothing when you die. If you got nothing in the middle, then you ain't lived no kind of life.

But I just keep driving, baby. Don't even know why.

Local Hero

Tom Pitts

"Vodka grapefruit."

"You still drinkin' that shit?" Taggart looked at Ronny, his upper lip curled into a sneer as he twisted a dingy bar rag into a wet glass. "I thought only old ladies order drinks like that."

It was the same drink Ronny had been ordering for years. Taggart had been making that same crack about it for years, too. Ronny watched Taggart go behind the bar and mix the drink. He always poured light, the son of a bitch. Every other bartender poured heavy for him—out of respect. Respect because he was a regular, respect for what he'd once been.

Taggart sat the drink down in front of him. "Here you go, ma'am."

Ronny didn't answer. He poked the straw in between his lips and sucked back the day's first swallow. He hated Taggart—hated him ever since high school when Taggart was just another loser getting stoned behind the woodshop. But things were different then. Taggart and his greasy buddies didn't even have the balls to speak to someone like him. Ronny was a local hero. He started, batted cleanup, was the closer, too. It didn't matter, he did it all. He made the front page of the paper; colleges and scouts were sniffing around. He was throwing pitches over one hundred miles an hour, curveballs a specialty. On the outside, right above the knee. He could draw anyone out, make them look like they were swatting at flies. *Low and Away*, that's what they all called him. Nobody came close.

"You decided to come back." Brenda set her tray beside Ronny and leaned into the bar. The comment was a running joke between them that had been running for years. Of course he came back—he had nowhere else to go.

"What are you doing here?" Ronny said. "I thought you didn't start till nine."

"Sheila's sick, so I'm picking up her slack. I been here since six."

"Shit, if I'da known that I woulda sat at a table instead of having to deal with this prick." Ronny hooked a thumb in Taggart's direction.

"Oh, he's all right," Brenda said. "Once you get to know him."

Ronny knew Brenda had been seeing Taggart for the last couple of months and it ate him up inside. Brenda was the one that got away. He'd overlooked her back in high school because he thought his luck was never going to end. Life was going to be an endless ride of pussy and money. That all ended one day in the top of the sixth when he heard his elbow pop. It all stopped, the girls, the offers—the respect. In the time it took to throw one pitch, Ronny's life was effectively over.

She touched his forearm lightly. "When you need another, let me know. I'll get it for you."

He started to say thank you, but she was already sliding her tray down the bar. He watched her move away toward Taggart. Bleach-blonde hair tied back in a ponytail, dark roots crowning her skull, she still retained her figure from when they were teens. She looked as good as the first day he met her. Brenda Beckett, the smart, shy girl whose wholesome good looks were easy to miss. Easy for Ronny anyway. It wasn't until she was serving him drinks that he realized how beautiful she was. And now she was with that piece-of-shit Taggart, with his long, greasy hair, smattering of homemade tattoos, and heavy metal T-shirts.

Ronny took in their exchange, noticed the warm look of supplication she offered him and the snide annoyance he returned. He lifted his glass and sucked on the straw till there was nothing but ice cubes left.

The night crawled on like so many nights before it. The same songs on the jukebox, the same stale arguments about what team would win whatever pointless game silently played on the TV, the same crowd of lonely losers who showed up every night like clockwork. Just like Ronny did. The time between drinks got shorter and who bought what got blurry. The vodka grapefruits didn't help the jukebox selection and they didn't quell the arguments, but they did help ease Ronny's focus, turning the night into a soft mellow hush, and that's all he was really looking for anyway.

Ronny let his mind drift. It was only six months ago Brenda was leaning on his shoulder. Her husband had left her with two kids and a hole in her heart. Brenda confided in him, about her sadness, about her poor choices in men. He was there for her, listening, comforting, playing the hero once again. Ronny thought he may still have a chance.

Benny the bar-back kicked everyone out at a quarter till two. Everyone but a few chosen regulars who were allowed to finish their drinks while Taggart wiped down the bar. Tonight it was just Ronny and some old drunk who Benny was already shuffling out the door.

"Ronny, finish up. You only got a few minutes," Benny said as he stacked the stools upside down on the counter.

Ronny gripped his drink like his life depended on it. In many ways, it did. The jukebox was dead and the only noise in the bar was Brenda and Taggart's arguing. Ronny turned on his stool and watched their animated exchange. She stood in front of Taggart, hands on her hips, defiant, while he spat words into her face, punctuating them with his long, bony finger.

Ronny felt a hand at his elbow. It was Benny, smiling cautiously. "C'mon, Ron. It's time to go."

Ronny slipped off his stool and set his glass on the bar. It toppled over and sent ice cubes skating across the mahogany.

"It's all right," Benny said, "I'll take care of it."

Benny must be good at his job, because the next thing Ronny knew he was standing alone in the parking lot, leaning on a car and feeling his jacket for a pack of smokes. He found it and fished out the last cigarette. The cool night air felt good on his skin, and Ronny stood smoking, gearing up for the long walk home.

He saw two silhouettes near the bar's entrance. Brenda and Taggart. They seemed to be arguing still, their hot breath blowing clouds of anger into the night air.

Their voices began to rise. Only Brenda's clipped curses were audible to Ronny, the rest a clashed crescendo of a lover's quarrel. He watched as Taggart's finger poked into Brenda's chest. After a few pointed jabs, she slapped him. Hard enough for Ronny to hear the smack across the parking lot. There was a pause, a cold breath between them, then Taggart shoved her backward. She stumbled on her heels, shaken and embarrassed.

"I told you," Taggart said, "I don't give a fuck what you think! I'll be home when I get there."

Ronny sucked in one last drag from his cigarette and flicked the butt into the darkness. He took two steps toward them. "Hey!"

"What do you want, fuckface? Bar's closed—fuck off."

Ronny started to speak, but the syllables tangled on his tongue.

Brenda pulled back her hand to slap him again, but Taggart caught her wrist and squeezed it tight. "Bitch, try that again and I'm gonna give you a fuckin' beating."

Ronny had heard enough. He closed the gap between them with quick long strides. "Let her go, Taggart, you fuckin' asshole."

Taggart let go of her wrist and gave her another shove. This one hard enough to send Brenda back onto her ass. As soon as she hit the gravel, Ronny moved in between them, chin out, chest puffed, giving Taggart his best hard-look. "Enough," he said. "Leave her alone."

Taggart seemed as though he was going to say something. His lips peeled back across his teeth forming a sick smile. But, instead of speaking, he punched Ronny in the stomach. Deep and hard. A gust of wind expelled from Ronny's lungs as he doubled over.

"What the fuck you gonna do about it, Low and Away? You drunk piece of shit."

Ronny was still doubled over. The pain had not yet registered, but he'd lost muscle control. He was winded and helpless, staring at the dirty ground. Then he felt something squeezing his neck. Fingernails, digging in. From his folded position, he still saw both of Taggart's fists, still balled up in front of him. The fingernails dug deeper and pulled him up and backward.

Behind him, Brenda's voice squealed, "Leave him alone, Ronny. This ain't none of your business."

His airway was pinched off by the lack of oxygen and blood blackened his vision. But in front of him he could still see Taggart laughing. Ronny tried to speak, but his throat was closed off.

"You like that, Ronny?" Taggart said.

Brenda tightened her grip, pulling him back, and Ronny stumbled into her.

Taggart reached out with both hands and grabbed Ronny by the shirt, yanking him away from Brenda. He spun him around and pushed him against a car.

Ronny felt the car's cold metal hood press against his back as he smelled Taggart's sour whiskey breath pour over his face.

"You wanna be a hero, Ronny? You like to get in other people's shit? You don't know fuck all. Your days are over. You're a loser, a drunk. Nobody wants your help, nobody needs you."

Taggart kept pressing and Ronny arched backward, feeling his vertebrae scrape against the fender.

"You think you're special? Because you can throw a fucking baseball?"

Taggart's full body weight pinned Ronny now and he let go of his shirt with one hand and dug a wood-handled pocketknife out of his pocket. Ronny saw Taggart flip open a three-inch blade.

"Low and Away, huh? That's what they called you? Such a stupid fucking name. I'll give you low and away."

Taggart swung his right hand down and stabbed Ronny in the lower thigh. The knife went deep, all three inches. The pain was searing hot and shot right up to Ronny's brain. His vision flashed white as Taggart pulled out the blade and drove it in again, on the outside, right above the knee.

Taggart stepped back and let Ronny slide off the car and onto the ground, spread-eagled and motionless.

"You don't come around anymore, Ronny. You're done. Banned for life." Taggart gave Ronny a sharp kick to the balls. "I don't wanna see you near this place or talking to Brenda ever again."

Ronny lay in the gravel, the warm blood from this thigh spreading across his knee, the nauseating pain from the kick radiating up into his stomach. He couldn't move. Taggart and Brenda towered over him. She didn't say a thing. Ronny did the only thing he could do. He nodded yes.

He listened as their footfalls crunched away in the gravel, and heard Brenda finally speak. Her soft, familiar voice whispering to Taggart, "It's okay, baby. Forget him. Let's go home."

Ronny lay there thinking. Thinking about his leg, how he was going to crawl home. Thinking about Brenda. What a bitch. Thinking about the Sea Sails Tavern. He was pretty sure he knew the waitress there. Karen. It was only a few blocks from his house. Hell, he could limp there tomorrow.

Glory Days

CS DeWildt

She walked into Nate's place and, goddamn, if I didn't want to weep. BOC was pounding out of the speakers and like the man said, I was burning. I watched her from across the bar, watched her scan the darkness for a familiar face. She looked uncomfortable and I knew it wasn't the environment, but the lack of attention she was getting.

I watched her step in, watched the men step in to meet her. I watched them try to hold her attention. One after another she left them in her wake as she powered through to whatever inevitable moment she was expecting. She found the only empty table in the place and hopped up on the stool.

"Connie," I said to the waitress as she passed. "See that lone girl in the corner? Set that sweet thing up with a Soco and Coke. Tell her it's from Stimpy."

Connie smiled and gave me a wink, left me to stare across the bar as Lindsay waited for someone to notice her. Goddamn, I hadn't seen her since just after high school. It had been fifteen years, but she was unmistakable. Still lean with a great rack you just wanted to bury your face into and then fall asleep on. She was a freak too, boy. She used to invite me over nights her folks went bowling. We'd have the place to ourselves and we wouldn't do anything but watch TV until we heard the garage door open and her parents' Volvo pull into the garage. Then Lindsay would pull me by the hand to the master bedroom. We'd squeeze under her parents bed and wait, no

sound but our breath, quick and shallow as we waited for her parents
to come in and turn off the lights. We'd listen to their inane pillow
talk, stifling laughter as they fretted about things like Lindsay's
grades and her little sister Allie's bed wetting. Then, when they
finally went down, Lindsay and I would undress each other with
silent care under the bed, fucking slow until it was time to bite our
tongues for silence.

Connie stepped to the table and delivered the drink I'd ordered.
I watched Lindsay look at the gift, smiling and curious as Connie
spoke to her. Then I saw genuine excitement as she simultaneously
sipped her drink through the swizzle straw and looked over the
heads, searching for the one she knew. I took my own gin and tonic
from the bar and waded through the crowd, trying to snag my own
inevitable moment. About twenty feet away her eyes found mine,
guided me to her and made each step more desperate.

"Ms. Thing," I said.

"My Stimpy Boy." She slid off the stool and threw her arms
around my neck, draping herself on me like a piece of clothing, and
it felt like a day hadn't passed. When she finally slid her arms from
my neck, she held my shirt and looked up at me.

"Good to see you," I said.

We caught up over drinks, shouting intimately to one another
over the coarse merriment of the patrons around us. Nate's was
beginning to fill up, but the noise, the music, it didn't matter to me.
I couldn't do anything but look into Lindsay's eyes and watch her
mouth make the words that my brain scrambled to decode, the
waves awash with drunken howling and a karaoke version of Bad
Company.

I learned she'd been married practically ever since I left. She said
his name, said he was in school with us, but I couldn't place him.

"What about you?" she said.

"Went out west. Tried to be a cowboy. Didn't work out."

"You married?"

I told her how Jenny had kicked my ass out a few months before. Told her I was using the time to visit my folks, let the familiar sights sweep over me, and bask in the nostalgia of youthful places. I didn't tell her that I was broke and being sued and that I didn't know how long I'd be in my parents' basement. I tucked those things away for down the road. Lindsay suggested we talk someplace quiet.

My car was someplace quiet. And while it wasn't under her parents bed it was a new experience for me, not fucking in the car, but I had never had a woman ride me to climax, the whole time spilling out every nasty thought she had about her husband: how he'd ruined her life, what a controlling asshole he was, how he was Facebook friends with their babysitter. Our energy was the opposite of the quiet nervous passion I remembered. It was fifteen years of desperate want come home. It was good.

Panting, she laid on top of me, dripping, and I tasted her sweat. Then I closed my eyes and imagined we were still eighteen. I tried to fool myself into believing that everything that had happened since the last time I saw her was nothing but a dream, a dream made real by the mind, real enough to fool the mind.

I pulled her close as we lay drying on the back seat. It was cramped but we didn't complain. We laid there silent until the temperature dropped and we could see our breath.

We left together, no destination.

"This is the first night I'd been out alone in, Jesus, ten years." She laughed at the statement, a private laugh that danced deep within her dreams and memories. It took her away for just a moment. Next to me, she sat balanced on the cusp of something poised to poison her soul. She shook it off and looked at me. Driving in the dark, the steady wax and wane of the streetlights, she was the same girl I knew. The fine lines disappeared, her crows' feet hidden in shadow and eye makeup.

"You're the last person I expected to see," she said.

"Me too." I took her cigarette and used it to light my own.

"Remember our game?"

I smiled. "Of course."

"You up for a dare? When's the last time you been dared to do anything? What's her name? Jenny? She one for the dares?"

I laughed. "No. She's not."

"No? No beer runs? No stealing the cancer kids' jar from the Quick Rip? Fucking in the most awkward of place?"

"What about your man?" I said. "Where is he tonight?"

She flicked her cigarette butt out the window, letting in a rush of screaming air before answering. "Camped out in front of the tube."

I let the words mingle in the air with the smoke. We drove without speaking for a long time, listening to Creedence and driving all the back roads we used to know. Every night we were on these roads, getting high, drinking beer and sickly sweet Southern Comfort mixed with fountain Pepsi from the Port Sheldon Street Amoco.

"Hey," Lindsay said. "Come home with me."

"Run away with me."

"I'm serious," she said as she unbuckled her seatbelt. She leaned over, draped herself on me, and pressed her nose into my chest. "I didn't know how much I'd missed you. Why did you leave? Fuck it. I don't care. When I saw you, it was like the most normal thing in the world. Like you'd been on vacation."

"It hasn't been one." I held the joint in front of her face. She opened her eyes and took it and looked forward into the night, her head still on my shoulder as she sucked smoke and let out her dreams in squeaks.

"Come home with me," she said.

"You're crazy. What's your husband going to say?"

"He'll probably say he's going to kill you."

"There you go. I'm feeling too good to die."

"So kill him first," she said. "I dare you."

She passed the joint, but didn't look at me. I smiled like a goon waiting for her to acknowledge her joke, but she left me there holding the tiny roach, burning my fingers as I let it smolder. And something about being with her, it was like my brain turned back into the mush it was at eighteen. Her idea didn't sound too bad. And it wasn't much different than Ricky. That had been an accident of course. We were all partying at this county road overpass out in the sticks, private, good forest to run to if the police showed up. So Ricky and me got into it and this little pushy-shovey, and he ends up going over the side of the guardrail. I saw him hit the ground, watched him come to and sit up face first into an oncoming car, first one we ever saw out there. Road had been closed as long as we could remember. Guy in the Cutlass just took a wrong turn, got lost and crushed Ricky.

I flashed my high beams at some idiot coming toward us and looked at the top of Lindsay's head.

"Where's your house?" I asked.

She didn't say anything for a bit, just nuzzled her head against my shoulder. I burrowed into her hair. Her shampoo smelled like all the reckless promises we'd made, back when we thought we controlled our future. It took me a long time to realize that the future just drags you through the now. Kick. Scream. You're going.

She led me around the back of the house, by the hand, and we were teenagers again. The weather was crisp and silent. The only sound was the crunching of frosted grass as we maneuvered in the dark.

We moved lightly up the wooden stair to the glass double door, stopping and watching Lindsay's husband sleep in his reclining chair. The room was lit with a single bulb, a warm yellow that seemed to smile, to blanket the man in a perfect kind of oblivion.

"Now what?" I asked.

Lindsay didn't take her eyes off her husband. "Now we do it. We'll make it look like a robbery. Blast him through the window, toss the place and get the fuck out."

"You really got this figured out."

"Been planning it for years, darlin'. Just waiting on you." Her eyes lingered on me as she turned away. She stepped on a small table and grabbed the gutter, stretched her arm over the roof, sweeping and searching. Lindsay gave a grunt of approval as she found whatever she'd stashed there. She stepped down and slapped the payload into my hand. It was heavy and wrapped in dishtowels. I opened the package and saw the weapon she'd hidden. The first thing I noticed was the rust.

"How old is this thing? Jesus Christ, where did you get this?"

Lindsay shrugged.

"It's falling apart in my hands, Linds," I said as the grip literally began to separate from the rest of it.

"Don't call me Linds. And it's fine. Just, I don't know. Be careful with it."

We looked up together, nearly smiled until we saw her husband, staring out the window. We remained frozen until we realized he couldn't see us, his view obscured by the reflection of the room he was in.

"Blast him, Baby. All six."

"Linds," I said. And then the porch light was on and I was standing face to face with the man I was supposed to kill. He stared at me for a moment, like the situation was just too odd to be a threat. Then I raised the gun and he saw it. Or maybe he saw it and then I raised it. And I did it. Messy. Noisy and messy.

Lindsay watched the body for a moment before elbowing past me and stepping through the shattered doorway, mindful of the glass and blood. "Wait," she said. "Stay here."

I wondered if anyone had heard. I looked over the back yard and I noticed for the first time that the house was set on a lake. A yellow pedal boat glowed in the moonlight, half on the water, half beached. It was late and I saw few lights around the shore. I listened for any kind of chatter and there was nothing. I stood silent and looked at the water as the warmth of the house rushed out behind me, making the rest of me that much colder.

"Come on," Lindsay said. I turned around and saw her head poke out from the hallway beyond the room, a few steps away from her dead husband.

I entered with the same care she had and followed her into the hallway. She checked to see if I was behind her and waved me into a room at the opposite end of the house. I stepped into the master bedroom and found her seated on the bed.

"Stop," she said with a wry grin. "Close your eyes."

"I need to get out of here Lindsay. *We* do."

"This will only take a sec."

I remembered the girl again, full of surprises. I grinned and shut my eyes tight. I waited. Time slowed.

"How much insurance is he worth?" I said, staring into the blackness behind my eyes.

"Tons," she said.

"You really think this is going to work?"

"Worth a shot," she laughed. "Open."

And then I got the joke. I really did. Even if I hadn't already unloaded with the crumbling thirty-eight, I don't think I was fast enough to get the draw on her. She already had a bead on me with a hand cannon of her own, barrel so wide I could put a finger in easy.

"Linds, listen—"

"I said don't call me that!" The barrel of her piece was stone still.

"Lindsay. Please. Don't."

"You put yourself here," she said. "Now deal with it. We're not kids anymore."

Queen of the Supermarket
Chuck Wendig

Cal loves Ginny Dell, loves her the way the cat loves milk, needs her the way a junkie needs shit in his veins, wants her the way a bird wants the sky.

She's over there by the conveyor, running onions and milk and Ovaltine across the winking red laser, *boop, boop, boop*, and sometimes she just stares down at it—the light up in her eye like the stare of a star, her berry-red hair cascading down around her face the way curtains frame a window.

Cal wants to have her, wants to take her away from this place. Wants to hold her close and smell her shampoo—Garnier Fructis; he knows that's what she uses because he knows her better than she thinks. That and this generic face-washing cleanser. And an acne rinse. It all adds up to her smell.

He hovers. Wishing he could smell her from here but he can't so he contents himself with watching instead. From behind the aisle with the apples and the pears and oranges. From around the corner where they keep the cookies. Everything is bright white under the store lights, everything is a hard smack of color that makes him feel dizzy, makes everything feel alive and insane; it's a circus and for a moment he feels like it's all gonna fall away—the whole store plunging into darkness while leaving him and Ginny up in the clouds. Like a coupla angels.

Ginny's got a boyfriend. Danny Reese. Punk-fuck kid, just buzzing around her like a fly buzzing around a flower. Doesn't deserve her. He's a nowhere boy, driving through life without any place to go, like everything is a dark tunnel with no end. Maybe Danny thinks Ginny is the light through the shadow but Cal thinks Danny's just a user and he'll get bored and break her heart and that's when Cal will have to break Danny's fingers. And his toes. Knees. Elbows. Leave the rest of him intact, a floppy octopus. Just a useless torso rolling around.

Cal checks his watch. He's gotta go. Shit. Shit! Back to work.

He gets in her line. It's a long line. Because they all know she's the queen of this place, the pretty, pretty teenage queen.

Cal puts just a few things on the conveyor—he can't afford much more than what's here, and if he could he'd put everything on the black belt just so he could stand there for a long time while she checked him out, *boop boop boop*, maybe giving him a chance to catch that shampoo smell.

But that's not to be. So instead he's got some canned asparagus, a box of store-brand Oreos, a tin of potted meat.

And then he's up.

And she grabs the asparagus—

Boop.

And she grabs the box of not-quite-Oreos—

Boop.

Then finally, the tin of meat—

Boop.

And he thinks, Jesus, she's not even gonna look up, she's just gonna stare through her hair at the screen and miss him entirely. And that's a helluva thing, a thing that would leave a pit inside of him hungry for the light—

So Cal tries clearing his throat a little bit.

Then again when she doesn't flinch.

Finally: "That'll be six bucks," she says, looking up.

Her eyes meet his.

Her eyes are almost gray. Not like a cloudy day. But like a silver watchband. Like a flashing nickel. Her mouth tugs into a little smile.

"Hey, Daddy," she says.

"Hey, Gin," Cal says. Licking his lips. "Still queen of the supermarket, huh?"

"Quit it, Daddy."

He laughs, a kind of nervous *heh heh heh*, and then he gives her his credit card with hands he hopes she doesn't see shaking.

He pays. He signs. She clacks her teeth, bored of him already.

"Bye, Daddy. I won't be home for dinner."

"Oh."

"Date with Danny." She shrugs.

"Sure, sure. I'll tell your mother."

And then he's out the automatic doors without even realizing it, and she's back there scanning some other customer's shit, and on the way out who does he see pulling into the broken asphalt lot but Danny Reese, that punk-fuck fly-buzz of a kid, and Cal thinks, *I got that 9mm in my glove compartment*, and so looks like Ginny won't get to have that date tonight after all.

Something in the Night
Mike Creeden

"Turn it up," Kenny said from the backseat. "So I don't have to think."

Rego glared in the rearview, arched eyebrows saying, *Really, little man?* But he tapped it up anyway, and Joe Strummer screamed louder about getting fucked up and violent.

Next to Kenny, Melissa gave a snort, but whether it was approval or mockery, Kenny couldn't tell. That was part of his problem: he never knew when he was being fucked with.

Kenny watched Melissa staring into the velvety darkness of Route 88, the ten-mile road that led from Fall River to Westport, from the vacant mills to rolling farmland to Horseneck Beach, where dreams came true. They had a case of beer on ice, and they were finally going to get what they'd been waiting for.

They'd paired up by weight class. Brenda, six-two in her worn-down heels and wide enough to spill some thigh over the bucket seat, sat up front with Rego, while Kenny and Melissa, the wiry and silent wannabe rockers, took the back.

These girls weren't biker chicks, Kenny told himself. They just hung out at a biker bar. The Depot—AKA, the Creepo—sat across the parking lot from Food Mart, the cut-rate supermarket where the guys worked produce. Sometimes, when he was out shagging carriages, Kenny spied Melissa with Doozum, the massive, aging biker with the long, gray ponytail. Rumor was he'd been sergeant-at-arms for the Sidewinders M.C. Now he was just the Neanderthal screwing the girl Kenny crushed on. Melissa came across tough, with her nose piercing and tattooed wrists, but Kenny knew she was more than just some biker skank. Some nights, when the girls got tired of eating BBQ chips and pretzels at the bar, they'd come in to the store to buy a sandwich from the deli, or an apple or some strawberries from produce. When she came in alone, Melissa would drift over to Kenny and wait for him to say something. The best he could do was quote song lyrics and movie lines. Melissa would stare with those dollar green eyes and wait. He'd choke on his lines, until one of them would make a joke about how bad the produce looked, then Melissa would flash an *it's OK* smile and take her banged-up apple to the register and leave.

Today was different, though. Kenny was feeling badass, slicing open orange cases with a fresh cutter blade, dumping oranges onto a pile, making a waterfall display.

Melissa came in alone. She seemed upset, lingered at the opposite end of the orange table. Kenny sheathed his cutter, stuffed it in his back pocket and walked around. And he saw the bruise.

Actually, he saw it before he walked over—that was the fucked-up part. Seeing her like that, the yellowing discoloration up near her eye, like another smacked-around Fall River girl—*that's* what gave him the guts to talk to her.

"What's up?" He pulled his cutter out and did some gratuitous trimming of the boxes on her side of the table.

She shrugged. "Same old shit."

Then Kenny found some stones, like some other guy had stepped into his smock. He said, "Yeah? Well how about we do some different shit? Maybe go for a drive?"

It took her a second to recover. "Maybe down Horseneck?"

Kenny nodded. Rego poked his head through the plastic curtains of the back room and watched them.

The new Kenny jerked his head toward Rego. "Bring Brenda, I'll bring him, we'll have a party."

Melissa looked out into the parking lot. "Yeah? How about tonight?"

♦♦♦

Brenda checked herself in the visor mirror then pulled it lower to look in back. "You kids OK? Don't do nothin' I wouldn't."

Melissa flashed a pained smile. She might have been anywhere from nineteen to thirty. She hadn't gone to Durfee, because with Kenny eighteen and Rego almost twenty-three, they had ten years of high school covered. Her accent was western or something, and she didn't look Fall River. She was pretty.

"God, all these crosses," Melissa said. "It's crazy."

"Look how dark this road is," Brenda said. "People driving on it, hammered out of their minds."

Kenny wanted to say you could ride it till dawn without seeing anyone, but he refrained, kept staring at Melissa. As they approached the light, Brenda said, "Drift Road," and tapped on her window.

Melissa looked up. "I know a house on Horseneck. Wanna check it out?"

Kenny felt a twinge of something, like an alarm going off, but he shrugged.

When Rego said, "All right," it was about as soft as he ever said anything.

Rego turned left on Drift, then right onto Horseneck, driving past the farms and toward the marshes that led to the rocky shore, and when Brenda rolled down her window Kenny smelled the salt air and it made him feel wasted. Melissa squeezed his knee and he leaned over into a sloppy kiss. He was just getting going when Brenda said, "Slow down. It's on the left."

They pulled onto a tire track road and drove fifty feet to a gate. Brenda got out, unlocked and swung it open, then walked to the car.

"Should we close that thing?" Rego asked.

"No," Melissa said. "Leave it open."

Half mile later, the house came into view. It was little more than a shack, but it had a front porch with some chairs and a barbecue pit. Broken-down motorcycles were parked near the house. Rego pulled up, nodded toward the bikes. "Whose are those?"

Melissa stared at the bikes. "Doozum's."

"He lives here?" Kenny's voice went up an octave.

Melissa shrugged. "He comes by once in a while."

"Will he be coming here tonight?" Rego asked. "'Cause I'm cool with going to the beach. Beach is feeling good to me right now."

Brenda cocked her head and flashed Rego a dirty smile. She wasn't bad, if you were into big. "You want to get sand in your ass or you want a bed?" Brenda leaned back into the seat and did something that made Rego's eyes bug.

"Let's go inside," Rego said.

Melissa led Kenny to a small bedroom in back with a mattress and box spring on the floor, made up with clean blue sheets and a quilt. On a poster above the bed, Keith Richards lay elegantly wasted, nodding out on a backstage floor with a scarf around his neck and a lifeless hand draped across his chest. In the far corner of the room, a worn recliner sat near a low bookshelf. Near the chair, a small table with a clean ashtray on it, on the wall straight ahead a wardrobe. Kenny knew that if he opened it, he would find her clothes.

"You live here, don't you?"

Melissa stared at the poster, her back to Kenny. "No. Why do you say that?"

In the house, a door closed. Outside, a car engine started. Kenny looked into the living room, before closing the door. "You seem comfortable here, and"—he gestured to the poster and the bookshelf—"this stuff seems like you."

"You don't know me," she said, walking toward him. "How do you know how I seem?"

They started kissing and fell onto the mattress and in a few minutes, the heat that had been lying in wait fell on them. They pushed against each other, sweating furiously. Clothes ripped off, thrown to the floor. The room smelled animal. He loved it. He was finally living. Then she pushed him off and got up onto all fours and faced Keith Richards.

"First time I have to do it this way. That all right?"

He'd never done it that way, so he pressed his stomach against her ass and fumbled around, as if he were too drunk to find his way in. She reached back and guided him. Grinding, Kenny stared at Keith, half expecting Richards to open his eyes and flash that rotten-toothed grin. Melissa moved easily and Kenny studied the taut muscles in her upper back as she braced herself. She whipped her head around as they went at it, and when the hair came off her right shoulder he saw the tattoo: *Property of Doozum, Sidewinders, M.C.* Off in the distance, he thought he heard the roar of a motorcycle. He listened for signs of life in the house but it remained quiet.

"Come on!" She reached down, stroked him. "Why'd you stop?"

She caught him looking at the tattoo.

"It's just ink. Words. Don't mean anything." She punched at him with her ass. "Come on!"

He tried to act like the guy he'd been earlier that day, in the store, and for a few minutes it worked. When the motorcycle pulled up, the sound hardly registered. When the front door slammed, Kenny told himself it was Rego and Big Brenda.

"They're having fun, huh?"

Melissa didn't respond. She looked at the bedroom door and poked her ass at him, rhythmically, like tapping her fingers.

Steps pounded toward the room. Kenny wondered why Rego would walk in on them. The door swung open and a flesh-covered refrigerator with the patchy gray beard and Geronimo ponytail stepped into the room.

Doozum stank of acrid, old man sweat spiced with whiskey and motorcycle grease. Melissa stopped bucking, but her hair kept swinging. When her hair stops moving, Kenny thought, I will be dead. Keith Richards dozed on.

"The fuck is this? Who's he?"

Melissa's juice dripped down Kenny's leg. His hand was on her waist; he felt her belly rise and fall with each breath. A drop fell out of her and hit the bed with a tiny pock. Where was Rego?

"It's all right for you to get your strange on," Melissa said, her voice harsh and nasty. "Well, tonight I'm getting mine on."

"The fuck you are."

In two quick steps, Doozum was at the bed and Kenny was staring at the giant thigh wrapped in worn, greasy denim. "The fuck away from her!"

The backhand was like a 10-lb. sack of potatoes to the face. Kenny's neck snapped back as he flew off the bed and landed in the pile of their clothes. He fumbled for his jeans and crawled behind the recliner as Doozum went after Melissa. She was still on all fours on the bed, as if waiting for someone to leapfrog over her. Doozum put a boot to her instead. It hit her in the rib cage, between her belly and breasts, lifting her off the bed and sending her into the wall.

"I can't believe you'd do this to me, you bitch."

Doozum stepped toward her, fist raised over his head like a club. Kenny stepped into his jeans and looked around the room for a weapon. The cheap furniture in this room was useless. All plywood and corkboard, it couldn't hurt a cat. Pulling up his jeans, he felt something in the back pocket. His box cutter.

"Stop!" Kenny shouted.

Doozum spun and stepped toward him. "You want to go first?"

He moved fast, and Kenny could see now that the guy was much younger than he'd originally thought, only about forty or so. Kenny flipped the recliner into the biker's knee, and when Doozum bent to swat it out of the way, Kenny leaned in. With a downward slashing motion, he swung the cutter at Doozum's face.

It was a pathetic swing, the kind you'd make to mock someone who didn't know how to throw a punch, but he got lucky. Doozum looked up at just the right moment, eyes bugging as the blade came at him, mouth slack in shock.

The razor cut clean through the ball of his nose. Blood bubbled out and a chunk of flesh plopped onto the back of the overturned recliner and lay there, like a bit of coughed-up meat.

Doozum made a gagging sound and reached forward. Kenny grabbed the ponytail and pulled. The biker fell and landed sprawled across the chair, which broke under his weight.

Melissa sat naked on the bed, legs splayed in front of her, eyes wide with surprise. Kenny threw her jeans and T-shirt at her and picked up his shirt and boots.

"Let's go!"

They stepped around Doozum, who lay there moaning, and ran to the door, pulling it shut.

In the driveway the motorcycle was parked where Rego's car had been.

"Where the fuck is Rego? Why did he leave me here?"

Melissa looked guilty, but more beautiful and alive than Kenny had ever seen her before. He'd be chasing that look for the rest of his life.

"I told him to leave us," she said. "Sorry. I didn't think it was going down like this."

Kenny looked at the motorcycle as he heard Doozum thrash inside the house.

"Can you drive it?" she asked.

"No, but I can push it over."

It was harder than he thought but he toppled the bike to the ground.

Doozum stepped onto the porch, blood pouring out of the red hole in the middle of his face. "You fucks!"

Kenny pointed across the yard. It was a half-mile of grass, then marsh, then the rocky shoreline. People would be there, parking, getting drunk, screwing by the water.

"Follow me," he said.

She put her sandals down, stepped into them and looked up at him with a smile.

He took her by the hand, and they tore off into the night.

Rosalita

Rob Pierce

So, I'm talking to Rosalita in this Spanish café, and—"Hey, will you guys shut the fuck up with those guitars? You gonna play all night *and* all day?"

The Ghost of Jim Toad

David James Keaton

Okay, remember that building where I used to live back in Nashville? Like most of those apartments, the building was old as fuck and sagging, but the decks were all new and straight lines, so it was like walking onto a lumberjack contest when you went out back. I was living there with Peggy, and you know how she was a talker, but I don't think we were used to sitting on a deck, smoking, talking smack, because otherwise we would have shown a little discretion about some of the shit we were saying out loud, Peggy anyway. But everyone was out there doing the same thing. Most of the people didn't have a nice, level-headed deck before to pretend they were normal.

We were on the third floor, right between all the neighbors. Below us was April and her creepy mom, Brenda, I think. I just call her Doris, because it rhymes with "Loris." You ever see those videos of the "slow Loris"? Bitch looks exactly like one but doesn't move nearly that fast. One time, she waddled out and showed Peg her bandages from her last suicide attempt, which invokes sympathy in some, but usually makes me imagine someone holding out a pile of dog shit and saying, "Look what I almost stepped in!" And April, she was never home. She bartended every night, and most of the time she was hooking up with some barfly and creeping in at dawn, nice and early so she could wake up Garbage Dog.

I'll get to that fucking monster in a minute.

So it was mostly just Slow Doris up there, creaking around, peeking down the steps that connect us since Doris used to steal Peg's cigarettes, too. And her green lighter, not that we could ever prove it. I ended up threatening the maintenance guy instead when I saw him smoking, might have got him fired since this was in a red state and the poor bastard was black. All I know is he never came back for his hammer, and it was a nice hammer. Oh well, collateral damage. Like he never stole a lighter before.

Now, on the ground floor was the main event. Some tall, skinny kid we called Hendrix after we caught him burning a guitar in the barrel the day we moved in. Actually, it turned out an ex-girlfriend had torched his guitar earlier, and he was just trying to save it, but all we saw was him waving his hands like a witchdoctor over the flames like Jimi at Woodstock. And Hendrix had this Chihuahua named Tom Joad, which we thought was kind of pretentious until we realized it was named after Springsteen instead of Steinbeck. Tom Joad was a gnarly little rat, yeah, but at least he wasn't Garbage Dog, so we kind of liked him. He was tiny and purple and green around the edges from some homemade Mariachi costume Hendrix forced on him in the winter, so Peg started calling him "Jim Toad' instead, because maybe Tom Joad had a Mexican buddy named Jim. Who can say? Still a hell of a lot better name than anything in *Grapes of Wrath*.

Wait, in the apartment directly above me was Cindy. At least that's what was on the mailbox. We never saw her. And above her are anywhere from two to five assholes, but they don't count either. Frat types, baseball caps. No idea. It just got noisy sometimes, or someone would be out in the backyard navigating the dog shit to play cornhole, and it was always them. They were funny at first, then after the third night we listened to them one-upping each other with finger-banging flashbacks or whatever, we lost interest. One time, I *thought* we were hearing an honest-to-Christ argument, full of passion and hate and betrayal, but, nope. It turned out it was the drive-thru at the McDonald's.

Or some girl Hendrix just broke up with working at McDonald's, yelling out the speaker trying to get his attention. The way the alley is set up, that shit is loud. I know he heard her.

But, yeah, Hendrix was a trip. When we were out there on the deck, we'd hear him down below smooth-talking some female, and the way he laid in, you'd be surprised to know that this skinny Mac Daddy punk was sporting a mouthful of chrome. Here he was, about a hundred pounds, almost six foot, voice like Al Green . . . and braces that filled every inch of his face. I kind of loved looking at him though. He was like a James Bond villain, or at least the villain's nephew. Every time I'd see him walking Jim Toad, I'd smile just to get one back and watch his lips work to cover those huge metal chompers. I didn't even realize they still made braces out of car parts. I thought that shit was all plastic now. He was a cool kid though, at first. Never really said, "Hi," but always said, "Say, 'Hi!' Say, 'Hi!'" Which was probably worse. But I figured maybe he'd get more chatty once the braces finally came off, like that kid in the movie who could throw a 90-mile-an-hour fastball once he lost his cast. I used to swear to Peg, or anyone else listening to us through the roof and floor of our deck, that one day I'd get him talking fast enough while he still had that smooth metal mouth of his, and I'd see those sparks flying for myself.

So I feel like shit after what happened. One night, way late, I'm sitting on my deck, watching the end of my cigarette flicker, watching for Slow Doris to come sniffing around to steal one, and I hear glass shattering somewhere in one of the apartments. So I creep down, and after seeing a giant hole in the door below us, I called 911. I wait out there until I see the cops come, flashlights bobbing around near the gas meters for awhile like the super sleuths they are, then I hear them finally roust Hendrix, who is hammered from a night at the bar breaking up with somebody of course, and I hear Hendrix say he was locked out and had to break his own door to get back in. It's the most I've ever heard him talk to a man, but the crime is solved. I start to doze off in my camping chair, and fifteen minutes later Hendrix is running up and down the alley and the McDonald's parking lot screaming, "Tom Joooooood! Tom Joooooood!" because either him or the police accidentally let the dog out during all the ruckus. Feeling guilty as hell and knowing it's a full moon (and realizing this is the widest I might ever see that mouth), I run down hoping for a laser-light show off those incisors. "Jim Tooooooad!!!" He's screaming so loud that I'd put three exclamation points on it if that was even allowed, so I know there's got to be sparks coming out of him by now.

As I put my boots on, I start to wonder. Is that the danger of metal in your mouth? All that hardware has got to be worse than a megaphone, almost battery powered. They say people can pick up radio stations on their fillings. How about broadcast from their braces? 57 Channels and nothing on but Hendrix. Turned out it wasn't sparks I got to see, just the street light reflecting off them, but it was still an impressive display of fireworks.

But I do try to help him, fully accepting my punishment of wandering the streets with this drunk kid, shaking bushes looking for his green Chihuahua with the goofy name, and this is what we're doing for three fucking hours. I have no idea if he knows it was me who called the cops, but I figure he must at least suspect it. But I'm not gonna bring it up, with him half-crying over his toad. I keep kicking around, and we jump every time a walnut drops from the tree next door, thinking it's Jim. Or Tom. Whoever. At one point, I wreck another neighbor's bush, uprooting it to look for something that was rustling in there like Cool Hand Luke signaling a piss. I point out my landscaping to Hendrix and say, "Is that him in here? I think that's him." But he won't even look over. He's on his cellphone with some ex, and he shrugs me off with a "No, not him, yo." I gut the whole stretch of Celery trees anyway, which is doing everyone a favor since they smell like jizz (an anomaly the landlord used to blame on Hendrix) but find nothing. No cat, no rabbit, no clue. Something had to be in there along that house, but Hendrix is too busy calling everyone he knows for some reason, crying into his phone for sympathy and refusing to make eye contact with me. I start thinking, "Yeah, he knows it was me who called the cops," and figure my work here is done.

And when birds start chirping and the morning in threatening, I notice that both the front and back door of his apartment are wide open, and I officially declare the rescue effort too flawed to be a part of. I go back up and climb into bed, trying to wake up Peg and tell her the story, hoping she'll tell me it's not my fault, but not really, and she's like, "Yeah, you fucked up."

Then it's a week later, still no Jim Toad. Then it's a month. Then we run into Hendrix at the art fair. He's with another girl, of course, and I get him talking about that night, you know, wondering who called the cops. It's weird, but he doesn't even talk about Jim Toad, that dog he was crying over right in front of me. Instead, he's just trying to figure out who was to blame. I lie and play along and avoid eye contact, but there's something about him that's off, and it doesn't hit me until later that his braces are gone.

This bothers me for some reason, and I start looking in the alley again for the dog, even splashing around in the little babbling brook next to the McDonald's drive-thru, figuring if a stray could survive anywhere for a month, it's next to a fast-food joint. I'm all over their lot every free chance I get, only stopping when a voice comes out of the speaker telling me I need a car to be served at the drive-thru. I'll want to say something about McDonald's being the biggest eavesdropping disappointment in my life, how maybe all my trips through the drive-thru were action-packed or something because all these motherfuckers ever did was order food or cry over their boyfriends, but instead I'll yell something about what kind of idiot puts a running stream next to a microphone?

And every time I thought I'd start forgetting about Jim Toad, I'd run into Garbage Dog, April's timorous monster, and I'd be thinking like the dad in *Stand By Me*, "It should have been you, Gordie." And it's true, it should have been Garbage Dog. So many nights I'd stare at Garbage Dog and his tumors and yelping and his slobbering happy face pushing the corners loose on our screen door, and I'd imagine sending him to a quiet place far away. Nothing violent like with my new hammer or anything, but maybe getting him in a headlock and sending him straight to Garbage Heaven, whispering in his torn ear the entire time, "Shhhh, shhhh. Tell Jim I'm sorry." Or maybe just, "Say 'Hi!' Say, 'Hi!'"

Seriously, if it had been Garbage Dog, I would have slept like a baby after letting it loose, instead of being responsible for the loss of the dog equivalent of a green, shivering naked old man. Not that it was ever restrained from shitting everywhere and anywhere anyway. Peg called Garbage Dog my spirit animal, and it's the closest I ever came to leaving her. Or adopting a dog.

Speaking of everywhere and anywhere, I know we have a walnut tree next door that's kind of noisy, and we live in an old creaky house with hardwood floors, but I know Jim Toad is still living on this block. There's just no way he's not around. How far could that Benjamin Button little fuck run without assistance? I never even saw him walk on one of their famous walks. He could have been trying to get his backpack to say, "Hi!" for all I know. And I never really cared for Steinbeck, but this experience has definitely affected my enjoyment of any Springsteen songs with a harmonica in it, which covers about six thousand and seventy-three of them.

I see Hendrix about five more times, and I try to bring up Jim, get some indication that he's still looking, that he even gives a shit. I even make sure I'm at that same art fair a year later, milling around in front of the booth where some hippie asshole spends her spare time covering dragonflies in scalding plastic to pretend they're amber paperweights. Hendrix loves those things, I guess, or maybe the hippie selling them, but not enough to drop forty bucks. He just hangs around her booth to fondle those big plastic balls, and when I see him again, I imagine Jim Toad frozen in one of those like he's stumbled onto a fortune teller, and there's a little movie projected on the dragonfly of Jim sizzling at the bottom of the McDonald's grease trap in the back of our alley.

I pretty much confess this time, saying, "Whoever called the cops, they may have been pretending to do a good thing, but it was really a bad thing, right? And they should feel bad?"

He says nothing.

"I mean you should feel bad, right?" Still nothing.

He keeps changing the subject, but not in that "It's too painful to talk about" kind of way. It's the "don't give a shit" kind of way. And his teeth are so straight I can't even hear him really. 57 channels and nothing on, for real.

So some time later, I can't remember when, I crawl into his apartment when he's sleeping, which is really easy since he's never fixed that hole he made when he broke in, and I take my new hammer and give him two shots with it while he sleeps. Just two for some reason. One to make sure he stays sleeping and the other to see if I can bring back the sparks. He wakes up between the hammer strikes, and even though he's conscious for about a second and half, for about the time it takes Bruce to suck in on that mournful harmonica between notes, I still have time to talk to him.

"I'm sorry I lost your dog, but can't you see we're bad people?"

The hammer hits his teeth, and I can see why the ladies love him. His smile lights up the room.

What Love Can Do

Peter Farris

My father built the house

From the ground up

And I remember my brothers and me

Pressing our hands

Into the cement foundation

Of a brand new swing set

To mark the occasion

Then he left us

And my mother raised three boys

All by herself

The hell we must have been

Roaming the woods and trails

Me and my brothers

All bruises and cuts

What's wrong with Momma? They'd ask me

Me being the oldest

Grownup problems, I'd say

Trying to explain why Momma sat at the kitchen table

Night after night

Crying into her hands

◆◆◆

The bank didn't care

They took the house

Our house

◆◆◆

I've been watching them now

For a few months

From a stand in the woods

She leaves at six

He at eight

♦♦♦

He walks around the yard

pulling weeds, cutting grass, planting flowers

She brings him iced tea

He takes her hand, kisses it, then rubs her belly

They stare at the house and smile

Our house

♦♦♦

I broke in through a basement window

Nothing was the same

The floors, the walls, the picture frames

Our pellet gun wars had left holes in the sheetrock

But they'd been patched and painted

Momma's bedroom had changed, too

The carpet gone

As was her leaky tub

The ceiling fan looked new and expensive

I opened a dresser drawer

And touched what I saw

Down the hall to Winn and Ryan's room

Where I closed my eyes, trying to see the pile of dirty clothes

Model cars, bats and balls and hunting catalogs

My brothers bouncing on their bunk beds

While Momma made supper in the kitchen

But the walls now were baby blue

And a nursery set had replaced those twin bunks

When I opened my eyes

It felt as if Winn and Ryan and Momma

Had never existed at all

♦♦♦

So I watch from the woods

And wait

Until the day

My binoculars are swapped

For a riflescope

Mansion on the Hill

Chris F. Holm

Love's a funny thing. Any poet worth a damn's spilled their share of ink trying to draw a cage that'd capture it. Half the fellas I grew up with spilled their own blood on playgrounds and in barroom brawls to do the same. And yet love don't seem as rare as that to me—or leastaways it didn't till today.

Time was, love came easy to me. Now all the sudden it seems like love and time are two things I ain't gonna see much more of. I guess at least I can say I damn sure felt its sweet caress, whatever else may come.

The first time I ever fell in love was in the back of my dad's pickup, parked out at the turnaround beside the power station on Mill Creek Road, down the slope from the sprawling old McDowell mansion. I was three weeks shy of sixteen, and three hours shy of the worst ass-whupping I ever got, on account of I was neither legal to drive nor allowed to touch my old man's truck to so much as fetch the mail from down our rutted dirt driveway.

Still, it was worth it for the hour I spent with Heather Bailey. And if my old man knew the half about what went down that warm summer night, he woulda beat me twice as bad.

I can still remember the roar of traffic from the highway, which sliced through the moonlit night just yards away—headlights strobing through the trees across our naked flesh as they passed. The brittle rise and fall of crickets in the silences between. My ragged breath. Her throaty cries. The steady hum of power lines above. God, the scent of her—soap and salt and some cheap teenager perfume that smelled like candy—mixing dizzily with the sweet pollen of the tall grass. Her lips tasting of stolen cigarettes and Southern Comfort. Me pretending to be old and wise while I stumbled terrified and shaking through the act.

Wasn't the deed itself that made me fall for her. It was holding her afterward, eyes closed, her body warm and still against me. I was overcome by the thought then that I could stay that way with her forever.

It didn't last, of course. At that age, nothing does. But three years later, I fell hard again, this time for a waitress at the diner out on 43. Sara, said her nametag, with no H. You might wonder is that important, but I say yes. I'm tryin' to paint a picture here, after all, and while I've met plenty of either spelling, it seems to me you can always tell to look at 'em just which they are, though Lord knows how.

This one was a no-H Sara through and through. And from the first time I saw her, standing over my table with her order pad in hand and smacking her gum like I was wasting her goddamn time just breathing the same air as her, I knew she was the one for me. She just looked so, I don't know, so sure and powerful, so I-don't-give-a-tiny-shit, I couldn't help but fall in love. So I flashed her my most rakish grin—you wouldn't know to look at me these days, but there was a time my smile was quite the panty-dropper— and asked her did she wanna take a ride with me when she got off shift. We didn't get but a couple hundred yards out of the parking lot before nature took its course . . . but then, it don't seem gentlemanly to tell you all the who-did-what-to-who that followed, or how her voice cracked as she called out, or none of that. I will say this, though: I lasted a damn sight longer than I did with Heather Bailey. Chalk it up to experience, I suppose, or maybe maturity—I wasn't in half as much a rush. But even still, it couldn't hold a candle to that first perfect time, that first perfect night, kissed by the hot breath of summer night beneath the mansion on the hill.

There were others after that, of course. A dozen, maybe more. Each of them my whole world, it seemed, for the short time we were together—then bleeding dry of color and detail in my mind's eye as they faded into distant memory. But never Heather Bailey. Never the details of the summer night we spent together. They were as fresh and true in my mind as if they'd happened yesterday. Even now, all I need to do to travel back to that perfect girl, that perfect then, is close my eyes.

It's funny to think if I were to pass one of the women who came after on the street today, I might not recognize her face, her curves, her lilting laugh—whatever it was that reached into the core of me and said, *That girl's the one.* But if I'm being honest with myself—and I think you'd agree the time for lying is long past—we both know that ain't gonna happen. Not that it matters—weren't any of 'em nothing more to me than a vain attempt to recapture what me and Heather had, albeit all too briefly. Heather's ghost lorded over the lot of 'em just as surely as the old McDowell place lorded over the fields and factories that sprawled below it, a glimmer of light and promise forever out of reach.

So if you want a why, Sheriff, that's it. Not for why I done it—that's for the headshrinkers to decide. But leastaways it's why I buried Sara and all those that followed right next to where I buried Heather, so they could lay still and perfect there together beneath the mansion on the hill.

Highway Patrolman

Ryan Sayles

She sits two shell casings on the top lip of the gravestone, steps back, says, "This is sort of a reverse of those husband and wife statues on a wedding cake."

I smirk and nod. See it in Mrs. Hopkins' eyes that she wants to take a piece of this granite cake and mash it into her husband's face. Sort of like stuffing all those promises back down his throat.

Her hair glances across her cheeks the way curtains will ripple like phantoms down a long hallway. She's beautiful, but it's like the brush that painted her had a hard streak in it.

"It's funny, you know . . . when I bought the headstone it was blank. Obviously. For such a simple thing as to tell the mason what Reg's name was and his . . . *dates* . . . I struggled. The room got fuzzy and no matter how many times I tugged at my collar it just choked the words . . . In the end I had to write it down. And now this."

I keep looking at the shell casings. Hollowed out. Empty. Like the marriage.

"Thank you for finding him, Mr. Buckner." Her voice trails off into the gentle breeze moving along us. It stirs the flower petals coloring the graves like graffiti. Reds and yellows and blues and whites shimmer, flapping every time God breathes along the subtle incline of the graveyard.

"It's what I do."

"You find ghosts? That's what you do?" She raises an eyebrow and coughs out a laugh. It adds a cynical note to a beautiful sound.

"I find a lot of ghosts."

Something about that word rips a seal under her eyes. She bursts out crying. The quiet graveyard catches a glimpse of her mourning. Like a selfish child grabbing every toy in sight, hugging them to his body.

Mrs. Hopkins turns to face a line of withering trees standing sentinel along the yard's border, their leaves shedding out of season, a little more death in a place already full of it. Her perfume tatters in the breeze and comes at me in tiny puffs, drawing threads between us. She smells like sugar and warmth. Her dress seam ripples in the wind, caressing against the polished surface of the gravestone, the fabric manipulated into fingers that follow the outline of the letters of her dead husband's name. Reginald "Reg" Hopkins.

I light a smoke. Wait it out. Stare at that reverse wedding cake couple. Empty casings from the bullets I launched at Reg's car three days ago when the motherfucker tried to run me over on a wet and humid street in the middle of a New Orleans slum.

◆◆◆

Three days ago . . .

The pictures hit the table in a *thump* that is drowned out by the terrible—and I mean *terrible*—zydeco music.

New Orleans jazz bar in the Big Easy itself. Live band filling the air with opossum screeches and hillbilly instruments set to a jazz swing. The place smells like an old shoebox stuffed full of people who own too many cats and sweat cheap alcohol.

"Two things, Reg," I say as I ease onto the stool next to him. "Did you know that the word *zydeco* is said to have originated from a French Creole saying which, when translated literally, means 'the snap beans aren't salty'?"

Reg Hopkins doesn't turn to face me. Instead he stiffens like I just raked his spine with a needle, then leans back just enough to show he has a tiny Derringer pistol aimed my way. Must not like hearing that name after all these years. "That's disputed," he says around the squat rim of a whiskey glass in his other hand. "Others say it means 'I have no spicy news for you.'"

I smirk. "Yeah, but that would mean some fool Creole made sense when he spoke, and I don't buy that shit for a minute."

"Who are you?"

"Name is Richard Dean Buckner. I'm former police, same as you."

"You wear a sheriff's badge back in the day? Been the only gun in a county full of restless good ol' boys?"

"No. Municipality. Drugs and thugs and murderers."

"Then you ain't like me. My name ain't Reg, and Richard? You can kindly fuck off."

I move slowly to avoid tempting him to send over a bullet. "The second thing I was getting around to, Reg, you're supposed to be dead." I pull the bottom picture out of the pile. The dude in it, a firm, young man, pride behind his eyes, starched deputy's uniform and campaign cover, looks a lot like this guy sitting next to me, minus thirty years, a lifetime of bourbon, and some good old-fashioned bar brawls solved with broken bottles instead of tin stars.

"Reg Hopkins, highway patrol—"

"I said *get*."

Next picture. "Susie Hopkins, married in 1965—"

"Last warning, *Dick*."

Third picture. "Why'd you do it?"

Reg doesn't shoot me. Which is good, because I'd come back from the dead to bounce his noggin off the tabletop.

No one calls me Dick. No one.

The Creole music drones on in the background and I can see the night from the picture play through Reg's weary eyes. Him being dispatched out to low marks all across the county to close off the roads. A grainy color photo of the ass-end of a squad car sticking up out of a swelling river. Wrong turn into floodwaters.

He grunts. Swallows his drink in one long pull, drawing down the booze like damned hands were coming up from his throat to drag the soul of the alcohol back in with them. The creases in his face deepen. His jaw clicks in place. Inhales through his nose, and it's gotta burn just as much as the booze going down.

Rubs his face, says, "Record rainfall that year. Like nothin' we'd ever seen . . . and I grew up there. Where'd you get these?"

"Susan hired me."

"So she gave 'em?"

"Yeah, from your accidental death file."

"How'd you find me here? New Orleans is a long ways away from up there." He wiggles his glass in the smoke-drifted air. The bartender sees it, nods. I catch his attention, raise two fingers. Another nod. Waitress fetches the glasses and swings by. "It's why I picked it. Far, far away."

I taste the bourbon. Watered down. "Susie has a friend named Carrie—"

"Susan." Reg says with the type of firmness I used when I shoved arrestees' faces into the ground. "Her name is Susan."

"I've heard it both ways."

"Don't care. That's my wife you're talkin' 'bout. Get her name right."

His wife, ha. The same wife he abandoned decades ago. I kill the drink to keep the ice cubes from ruining the flavor of weak alcohol. "*Susan* has a friend named Carrie who came down here on her honeymoon. You know her?"

"Carrie? Carrie Bendleson?" Reg waves a dismissive hand through air, swatting at whatever fly this Carrie must be. "Carrie . . . oh, who cares. Does me no good to call her a slut or anything else. Lord knows she latched onto anything in that county that looked like it was headin' outta state. But she always came back, short a wedding ring and some self-respect. She's been married three, four times." Reg drinks. "Saw me, eh?"

Next picture out of the pile. Reg stabs a finger onto it, drags it near. There he is, a month ago now. Pulling a trash cart out into a dumpster behind a hole-in-the-wall restaurant. An apron that was white six or seven years ago when he first started cooking. Before the catfish guts, before the peeled shrimp. Before the seasoning and spattered oil.

"What're the odds?" he asks, seeing himself through the eyes of an accidental voyeur.

"Astronomical," I say.

"So what now? You gonna take me in?"

"Nah. Susie just—"

"*Susan*, you sonofabitch."

"My mistake," I say, watching the gun harder. "Susan just wanted to know why you did it."

Reg stares at himself in that picture, throwing trash. He looks at the young man in the other photo, now hollowed out. Dead and buried along with the life he gave up to mop grime and smell like okra in a swampy Creole kitchen in humid Louisiana hell.

"Why'd I fake drowning in an overrun river? You tell her I did it because I hated that life. Hated every fiber of it."

"Because of Clint."

"Don't be sayin' that boy's name 'round me. If you wanna fight, if you wanna get shot, keep sayin' it."

I lean back. Feel the weight of my own iron. My fingers tickle the handle. Word was Reg used to be a good deputy, but now, decades have dulled his senses. I can tell. Plus, he's starting to slur. Swaying in his seat.

"Susan told me once that she loved my kid brother first. My no-good kid brother, Clint, that *I*"—he stabs a self-righteous thumb into his chest a few times—"had to keep rescuin' from his trouble. And then he comes back and kills that boy in the bar? Makes me have to come after his ass? That's his thanks for all my troubles? *That's* why I was the law? To finally arrest my own no-good kin? And *my* wife loved *him* first? You tell Susan I hated every damn fiber of it."

"I hear Clint was a good guy in everybody's eyes but your own."

"Clint ain't no good. I been tellin' folks that my whole life."

"What if he's mended his ways? Become a good man."

"I wouldn't believe it if I saw it." Reg starts to look mean.

"He's back in the States these days."

"You accusin' me of lettin' Clint get away?" Reg snarls.

"I wasn't there. But the story is, yeah, just you pulled over and let him get to Canada."

Reg stands up. Gives me his full size. His eyes give him up. Behind the bleary windows to his soul, I see his confession.

I stand as well. It's not even close. "If I'm connecting the dots correctly—and I'm sure I am—after you let Clint go, the guilt ate you. I understand. You're the law and you have to put your own brother away for a dead man. But you gave up and let him go. One day when you can't take it anymore, you fake drowning and come down here to start a new life. That about the size of it?"

"I done an honest job."

"You let 'em go."

"I done an honest job," Reg says, trying to convince himself more than me, and the music stops playing when he opens fire.

I hit the purse gun with one hand and his ugly face with the other.

A .22 round goes wild into the seedy club and adds just one more hole to the décor. Reg stumbles back and I charge in. Three Cajun shitbirds jump up and tackle me. Reg thrusts through the cigarette smoke fog and all I see is a swirl where he was. I throw a couple of elbows and get to my feet. Out the door to a naked street.

I race into the middle of the dead road and turn this way, then that. No Reg. Cars line the curb, rusty, jalopy teeth along the concrete jaw of the block. I turn back in time to see those three Cajuns popping out of the front door.

All that noise pours out the entrance but I still hear squealing. I spin. Car. Reg behind the wheel, no headlamps. Gunning down the street, twenty feet away.

I roll. Feel the wake of rushing air yank at my lapels. I heave out my iron and light up Reg's bumper with two shots before he bounces off two parked cars and rockets away. Up on two wheels, he takes a corner, and hurls off into the night.

Reg has run this play before.

♦♦♦

Susan Hopkins stops crying as a truck pulls up alongside the graveyard.

She stares at the wedding cake bullets for a moment and inhales deeply. Cleansing. Guilt, like so many emotions, can be a cancer. Her first husband was a good man who got eaten alive by it. She was left holding the bag. Now she has to bury him all over again.

Susan furiously swipes at the bullets and sends them flying off into the abyss of a world past us, spent brass twinkling in the light before they disappear forever.

She turns and her new husband walks up, soft footfalls in his respects. He smiles, looks like a different man from whatever he must have been before now. Susan folds into his open arms, says quietly, "Reg is still alive."

"Nah, baby. We buried our Reg a long time ago."

"I suppose you're right." Susan looks at me, smiles. "Thank you, Mr. Buckner."

I grind out my smoke and nod. "You going to report this to the locals? See if New Orleans police can pick him up?"

Susan shakes her head. "No. Let him stay dead."

They start to walk off and I shout after her. "Mrs. Hopkins, is it Susan or Susie?"

She smiles brightly. "I've heard it both ways."

Clint, healed and a different man, arm around his wife, shoots me a knowing look. "Susie. I call her Susie." They get in the truck and drive off down a country road. Out here, that road looks like it will stretch on forever.

I sit a single live .44 magnum on the gravestone. Let Reg use it on himself when he finds out his kid brother came back and his wife claimed her first love.

Wreck on the Highway

Brian Panowich

I shuffle a crooked cigarette out of the pack and carefully drop it into my mouth. Of the three left in the box, it was the only one not broken. I was favored by the gods.

No light. Shit.

I should have known better. I just let the damn thing hang there, and stare out the window. The sun is coming up, although from this angle it looks like it's coming down. I have a perfect view, as if the skyline adjusted itself just for me. I wouldn't give a rat's ass about a sunrise right now if I didn't have this sudden forced moment of peace. I think about how many times people wake up to that big ball of fire smiling at them, and nobody gives a good goddamn? They just keep running in the same circles, making the same mistakes, competing for the same nickel.

Like me.

I look at Frankie hanging next to me. He's sleeping through the moment. I let him. He wouldn't give a shit anyway. I try to remember the last time I watched a sunrise, but it's hard to think. My head is still foggy. I'm pretty sure, the last time was from the hood of Choctaw's Camaro just south of Bull Mountain with . . .

Hillary.

Aw, Hill baby, I'm sorry. I fucked everything up again. But you knew I would, didn't you? You knew there was no such thing as *one last time*. That's why you said goodbye when you left. You never used to say goodbye. I should be sitting in your kitchen right now, drinking your weird new age tea, watching the sun come up with you. Not with Frankie. Not like this.

There's a scarecrow just past the edge of the cornfield to my right. He must have been on his coffee break a few minutes ago when I needed him. Way to go, asshole. Nobody takes pride in their jobs these days. Nobody cares. Well, you don't have to worry about it now, buddy. That's a little over seventy-five grand blowing all over your hometown, so maybe now you can climb your lazy ass down off that post and retire. Go tell Mrs. Scarecrow you hit the jackpot on the back of some poor bastard's bad luck.

Speaking of poor bastards, Frankie's head is starting to look like an eggplant. I pull my knife from my jacket pocket, and cut his seat belt. He falls straight down with a hard thud. That woke him up.

"Gimme a light," I say.

He doesn't even hesitate and try to get his bearings first. He digs a Zippo out of his pocket with his good hand and tosses it over. I light up and the rush of smoke is a stream of battery acid down my throat.

"The fuck happened?" Frankie says.

"A bird, I think."

"A bird?" He tries to right himself by grabbing at the back seat above him, but can't. He's busted up pretty good.

"Yeah, a big one."

He tries to laugh, but it comes out as a thick, wet cough that sprays blood all over the roof below us. He ain't got long. I put my cigarette to his lips and he takes a grateful drag.

All better.

"Where's the money?" he says.

Now it's my turn to laugh, as I look out the window and see the bills scattered like confetti all over the two-lane road.

"Frankie, my friend, I think we went through a lot of trouble just to end up paying off some farmer's bank loan."

More laughing. More coughing. More blood.

I ask him if he can see the sunrise. He doesn't bother to answer. I knew he wouldn't care. Hillary would. That's all that would matter to her right now. She'd hold my hand right up to the end, which is pretty close now, because I'm beginning to hear the sirens.

I keep my gun in my boot, but I can't reach it. My legs are so twisted up; I don't even think they can qualify as legs any more. I'd be hysterical, screaming in pain right now if it wasn't for all the Oxy pumping through me. Thank God for the miracle of prescription meds.

"Can you reach your gun?" I ask. "Mine's stuck."

No answer.

"Frankie?"

No answer. He's gone. Shit. Sorry, buddy.

I take one last drag and tamp out the bloody butt on the asphalt. Then I reach over and pull my dead friend a little closer until the .38 in his armpit shows itself.

The sun is high above me now. It's a new day. The sirens are all over the place. I tell Hillary I'm sorry one more time and put the snub-nose to my head.

I'm never going back.

No bullets. Shit.

My Hometown
Matthew Louis

There's a tavern or two like Jericho's in every decomposing podunk in the United States. These dim watering holes, it seems, will always keep the neon glowing, even as all their fellow travelers along the old drag go dark and stay dark going on five, ten years now; even as plywood nailed over doors and windows blocks any dream of a Main Street revival and the *For Lease* placards fade with dust and sun-bleaching and begin to look like grave markers.

. . . Even as some forgotten farm road is rezoned and consumer amusement parks spring up and the beer and whiskey drinkers begin to haunt the production line drink pits at Applebee's and the Outback Steakhouse.

. . . Even as the disgusting tattoo parlor opens up where Sorensen Realty used to be, and a pot-head emporium is right on the corner—first thing anyone sees when they come off the freeway—and four—count 'em, *four*—goddamned taco shops all seem to keep doing business after the Super Burger and the Kountry Kitchen failed.

No matter. Just like in 1984, when Reagan was going to keep all this from happening, when America was going to return to the Old Ways, Jericho's opens at eleven. The TV pops on from remote control pressure and, in supreme boredom, begins its daily FOX News marathon. A plastic toggle ignites the hanging lamp over the pool table and a bank of lights overhead comes alive and makes a disinterested effort against the murky atmosphere. Jerry Coburn, seventy-four this year, shuffles in his groove back of the bar, mechanically working his dank rag over random surfaces, and the regulars and odd passersby stir somewhere, distracted and decrepit wolves feeling the attraction of distant soul-nourishment, drawn by the faint scent of ready beer and dirt-cheap cocktails, moving in circuitous routes and uncertain patterns to gnaw the bones of the last decent carcass on the downtown landscape.

Bob Mantoni comes in at 11:20 or so, says "How goes it" with no expectation of an answer while Jerry gets a bottle of Bud out of the icebox on reflex. Almost impossible to believe the two old men went to high school together. Pompadours, Elvis sideburns, and magic hotrods made from Model Ts and early Mercurys; Greek gods in cuffed jeans and white undershirts. Between the two prodigies and the long-dead third musketeer, Davy Felhorn, they *owned* this town, could boast a thorough ass-kicking of anyone who crossed their crew, and a thorough going-over of all the worthwhile pussy that shared a yearbook with them at Carleton High. That was, at any rate, the history that came to life around the time the last trickle snaked down the neck of the fourth bottle of Bud.

Mantoni, his head adorned with a fading ghost of the dense, black, lacquered pile of hair that once stood at the northern border of his face, tilts his beer toward the TV. "You hear what the baboon did now?"

The men have a sort of game, when company in the bar isn't too mixed, of using various simian descriptors to refer to the president.

Coburn slices a look at the other old timer. "You already drunk, Bobby?"

"Ah, nothing really." Mantoni tosses a hand, shifts his dentures in his mouth and clenches his jaw to set them. "Had some in the bottom of the bottle so I killed it. Look at this shit." He redirects Coburn's attention to the television. "A pen and phone, that fucking monkey says. That's how the country's gonna be governed."

Coburn shakes his head, staring up at the TV where a gorgeous, statuesque blonde talks in understated alarm while quasi-subliminal messages and space-aged graphics swirl around her. "Blow fuckin' 'Taps,'" the bartender declares. "Country's dead. Been dying since the sixties and now it's just flat *over*."

Mantoni grunts and both men involuntarily begin thinking of the latter-half of the 1960s, when things started to deteriorate in earnest, when Carleton's young people started looking like scarecrows and gypsies, and when the town's blacks started getting attitudes. Both men tense, simultaneously remembering the carload of blacks—*just as good—hell, better—than* you *honkey-ass mothuhfuckkas*—beside them at the red light at two a.m. The three musketeers were all married by then, working and making their ways, but on a Saturday night they liked to act out at the bowling alley, liked to pretend they were still the biggest news in Carleton.

It was Fellhorn, the star linebacker, who had not quite been passed out in the back of his own brand new Impala. The challenge and derision in the blacks' voices had plumbed through the beer-numbed layers of the man's consciousness; his eyes had peeled open and he'd clawed upward, growling words the blacks would have been surprised not to hear. Neither Coburn nor Mantoni could have guessed that Fellhorn now kept a sawed off shotgun beneath a folded blanket behind the driver's seat. The blast, from the open back window, four feet from the target, was gargantuan, bright and vicious, followed by gasping and screaming over a Motown soundtrack. The blacks' new blue Cadillac began drifting into the intersection as the driver was incapacitated by injuries or panic or both. Coburn was behind the wheel of the Impala, and he pushed the gas all the way down.

Lee Hicks, a twenty-three-year-old laborer at Wellingford Textile—who had been sitting in the passenger's seat in the Cadillac—was killed. David Christopher Fellhorn was knifed to death outside his father's grocery store, as he approached his Impala, three weeks later. The black youth who killed him, nineteen-year-old Adonis Hicks, was shot to death by the elder Fellhorn while trying to flee the scene.

It was concluded, more or less correctly, that Davy Fellhorn had killed the older Hicks brother, and that the younger brother's knife attack had been an act of retribution. Nobody else involved came forward and Coburn and Mantoni were never so much as questioned by the Carleton PD.

♦♦♦

The FOX News extravaganza continues. Mantoni finishes his Bud and Coburn collects the empty bottle and plants a fresh one. The old men say nothing for long moments, but continue to think along parallel paths, each identical reminiscence tipping the domino of the identical next thought until they arrive at the same conclusion, which neither of them bothers to say aloud.

Daylight intrudes. The street door gets half-hearted glances as the silhouette enters. About time for a couple lunch drinkers, maybe another veteran of better times. The first thing they notice is the clack-clacking, and they look again to see the stiff yellow cowboy hat, the elaborate mustache, the glowing white shirt with embroidered filigree tucked at a pinched midsection behind a heavyweight-champion-sized belt buckle. The Mexican is about forty, tallish, wiry and sallow, with pronounced cheekbones.

Mantoni mutters, "Shee-yit."

Coburn deposits a cocktail napkin in front of the man, says, "What can I do for you?"

"Un bee-ear, amigo."

"What kind?"

A pause. "Half Dos Equis?"

Mantoni leans away a little and studies the man. He clears his throat. "You a character out of a book, buddy?"

The Mexican looks at the old man. Blinks.

"You know—Hemingway? The noble bullfighter? Ain't that what you're dressed as?"

Gold, silver and white teeth are exposed in a polite smile. "My Ingleesh—he's not so good."

Mantoni nods and smiles, the wolf smile of the old days. Coburn looks at him, not disapprovingly. Something is in the air today.

"'Course your English, 'he's not so good.' Why bother to learn English? Pretty sure I woke up this morning in fuckin' Mexico, right?"

The Mexican waves a hand. "*Aiee! Pinche viejo boracho!*"

Mantoni winks at Coburn, reaches out and slaps the Mexican on the shoulder. The Mexican stiffens.

"You said it, pal." Mantoni nods. "You like this Barack Obama?" He points at the TV. "He's gonna bring your whole family over here, right? Town where I grew up? Town where I raised my kids? Town my daddy fought to keep free?" Mantoni continues to smile. "Gonna be nice, ain't it, when my hometown is just like the wetback shit-hole you left?"

Salvador Salas swallows, his sinewy neck reddening, but he can't respond because, as the old man has surmised, the Mexican has no idea what's being said. He understands exactly what he's wandered into, however. He's been a courier for various drug syndicates in Latin America and his native Mexico for decades, and he's been in more tense and hateful situations than he can count. He has, he muses, gutted men for less. He has a trigger, he knows, that once tripped will result in blood on the walls.

His fortunes made, his documents evidently legal, and his seventeen-year-old, pregnant wife and three children here, it's

Salvador Salas' plan to open a cantina on this street. He's only come into Jericho's out of idle curiosity, out of a businessman's instinctive desire to establish cordial relations with someone in the same industry. He had planned on slapping his chest, smiling and announcing, "I make bar on corner!" To which he would expect, at the very least, some form of polite acknowledgement.

But, he laments, this stinking old *alcoholico* is not going to allow it.

Mantoni accepts another fresh beer from his old friend. Takes a pull. The Mexican has turned around on his stool and is calmly surveying the room, elbows hooked on the bar edge, Dos Equis dangling from his fingertips.

"Just look at this guy," Mantoni says, making an effort to be indiscreet. "The blacks clear out when Wellingford goes tits up, and maybe, just maybe, I think my daughter and my grandkids might have a good life here, and now we got *this*. Worse than the blacks, if you ask me. Coons don't do nothing 'less you give 'em the means. These guys are just smart enough to hold down the real estate on their own—for just long enough to ruin it."

Coburn sees Mantoni glaring at the side of the Mexican's face and says, "Let's cool it, Bobby," but his words have the opposite effect.

"You think it's funny, spic?" Mantoni says, first knocking the Mexican's hat askew, and then shoving the man's shoulder, precisely the way Coburn saw a far superior Bobby Mantoni pick fights fifty-five years before.

The next few moments play out very quickly. The Mexican slides off the stool and has a look of benign focus on his face as he simply hooks a chrome boot-tip under a leg of Mantoni's stool and sweeps. The operation results in the old man dropping as if through a trap door. Coburn is shouting, "All right! All right!" as he produces the 9mm Smith & Wesson he keeps stashed next to the icebox. The

Mexican puts up both hands and wet metal glints as he smiles. He's talking with strange casualness, in Spanish, nodding along with his explanation, when the bartender interrupts him with, "Goddammit, Bobby, siddown!"

But Mantoni unfolds his buck knife as he stands. His dentures have fallen out and he pushes his tongue behind his upper lip as he sneers, his collapsed face bulging and twisting into inhuman shapes.

The Mexican watches the knife, managing to maintain a calm air as he passes the bottle of beer to his left hand. He straightens his absurd hat with a flash of dirty-looking, oversized knuckles. As Coburn watches and aims, there's a barbarian, Mongol aspect to the man—alien, with subtly slitted eyes; a too-lean, always-hungry shape, like a dog that lives off garbage. His circus outfit, a bad joke that must be taken seriously, completes the raw insult of his presence. Coburn thinks of the street outside as he squeezes the trigger, thinks of gliding past the rows of thriving businesses in his LeSabre with Jerry, Jr., five-years-old, sitting on his lap and taking a hand at steering, not squealing but gripping for dear life and concentrating like a little soldier. He can see the fresh white, blue and red paint on building after building, the immaculate sheen of the display windows, the uncracked sidewalks, free of debris . . .

The bullet, aimed with firing range efficiency, seeks out the heart, and the Mexican is dead instantly. Beside him Dos Equis trickles on the tiles until the liquid sits level in the bottle.

Coburn is breathing hard, a painful pulling in his chest.

"He came into your playth," Mantoni says, fitting his dentures back into his mouth. He clenches his jaw once and jerks his knife blade between himself and Coburn. "We just wanted to be left alone."

Death to My Hometown

Christopher Irvin

The weatherman on Channel 5 had been forecasting snow each day for a week, but all Detroit received was gray clouds and a bitter cold that made the abandoned city streets even more lifeless. But today the weatherman was certain: the reformed Motor City would be covered in a thick blanket of white powder. "Stay indoors," he warned. "We're looking at possible blizzard conditions, folks." His delivery was poor and riddled with anxiety that even his bleached smile couldn't hide. But few took notice; the city had been asleep for years.

Riggs woke on the couch, blinking his eyes in the glow of the television, busted watch buzzing on his wrist. He stretched his cramped muscles and polished off half a lukewarm Pabst left over from the Red Wings' loss. One of the few promising things left in the burned-out city, the Wings were turning sour like his beer, quickly becoming a "maybe next year" team. No playoff beard this year, that was good as guaranteed. He tossed the empty into the sink, cracked a fresh can from the fridge. Finished it while he gathered up his keys and fit a hat over his sleep-mangled hair. The barbershop around the corner folded over a month ago, making him long overdue for a cut and a shave. He threw on a jacket and cut the thermostat from sixty to fifty. Just enough to keep his mind off the pipes.

The wooden stairway in the crumbling brownstone creaked beneath his boots as he made his way to the street from his third floor apartment. There were no neighbors to worry about waking with his descent. They'd long since fled in search of a home with something to offer. When Riggs showered he could hear the phantom cries of their babies. Sometimes he caught the scent of a woman's perfume in the couch—his couch—they'd left behind. He didn't blame them; they weren't born here.

Outside in the darkness, the wail of police sirens greeted him, speeding toward sections of the city that still possessed enough life to warrant an emergency response. A sliver of moon hung barely visible in the sky, and would for another hour or so. It was how Riggs preferred to work—in and out before the sun could garner him much attention. His gruff demeanor portrayed a man who went looking for conflict, but in truth he did his best to avoid it.

His battered tow truck was parked on the street near the last functioning streetlight, the rest having been shot out over the past year. Complaints to City Hall fell on deaf ears. No budget for bulbs when politicians were too busy banking dough for their friends. He'd left the truck near the light, but not under it—the sentinel was a beacon to drunk drivers. Like a bug zapper, it drew them in on a weekly basis. Most narrowly avoided the trap, but occasionally he'd find a fresh coat of paint etched onto the reinforced concrete, along with salvage of what used to be bumper, headlight and side mirror. Once in recent memory a man had taken the pole head-on, coming to rest on the neighboring steps after sailing through the windshield. It took a few calls and half a day but paramedics eventually cleared the scene.

Riggs turned on the engine and let it warm the cabin while he sat shivering in time to the rumble of the diesel. When his cell rang, he put the truck in drive and pulled away. His mother, calling from her home on the other side of the city where she waited to die. On most mornings they'd chat, but not on workdays—she didn't approve of his business. "Bringin' people bad news ain't a way to live, son." "Buzzard," she'd called him once while in a particularly bad mood, "flocking to a dead carcass." He'd told her, like he told himself each morning, "I'm just helping to clean things up, Mom." The only bright spot in her day was a four o'clock sherry with the ladies. That and her chat with Riggs, though she'd never admit to her enjoyment.

He cruised across Midtown, checking his brakes through red lights, passing block after block of boarded-up windows, churches abandoned by their congregations and forgotten. Stopped for caffeine at the 7-Eleven on Brown because cops need coffee too, and their presence kept the junkies out. An officer slept in a squad car parked in front of the convenience store entrance, bumper freshly tagged with spray paint. Nothing safe, nothing sacred.

Riggs followed a detour through Poletown East, past the warehouse where last winter a homeless man drowned in an elevator shaft. Spent three weeks frozen in ice while his friends huddled around a nearby burning barrel. They took his shoes and socks.

Even before the recession Riggs had spent years here, scouring the forgotten blocks for tricked-out sports cars and luxury vehicles, serving as the long arm of the banks, collecting on broken promises. And like so many men before him, he comforted himself with the notion he was only following orders. There was nothing left here, but the city was still hungry and so it gnashed its eager teeth for the suburbs. Riggs turned onto Route 75 and headed north for 8 Mile Road, leaving the broken heart of the city behind.

The blight followed him like a fungus, swallowing the suburban grass, wrapping entire streets gutted by fire in darkness on both sides of the highway. It was on those early morning drives that Riggs saw the true cost of his hometown's fall, and questions grew in his gut over whether it would ever recover. The wind picked up as he crossed 8 Mile Road, buffeting against the truck like some unseen force field testing him.

The minivan he sought was only a few miles off the ramp, nestled in the driveway of a small home surrounded by McMansions, the result of tear-down flips and excessive additions. The bungalow was unkempt, lawn becoming jungle, driveway riddled with cracks. A rusted basketball hoop without a rim hung over the garage. Riggs swung wide and threw the truck into dreaded reverse, the warning beeps as he backed up like an air raid siren in the sleepy subdivision. He gunned it, parking within inches of the car. By the time he hopped down to prep the hookup, bedroom lights were already on. Two more steps and the living room lights followed suit, revealing the silhouette of a slender woman hugging a child tight to her shoulder. Riggs muttered to himself to hurry up, but his fingers were numb and slow, refusing to cooperate. The windows of the minivan were blanketed in smudges from curious little hands. Any moment now and the husband would charge out of the house, full of rage and despair. *Don't kill the messenger.* Riggs had uttered the phrase so many times it now came out on autopilot, devoid of emotion.

The flurries started, fat and thick as marbles. He let out a sigh and watched the moisture from his breath coat the window. Drew a smiley face with his finger, then wiped it away. The woman stood still as a statue, muted in shadow. There was no man coming to argue, barter and plead. No one to save the day. He wondered if he could be that man.

He looked away from the house. The storm worsened, the street disappearing under a white blanket. It could be dangerous to tow in the coming blizzard, he reasoned. He rubbed snow off the minivan like he'd run his hand through the mess of a young boy's hair. Before he could talk himself out of it, he returned to the truck without so much as a nod.

At the end of the street was a great park with three baseball diamonds. He pulled over and turned off the engine. His body shook, but not from the cold. The snow billowed in the wind like sheets on a clothesline, hiding the field and the skyscrapers that rose in the dawn. It filled the cracks and buried the grit. It felt good. All they needed was a little snow.

As he drove away, he wondered if it could cover the fresh scar he'd left behind.

Nebraska
Paul J. Garth

They fled across the prairie, from the river valley to a small town flanked by grain silos, and then farther west, her hand wrapped tightly in his. They traded out the car. Took another and swapped the plates, a trick he'd heard one of his brother's friends had pulled up north. They drove on roads that curved through low fields, past abandoned barns and houses with windows shot out. He talked about everything and nothing at once, the soft timbre of his voice calming her as they rode together, the land passing by.

At night, she held him and promised she'd never leave.

They left together in the morning.

"Baby?" he said, guiding the car over thin highway roads. "I was thinking. About a stoop or something, a place we can sit and talk at the end of the day."

She opened her eyes. Blinked in the summer light. On either side of the Cadillac, the land lay golden and flat. Fields of corn and soybeans flicked by, there and gone in a breath, a gentle curve on the horizon that suggested hills farther west. Her hand found the cross that hung from her neck and she gripped it tightly. "Red chairs," she said. "With flowers next to the steps so they're beautiful to walk up."

He turned to her. Found her wet, gray eyes and whatever gave him peace. "We'll have dinner there. And a little silver bucket to throw the tops of the beers in."

The thought of the porch and their time on it caused a sense of wonder in her. Could they really have it? After every thing they'd done? She pictured him digging holes for the plants. On his knees, shirt off. She could almost taste the sweat rolling off his back.

"Every night?" she asked.

He looked back to the road, checked his speed. "Not every night," he said, smiling. "We'll have to get you a good kitchen too, for when winter comes."

She smiled at the thought.

◆◆◆

They only went a little ways each day. They were being looked for. Probably across the river where his family was, he told her. But still, they had to be smart.

Every morning they drove aimlessly, following back roads and tracing the edges of fields looking for a place they would feel safe, a place that felt like home.

She watched him as he gassed up the car, his body taut and powerful as he moved across the gas station parking lot to pay. He'd come alive since they'd left. Guided by something she'd never seen. The way he moved, talked. She could see him thinking behind his eyes, gears smashing until something came out the other end that was sharp, smart, and dangerous. He'd become the man she'd known he could be, and she was proud of him.

He stood outside smoking, while she gathered food for the rest of the day. Inside the station, the clerk asked her where they were headed.

"Home," she said.

♦♦♦

They found a cinderblock motel and checked in paying cash. The TV in their room played static and the light in the bathroom flickered.

In bed, he played with her hair and whispered that she was beautiful. He told her how much he loved her and that when they were settled he wanted to try for a family again.

"But what if it doesn't work?"

"We'll make it work."

"But we couldn't last time."

"We weren't ready." He smiled at her. "Besides, we didn't try hard enough."

His words drew her in, excited her, and they made love.

Afterwards, cooled by sweat as he slept, she lay there, hoping desperately that his seed would finally take root. That it would grow, healthy and strong. It had to happen. God had already taken from her once. She rubbed her hands over her breasts and stomach, willing them to grow.

She dreamed of damnation and the plains alive with fire.

♦♦♦

They left at noon. Turning off the highway, he steered over county roads. There was no radio and he was quiet as he drove.

"When we find it, we'll know, right?" she asked. "Do you think it could be today?"

"I don't know," he said.

As he drove, she imagined what it would be like. Small, she knew, a place tucked away from the main roads where people could become new. In high school, she'd worked as a waitress and she'd been good at it. There would be a diner. A little one where she would wait tables and get to know the regulars who would tease her as she refilled cups of coffee. Down the street a church would sit next to an old barbershop and the only realtor's office in town. He would work as a mechanic and come in for lunch every day, eating hamburgers and watching her ass as she walked away.

She described it to him, their perfect place. He didn't respond, just sat awkwardly in the seat, the knuckles of his hands bled white as he gripped the wheel.

"You think that sounds nice?"

He shrugged.

"How 'bout this?" She reached over and began to stroke the inside of his thigh.

Gently, he took her hand and moved it away.

"Running low on gas," he said. "Gonna have to do it again."

She sat up straight in her seat, turned, and looked out the window. She wished they knew where they were going.

◆◆◆

When he found an area that was straight and flat, he pulled over.

"We're getting closer," he promised. "This's the last time. I know it." He kissed her long and deep, his lips opening her mouth. She nodded at him.

He rifled through the trunk before disappearing into the green stalks that lined the road, while she took position at the front of the Cadillac. She tied up the front of her shirt, exposing stomach, and rolled the legs of her shorts and waited, rocking her hips from side to side, knowing he was watching.

The sun beat down. In the late-afternoon heat, shimmers rose from the ragged concrete. It was a long time before she finally saw sign of another vehicle, a glint of light reflecting off glass in the distance.

The vehicle grew closer and revealed itself, an old Taurus, white and rusted around the wheel wells. She waved as it stopped and turned off, the ticking of the engine unexpectedly loud.

The driver exited the car. Tall and thin, with brown skin and long hair tied back. An Indian, she realized, probably driving somewhere from the Reservation.

"I had some trouble," she yelled.

"Honey, I know what that's about," the Indian said, moving closer to her.

When she heard the voice, she realized she'd made a mistake—the Indian was a woman. She came closer and smiled at her gently. "Let's see what you got here," she said.

He came rushing from the corn, the shotgun level and unmoving. Her face melted into a look of surprise as he pulled the trigger.

There was a loud click. He looked confused.

The woman turned and ran.

Desperately, he pumped the shotgun again and pulled the trigger, but nothing happened. He threw the gun to the ground and took off running towards the car. "Fuck!"

The Indian woman had already made it halfway back to her car.

They were almost next to the Taurus by the time he finally caught up with her. He grabbed her by the back of her shirt but she turned and struck him with an elbow. He fell, pulling her down with him into the tall grass of the ditch.

The woman landed on top of him. Her hair wild, she threw fists at his face. Both of them were screaming. Trapped beneath the woman, he tried to throw her off. He reached for her neck. Punched at her face. But the Indian stayed, latched, and smashed his throat with her elbows.

She ran to him. Stumbled over the ground, tearing flesh from her palms. She knew his face had gone bloody and he was yelling her name. Screaming for help. She lifted herself. Blood pulsed in her ears and she realized she was screaming as well. A chunk of concrete sat loose in the road next to where she'd fallen. She stopped. Grabbed it, and ran towards the woman, the shard of road raised overhead.

She tackled the Indian. Hefted the concrete and swung it down and into her skull. The reverberations rang up her arm and she felt something in the woman's head give and then break. She swung it again. And again. Until she was sure.

♦♦♦

They lay in the prairie grass, both their faces slick with blood, the Indian woman's body a few feet away, attracting horse flies. Blood drained from her, and the soil soaked it up greedily. Above them the sky was blue and bruised with streaks of purple. The first stars had begun to appear in the east, but the heat of summer still pressed down. She squeezed the cross on her necklace and then found his hand in the grass and held it for a long time.

He moved his other hand to her face and made as if to wipe the blood away.

She stopped him. "Don't," she said.

When the moon began to grow, they stood. She went to the body and rooted through the woman's jeans for her car keys while he went back to the Cadillac and gathered their things. She made it back to the Taurus first and opened the door.

In the backseat, strapped in a cheap car seat, a baby sweated and looked at her with wild, thirsty eyes. She screamed for him, desperate not to lose something she'd wanted for so long. They found a water bottle in the backseat. She removed the baby from the car seat and cooed to it. Whispered that everything was going to be all right. Eventually its crying stopped.

The baby's skin was hot to the touch and she slowly showered it from the bottle, the water mixing with the blood from her hands, slowly trickling over its forehead.

She could feel him looking at her from across the car. "This is it," she said. "We can have a family now. Please. Please. We have to take it with us."

He took a long time to answer. "If that's what you want," he said, smiling.

She jumped in place and squealed, joy overtaking her, the child wrapped tightly in her arms.

She carried the baby to the passenger seat and she sang to it as he moved their belongings from the Cadillac. Finally, after he'd switched the plates and deep twilight had fallen over the fields of Nebraska, he started the Taurus, turned it carefully on the small county road, and began to drive west.

The rhythm of the road rocked the baby back to sleep, its head resting between her shoulder and neck, and she could feel its heart beat against her own.

Quietly, so as not to wake it, she began to talk about the stoop and the diner and the roses by the steps again, before beginning to talk of the nursery they would need when they found a place to settle. They were heading home, she knew, even if they didn't know exactly where that might be.

Pictures on the Edge of Town

A Collection of Images by New Jersey

Photographer Mark Krajnak

www.jerseystylephotography.zenfolio.com

The Iceman

Les Edgerton

I shot her.

Twice.

The first time so she'd feel it, get the picture.

I wanted to talk to her a bit before I finished.

I told you, you didn't know me, I said.

You kept giving me that stupid grin and saying—I lived with you for twenty-five years. I know you.

But you don't, I said. See?

Then, I shot her the second time. The first time it was a gutshot and the second I put a hole in her forehead.

I imagine she believed me now, I thought. For a few seconds anyway. Between the first bullet and the second.

She never said anything, either time. But then, she didn't need to. Her face said it all. She realized I was telling the truth.

After the second shot, the one that quieted her for good, I sat there a while, waiting for the emotion to come, but it never did. Not even a general feeling. Nothing. Nada. That was what I was trying to tell her—had always been trying to tell her.

I sat there, in the chair across from her. From what wasn't her any more. Now it was just a body. I thought about what memories I'd carry with me of her after twenty-five years of marriage.

All I could come up with was our nightly routine. At nine sharp, each evening, we'd turn off everything downstairs and come up to bed. I'd go in the bathroom first, and sit on the stool, lid down, and read something, usually a novel. I'd have my last cigarette of the day. Take my pills. Open the window so the smoke would go out. If it was summer, I'd close it before I left to keep the air conditioning in. Same thing in the winter, for the heat and furnace. Those times when neither was on, I'd just leave it up.

I'd leave a cigarette for her on the sink counter. We kept a lighter there, all the time.

I'd go to bed, turn down my side and climb in. She'd usually have the TV on, the remote tossed on my side of the bed. That was because she'd go to sleep before me. I was a night owl. From my days in the joint. I couldn't go to sleep without TV or some kind of noise going on. Since our neighborhood was quiet, it was the TV's job to get me to sleep.

She'd go in the bathroom and smoke the cigarette I'd left for her.

You may wonder why she didn't have her own. Years ago, she'd quit. Only she hadn't. She quit buying cigarettes. She smoked mine.

Depending on the day of the week, she'd have whatever she liked that day on. On Thursdays, it was always *Cops*, either a rerun or a new episode. If *Cops* wasn't on, it would be Court TV for a long time and then IT. Both featured murder cases.

After she finished her cigarette, she'd come in, turn down her side, throw the covers off and lay there. For what seemed all of our married life, she had heat attacks as soon as she came to bed. Menopause, she said, but it was sure a long menopause. It lasted for at least the final fifteen years of our marriage.

Until I shot her. Twice.

It just irritated me, her saying she knew me.

Now she does.

I went and pulled the blanket up over her face. You see, I said to her. I really was the Iceman. You should have believed me. All I ever asked from you was respect.

I went into the bathroom and there was the cigarette I'd left her. I smoked it all the way down.

No sense in letting it go to waste.

We Take Care of Our Own

Todd Robinson

It was Anquan's 14th birthday, but nobody seemed to care. Not even Anquan.

There was a flimsy paper banner over the window from the Dollar Store on MLK Boulevard, lots of food, a cake. Colorfully wrapped boxes sat under the banner. None of it was for Anquan.

Still, Anquan was excited. He did his best to keep his hands from shaking. Lord knew that he even felt a tear or two welling in anticipation.

It was almost too much. Shawn was already an hour late.

But he had to play it cool. Bad enough Uncle Rob called him "Little Man" in front of Terique, who just covered his mouth snickering. Quan knew he would pay for the comments later.

"Here he comes!" came Terique's voice up the project's stairwell.

Quan's mother burst into tears. Uncle Rob grinned ear to ear and started an excited pace within the small confines of their apartment.

Terique came busting in, his oversized jacket covered in loose flakes of snow. "He's comin' up the stairs right now."

Quan took a deep breath and rolled his neck. *Stay cool*, he told himself over and over.

Then, there he was. A good two inches taller than when he left. Shawn's grin lit the room when he walked in.

A cheer erupted in the small room. Baby Tanya startled at the noise and began wailing, the sudden clamor too much for her two-and-a-half years to handle.

The room was a flurry of sound, tears, and embracing. Shawn was nearly driven out the door when Mama and his baby mama, Cherice, assaulted him with their affections. Uncle Rob smacked Shawn on the back. Tanya screamed fearfully until her daddy lifted her high and gently kissed her tear-streaked face. The baby stopped crying, puzzled for a moment as she remembered his smile, the smell of her daddy that she hadn't inhaled since he signed up and shipped off for Afghanistan.

Despite the roiling joy inside him, Quan did, in fact, keep it cool. He felt Terique's eyes on him, knew his best friend's lip was curled in that sly smile of his. Terique would be waiting for the slightest crack to bust his chops, preferably in front of the girls.

But then Shawn stepped from their mother, handed his daughter back to Cherice. He stepped to his little brother.

"You got taller," Shawn said, warm smile on his face.

"You did too."

"If I was gone much longer, I'd be looking up at you."

That wasn't true. Might never be. At 6'4", Shawn had inherited their father's height. At 5'3", Quan not only inherited their mothers' features, but her slight nature.

Quan shrugged. "Soon enough," he said, although he didn't believe it himself anymore, even as he stared down at his brother's military-issue size 15 boots.

Then, before he could steel himself, his brother's arms were around him, pressing him close. And for the first time in a long time, Quan felt safe as a fourteen-year-old in the Grant Housing projects could.

♦♦♦

"Nigga's trippin,'" Terique said, the stem of a Slim Jim poking between his teeth.

Terique and Quan watched Shawn lace through defenders for an easy lay-up. Watched as Lamarr Washington shot looks down at Shawn's brand-new Air Jordan V's before swiping at the back of his teammates' heads for letting Shawn score another easy two. The sneakers, called "Bel Airs," were a gift from Uncle Rob. Normally new kicks would've been beyond the realm of possibility for the family's budget, but Uncle Rob used his Foot Locker managerial discount to snag them for his hero nephew.

Once word spread about Shawn's return, his homeys threw together the afternoon game between the self-titled Grant Regulators and the Manhattanville Playas. The two projects had a rivalry that on occasion had erupted into violence, but the basketball teams, informal as they were, had been playing each other for years. Not without tension, but miraculously without violence.

The younger boys, Quan and Terique among them, spent a good part of the morning clearing off the court, using pieces of cardboard to push the snow off the lines.

Terique didn't care about the violence-free history. He was more concerned with the current attention that Lamarr was giving to Shawn's new kicks. "Don't like those looks, brother."

"He's just tripping," said Quan.

Shawn stole the ball from one of the smaller Manhattanville ballers and nailed a long three-pointer. Lamarr shoved his own player violently, the smaller boy nearly face-planting onto a pile of slush even as the Regulators flurried Shawn with back slaps and high-fives.

The Manhattanvile squad enjoyed an easy dominance for the last couple years due to Shawn's absence, Lamarr being the six-foot-three cock of the walk. Not quite tall enough or athletic enough to turn his considerable high school skills into something more, he'd continued his authority the only place left to him—the housing courts.

While he and Shawn had been court rivals, Lamarr had let the last two years make him lazy, his size being enough to overpower casual players. But the two years that Shawn had been in the Army had fine-pointed his skills. Their differences condition-wise were obvious.

Shawn seemed oblivious to his rival's seething.

Terique wasn't. "Yo, your brother needs to lay back. He don't need to humiliate a brother."

"He's just playing his game. Not his fault Lamarr turned into a fat fuck."

Lamarr hadn't exactly grown fat but he certainly had gotten softer. And Anquan would be lying to himself if he said he wasn't enjoying his big brother's performance with pride.

Shawn was dead five hours later.

Nobody heard the shots, or at least nobody said they did.

The police found him in the fourth floor stairwell of Cherice's building.

From a deep sleep, Quan heard the phone ring.

Then his mother's scream.

Shawn was stripped of his wallet, his down jacket . . .

. . . and his sneakers.

The next night, Quan's uncle stood in front of the building with all the local politicians and community activists, decrying the violence that had beset his family; that had been a stain on the community.

Quan knew what time it was. The violence in the houses went back decades. It wasn't a stain any more. It was a permanent part of the projects, no less than the bus stop. A stain could be scrubbed out. That shit? Might as well toss a frame 'round it and call it décor.

His mother was in the apartment, wrapped in Shawn's blanket, doped to the gills. She hadn't spoken or eaten since the phone call. Uncle Rob had to identify Shawn's body.

Quan sat in the stairwell, eyes dancing at the thick candles, Jesus printed on the glass, the flowers, the teddy bears left at the site of his brother's murder. Fucking teddy bears, like Shawn was a four-year-old caught in a drive-by.

But mostly Quan stared at the blood on the wall that hadn't even been washed away yet, the dangling pieces of yellow crime scene tape that the disaffected cops left behind after their preliminary "investigation."

To them, Quan figured, Shawn was just another in a long line of dead niggas that got wheeled with a blanket over their faces from the projects, an occurrence too regular to be worthy of attention.

◆◆◆

People came and went. Some left totems, a few just shook their heads, muttered something along the lines of "damn shame" as they passed.

Damn shame.

"You know." The voice came floating up the stairwell like a devil from the depths. Terique tossed a bag of Skittles at Quan's feet, offered a bottle of Fanta that Quan didn't reach for. Terique shrugged and cracked the cap himself and took a swig of pineapple soda.

"Don't know nothing." Quan's lips felt numb even as the words passed through them.

"Yeah, you do."

Quan wrapped his brother's hand-me-down coat around himself. He leveled his eyes at Terique. "I don't know nothing."

Terique shook his head and let loose a *pssssst* as he looked over the ghetto memorial. "You bein' stupid."

"What am I gonna do, 'Rique?"

"Well, when you decide what you do and do not know, and what you want to do about it, you let me know." Terique slid his hand under his jacket and moved the pillowy coat enough for Quan to se the duct-taped grip of a snub-nose sticking out.

Quan lept up and pulled his friend's jacket close. "Damn, nigga?! You stupid? Cops are all over this place."

Terique stepped back, his arms wide. "Don't know about you, but I don't see no cops anywhere. Cops don't give a fuck about another dead Grant Houses nigga. You know that. I know that. You holla at me when you decide you care enough."

"Fuck you, 'Rique."

"Fuck you too, brother. Fuck you too."

Shawn was buried two days later.

Time passed.

The snow melted.

Life went on in the Grant Houses.

Nobody got arrested for the murder of Shawn Pederson.

The one lead they had lay on the missing shoes. But nobody in either of the projects could rock a size 15 without looking like they were wearing clown shoes. Not even Lamarr, who had a similar build, could work the shoes with his thirteen-wide feet.

Fewer and fewer people seemed to give a fuck.

Cherice moved to Atlanta, taking Tanya to live with her aunt and cousins.

Uncle Rob kept up the good fight, trying to hold press conferences, even when he was down to one community blogger showing up. He tried to throw one last Anti-Violence march in Shawn's name, but he just stood in the rain alone that March afternoon. Quan watched his head drop from the corner. Saw defeat in his uncle's slumped posture, the ink on the picket sign bearing his nephew's image running down the cheap cardboard until it looked like he was screaming, melting in the rain.

Not even his mother could drag herself from the Xanax womb she'd kept herself in since the first night she'd learned that her baby was gone.

Two days after Uncle Rob's final attempt at awareness for Shawn, shots rang out at the Manhattanville Houses. Three hit, two dead. All three victims aged sixteen.

The marches started up again. Pleas for peace echoed through the projects for an end to the violence, most of the voices booming through the same megaphones that had decried Shawn's shooting. But once the new violence had erupted, no one remembered a nineteen-year-old veteran who had fallen three months earlier.

The city grew warmer.

Life went on.

For some people.

Quan grew an inch in three months. Once his toes started curling in his worn Adidas, he scrounged what he hoped was enough money from his mother's purse for new kicks.

"Hey, Little Man," Uncle Rob said as he walked into Foot Locker.

"I need new sneakers, Uncle Rob. Can you hook me up?"

Uncle Rob's smile fell—only for a second—at the memory of the last time he'd bought his nephew a pair of shoes. The smile quickly returned to his mouth, but not his eyes.

Quan was still seven dollars short, even with the discount, for the pair of hideous neon green Reeboks, the cheapest in the store.

Quan was happy enough to relieve the cramping in his feet until he ran into Terique by the courts. Terique covered his mouth, made his *ksss-ksss-ksss* sound of laughter as Quan walked by.

"Damn, nigga! You get those from Oscar the Grouch's Goodwill?"

"Shut up, Terique." But even Quan had to crack a smile at that one.

Quan's eyes wandered over to the courts. Lamarr was once again the king, bullying the other players as he drove the lanes.

"I see you looking," Terique said.

"At what?"

"Nobody gonna be dumb enough to wear your brother's shoes on home turf."

"No. I guess they ain't."

"You know what I think."

"Yeah."

The game ended fast.

"Shit," Terique said. "Chalk another for Manhattanville."

Lamarr's teammates all celebrated, but packed their gear quickly. You didn't talk too much shit on enemy turf, especially since the last round of shootings.

Quan heard Lamarr tell his boys that he was off to work.

"Yo 'Rique. You got that twenty dollars I lent you?"

Quan kept back, but followed Lamarr to the A train. Quan kept his hoodie up and stayed one car down. When Lamarr exited at West 4th, Quan got off, too.

The station opened onto the legendary street courts where Anthony Mason and Jayson Williams carved out their toughness. Though no tourney was happening, an impressive assemblage of size and aggression were playing in The Cage. Lamarr called out a couple names, who in turn gave him a greeting, but he never broke pace.

Quan followed him down to MacDougal, where Lamarr stopped and rang a buzzer next to a falafel joint called Mamouns. Quan stepped in line with the patrons, but never took his eyes from Lamarr.

The fuck was Lamarr going?

Quan bought a sandwich, ate it slowly as he waited. 'Hood rumor said Lamarr had himself some downtown Albanian pussy that he'd met while bussing tables at the Jamaican restaurant on 3rd.

A half-hour later, Lamarr walked out, freshly showered, wearing his work uniform and holding hands with a pretty white girl with wild hair. Quan kept his head down as they passed in front of him. The girl said something about Lamarr coming over after four. Quan couldn't place her accent, but she sure wasn't American, much less a hoodrat.

Quan was so impressed with the second life that Lamarr had for himself downtown that he almost didn't notice the slightly-too-big Bel Airs on Lamarr's feet.

Almost.

◆◆◆

Quan killed time by walking through Washington Square, feeling especially black amongst the nearly all-white NYU students and young hipster families. He found a fancy movie theater and paid the rest of his cash to see some bullshit about French lesbians. He walked the same blocks over and over, never straying too far from the Jamaican restaurant, watched Lamarr clearing dirty dishes through the street-facing windows.

At midnight, he called Terique.

At two in the morning, he saw the restaurant's lights shut down.

A half-hour later, Lamarr walked out and down Sullivan to a bar on Bleecker. Even though Lamarr was still shy a year of drinking legally, there were enough bars in the neighborhood for one or two to look the other way.

Quan looped the block.

At a quarter to four, his cell vibrated.

Here he come

Quan quickened his pace back over to Sullivan.

The street was empty.

Lamarr's long shadow weaved up the block.

Where the fuck was Terique? Lamarr was twenty feet ahead of him. Quan could hear Lamarr drunkenly mumbling an old Tribe track.

A voice came up from the recessed stairs of the VFW as Lamarr passed. "Got a light, brother?"

"Depends," Lamarr slurred. "Whatchoo smokin' and what you willing to share?"

Terique chuckled his *ksss-ksss-ksss* and held up the thick jay.

"Damn," was Lamarr's final word on the planet.

As he pulled the pack of matches from his pocket, Quan pressed Terique's snubby into Lamarr's ear and pulled the trigger.

One loud bang.

Skull and brains erupted from Lamarr's other ear, and he pitched forward into the VFW stairwell. What remained of his head crunched on the stone steps.

"Boom, nigga!" Terique shouted. "Bounce!" Then he was gone.

Quan didn't run. On quaking knees, he walked down the steps and dropped the wrapped gun next to Lamarr.

Gently, he removed his brother's sneakers from Lamarr's feet. Being a little too big, they slipped off easily. When the second shoe came off, the rolled-up sock stuffed into the toes tumbled out, plopping into the spreading pool of blood.

They were still too big.

They were still too big for Quan, too.

But Quan was still growing.

My Best Was Never Good Enough

Keith Rawson

The first time, Darrell walked down the street swinging a cinder block, whistling, putting it through windshields. Not all the way through. He'd swing down hard, spider-web the windshield, move on, car alarms following his easy pace. He made it two blocks, twenty-five or thirty cars. He wore himself out, bent over at the waist, the block between his feet, shirt off and dripping sweat. The cops took him gentle, and we didn't see Darrell for six months.

♦♦♦

My parents kept saying he was acting out. His parents were no good. We all heard them every night. Their windows and doors thrown open. Breaking glass and screams, Darrell's dad running out onto his front lawn the summer before the cinderblock, with his head gashed open, his wife coming after him with a fistful of glass. Nobody understood what she was saying; she was speaking in tongues, pointing with a jagged neck of a Rolling Rock bottle. Darrell's dad telling everyone to stay back! Stay back, he'd handle it! None of us saw or heard Darrell during the fights, but we knew he was there, watching. Nobody blamed him for the cars; he was acting out.

♦♦♦

The second time, Darrell had been back six months from wherever they sent him the first time. He didn't talk much or hang out. But we were all freshmen, so none of us talked much or hung out with anyone. Darrell was in 4th period shop along with all the other boys making plastic key chains, just like all the girls were in Mrs. Mulroney's home economics class, burning macaroni and cheese. Darrell was at the band-saw, cutting his chunk of multi-layered plastic into a five-point star. Mr. DelVicci was helping Darrell with the cuts. Standing behind Darrell, his rough hands over Darrell's, guiding his fingers.

The boys who were there said they didn't see nothing, just DelVicci on the concrete with the chips of plastic and wood shavings, a pool of blood spreading from his two missing fingers, and Darrell kicking him in the chest. Dale and Bobby pulled him away, said they had to lay on top of him. Bobby said Darrell tried to bite him on the neck. Principal Shaver called the cops, but Mr. DelVicci wouldn't press charges; too many people already knew he was a fag. Darrell didn't come back. Either he was kicked out or just didn't bother showing up, no one really knew, and I never bothered to ask him.

♦♦♦

Mom and Dad divorced. Neither of them were screamers; all their problems were behind their bedroom door, harsh whispers drowned out by the television being played too loud. They divorced but still stayed in the house together, Dad moving into one of the empty rooms originally meant for ghost siblings. Being roommates was a better fit for them, not that I noticed any difference. Children don't notice if their parents love each other, and they barely recognize hate unless they see their moms walking around with missing teeth and raccoon eyes. They both worried about me, once an hour asking:

How're you feeling?
How're you feeling?
How're you feeling?

They were waiting for me to act out. They wanted it, my moment, and I wanted to give them their show. I didn't know how. I am, was, the quiet girl. I started watching Darrell. He knew the movements, the angles. He'd show me how to provide them their guilt.

♦♦♦

The third time was the year after graduation when we all pretended that we wanted to go to college. It was October and still 100° outside. But we all wanted out of the air conditioning, so we'd sit out on our front lawns and trick ourselves into thinking it was cooler.

Darrell's mom charged out of the house, Darrell at her heels, both of them ranting, a strange Christ tongue only they could understand. Darrell's mom was squat, thick, her eyes perpetual unblinking iron skillets. Dad called her the linebacker. She scared us all even before she started unraveling. Darrell was twice her height, rail thin, yet he flinched with her every word, but he didn't back down. Half way across the lawn, she turned on him, ran her fingernails down his cheeks, skin clotting under them. She made this sound, I don't know, like the time one of the neighborhood strays crawled up inside dad's car and he turned it over, the body wrapped in the fan blade. That.

He stood bleeding from eight runny scratches, eyes watering; not so much tears, but like hay fever attack, like he was allergic to his own blood. The first punch was sloppy, a shaky right hand, the fist loose, unsure of where it should be going until it made contact with her nose, the knuckles digging deep, a squelch of bone made rubbery and broken. After that first punch, the ten or twenty that followed knew exactly where to fall; Darrell was a natural. The police didn't come for him this time. No one in the neighborhood seemed to care about the beating, or they secretly admired it, picturing themselves in Darrell's place, finally giving the crazy bitch what she deserved. Or maybe they pictured her as their wife, or child or boss, whatever. Darrell went to live in the park afterward wearing only the blood-speckled clothes on his back.

♦♦♦

Central Phoenix Park is no man's land. The city cleans it up once or twice a year, usually when the natives hold their annual POW-WOW. Other than that, it was a quilt of pissy drunks, dopers, and other people like Darrell. You had to watch out for the people like Darrell. The drunks and junkies were like rats; you could scare them away by stomping your feet and yelling, and they would scatter. But the people like Darrell, they have no boundaries. The idea of possession is alien. Everything belongs to them. I would bring him things, food, sweaters, blankets to keep warm. He would smile, thank me, ask me my name sometimes.

"Amy," I would say, a little sad.

The people like him would take the things I brought him. He wouldn't say anything. He'd smile, tears trickling from the corners of his eyes.

♦♦♦

The fourth time it was February in the park. Winter in the desert isn't really cold or wet like it is other places. It can get cold, but it normally doesn't get deep in your bones. There are exceptions. I found Darrell early in the morning a couple of hours before I had to be at my summer job, which had turned into my winter job, which had turned into my whole life outside of Darrell. It had rained the night before. A cold January rain.

He sat under the monkey bars in the wet sand. Someone had taken the old jacket of my dad's that I'd given him. Or he'd forgotten it somewhere. He shivered, his whole body trembling. He looked up at me, lips split, scabby, one of his front teeth cracked in two, going gray. Raccoon eyes, broken nose. One of his people must have come after him.

"Amy?"

It was a good morning for him, mentally.

I squatted down in front of him, unslinging my backpack, opening it, handing him the Tupperware full of chicken noodle soup still warm from the burner. He could barely hold it, his fingers thick and blue, crusted cracks in the knuckles in the shape of teeth. I wondered if he'd done the damage to himself.

He hadn't, and I didn't notice the person who did until he was right on top of me, yanking me up by my armpits like a toddler. I dropped my weight, but he was so strong, so large, and stuffed into my father's old jacket, the seams ripped, white polyester stuffing falling in tufts. I tried curling into a ball, making myself into a rock, a boulder. I was never so scared. Thinking about being beaten. Thinking about being underneath him as he tried to push himself inside me.

Darrell threw his body at the gigantic man and I dropped. Darrell pinned him to the wet ground and brought his doubled fists down on his head. It was five minutes after Darrell tackled him that I noticed the wet sucking sound when he hit him. Noticed the blood. I stood up and put my hands on his shoulders, gentle. He jerked around, his eyes pie pans, like his mother's.

I willed him to his feet, pulling him to me as we walked away from what was left of the thing on the ground.

♦♦♦

I won't tell you about times five through sixteen. I do my best to try and keep him calm, safe. I do my best, but sometimes it isn't good enough. So I won't tell you about those times. They're none of your business. They belong to me.

Streets of Fire

Isaac Kirkman

I. THE GOD-SHAPED GHETTO

Twelve-year-old Sebastian sat sullen before the library computer, staring at his seventeen-year-old sister Aurora's Facebook page, hoping that she had checked her messages. But there was nothing, hadn't been in a long time.

With his left hand he clicked from profile to profile, searching his sister's former classmates' walls for signs of her. Beneath the desk, he clutched his backpack as tightly as his sister had clutched his arm when she pulled him through the smoke of their burning apartment. Since then he'd had burn marks on his arm, except for the part his sister touched. She was the same way; each had a scar-free area in the shape of the other's hand. But unlike Sebastian, whose body remained unscathed, hers was wrapped in third degree burns the shape of cherry-blossoms in windblown bloom.

It had been five winters since the fire. Five winters since their father became a heartbeat connected to a machine. Five winters since their mother became a headline in a newspaper that fresh fish were wrapped in, kennel cages lined with. Five winters since their pastor uncle took them in and everything changed.

Sebastian lifted his Urkel-thick glasses, and rubbed his eyes. Though possessing a cerebral, dream-like intelligence, Sebastian had an overbite that gave him the dazed look of someone perpetually walking into a prank. Always anchored to a book, he often left his hair uncombed and his pants inked-stained.

He finished scanning the comments and clicked the next profile, shifting nervously in his seat as the homeless woman sleeping in the corner moaned mournful, almost sexual sounds. His eyes returned to the grinning photo of his uncle standing behind the church lectern. It angered him that his aunt and uncle had deleted his sister as a friend after they kicked her out. They said they had to set an example for the church, that they couldn't have a drug-using Jezebel in their house. After her exit they stripped Sebastian's room, removing his computer and anything that would be a portal for the devil. Nothing left but the bed, a Bible, and a desk. But unlike his sister Sebastian knew how to hide things. He knew how to walk soft and silent in his dirty thrift-store sneakers. He knew how to stay off their radar.

Sebastian skipped past his uncle's profile, trying to catch his sister's trail. Unlike his sister he wasn't a street kid, nor was he social like her. He was introspective. He hid mythology books and comics from his uncle, not weed and liquor. When Aurora was his age she was tagging trains and running off with boys; Sebastian preferred the solitude of his YMCA archery class and model plane kits. But when some older street kids broke his bow last year, he drifted deeper into the written world of ancient gods and heroes.

Wall after wall he scanned, searching comment feed after comment feed for his sister's presence. Sebastian had heard rumors on the corners where his sister copped, stories from the boyfriend who turned her out. A few months ago, Sebastian had seen her hop into a car only a few yards away from him, but she was too doped up to hear him call after her. Beyond that corner where he'd last seen her, Sebastian had no idea where she turned tricks or even where she crashed when the opiate sleepwalk wore off on the River Styx.

The sleeping homeless woman turned and groaned again. Every time she let out a sleep terror murmur, Sebastian tensed up, looked around rapidly and clutched his backpack tighter. He unzipped the bag and slid his hand inside, fumbling through his loose Spanish homework and his sister's wrapped Tarot deck, pushing aside his favorite book, *Bullfinch's Mythology*, wrapped in a Bible sleeve, to the 9mm semi-automatic pistol, stolen from his uncle and resting at the bottom like a sleeping Cerberus.

His fingertips lingered but his attention shifted when he saw his sister's name in a comment on the Facebook wall. There was a video link. He immediately clicked play. On the screen his sister leaned into a station wagon window, asking them if they wanted to fuck, before the teenage passenger screamed, "Thirsty?!" And then busted his full Big Gulp soda against the side of her head.

As the Vine video repeated in six-second loops, the hateful comments poured in below. But Sebastian's eyes were locked on the mailbox address in the frame. It was the same block where those street kids, Li'l Mike and Lanky J, broke his bow. The footage was minutes old. His eyes shifted to her face as she leaned towards the car window. Gaunt, more like a lost child than a young woman.

Her face, untouched by the fire, had a dark bruise that flowed from the right side of her cheek down her neck like the surface of a rain-swollen creek on a starless-night.

With trembling hands Sebastian logged off his account. He sat there, head bowed as if he was melting, like his torso and head were the dripping wax wings of Icarus and his sister's tears the sun.

All around him, students checked out books; the transients and the junkies stirred awake. In the shifting commotion he bent down, and slid the 9mm out and into the kangaroo-pocket of his hoodie, then slipped on his overcoat. Zipping shut the bag he paused at the sight of a Tarot card sticking out of his sister's deck. He removed and flipped it over.

The Tower.

An image of a lightning bolt shattering apart a castle, faces inside screaming and falling into the black oblivion.

II. THE LOVE EQUATION

Returning the card to the deck Sebastian felt a cold vespertine wind roll across knuckles, blowing from the opening and closing library doors. He zipped his coat, patted the 9mm through the layers, and slipped his backpack on. As the night rolled in like a river, dragging the sun away in its torrent, the transients continued to rise from slumber, rising up out of nooks, from behind shelves of arcane books, emerging from hidden library alcoves, gathering their gear like tired fishermen. Sebastian slid his hoodie over his head, exited the library, and descended the steps into the night, an Orpheus. All around him a grim mist fell.

He moved swiftly down the city street, his attention flickering to the library vagabonds who poured out in the same direction, searching as they moved. They made him nervous, for they held the same ghetto secret in their heart that he did; and that desperation was more dangerous than the confidence of a million cock-diesel thugs. He avoided their eyes, which smoked like the charred husks of his family's old doorway.

Spreading out around Sebastian they surveyed the watery night, pulling change from the fountains like worms from soil, searching for enough to hook schools of fish in their dealers' river-deep pockets. The cannabis goldfish. The crack piranha. The OxyContin eel. The St. Ides barracuda. All the junkies eyeing Sebastian as they snatched up minnows of cigarette butts.

With head down, Sebastian picked up his pace, moving swiftly down the street. Only a few blocks remained. Above him traffic lights swung like hanged men. The pre-storm roil made the neon lights expand into otherworldly visions, Technicolor shades floating through She'ol. He ducked through a back alley, avoiding the blue lights of the police who drifted through the streets like poltergeists, hungry for something to possess.

Sebastian paused by a boarded-up check-cashing store. Using the bullet-chipped brick corner for cover, he leaned around, peering at the old duplex house from the Vine video. There was no sign of his sister, but he recognized the two corner boys, Li'l Mike and Lanky J, hanging out by the mailbox, talking to a drunk older man.

Feeling sick, he steadied his shaking hands by sliding them into the pocket and gripping the pistol. Calm flowed through his body like the touch of his sister's arm as the burning roof fell. And like his sister stepping into the fire, Sebastian approached the group. Li'l Mike, eighteen, thin but with muscular, tattooed arms knotted like bonsai trees beneath his coat, distracted on his cellphone, puffed away on his blunt.

Though Aurora would not acknowledge to others or even to herself that Li'l Mike was a pimp, he had no problem referring to her as one of his hoes. Li'l Mike's friend and partner, Lanky J, negotiated with a drunk john on the steps. Behind them, through a dirty living room window, Sebastian could see his doped-up sister slumped on the couch.

Lanky J chugged from his brown-bagged forty-ounce, eyeing Sebastian, then bumped Li'l Mike. "Look, Mike, it's dirty Urkel." Pulling back an imaginary string from his malt-liquor bow, Lanky J squinted his cheeks and made a bucktooth face, imitating Sebastian's overbite. "Dirt-Kel-Hood!"

Li'l Mike leaned in, cell phone in hand, and blew blunt smoke in Sebastian's face.

"What the fuck you want, faggot?"

Sebastian slid the 9mm out and pointed it at Li'l Mike's head.

There would be time in the future to ponder how a bullet can strike like Rosetta Stone and translate life into death, but as Sebastian double-tapped and blew brain and blood lilies out the back of Li'l Mike's head, light and bone whirling like cherry blossoms, all he thought about was holding his sister again, the way she held him when the ambulances came. Sebastian turned and pointed up at Lanky J, his mouth still gaped from caricaturing Sebastian, and pulled the trigger. The drunk john tried to flee, knocking over trash cans as Lanky J's face bloomed into wet, meaty petals, teeth flying out of his mouth, bees drunk with blood-pollen. Honey-colored malt liquor from the broken bottle snaked into the pavement cracks.

Forevermore in the ghetto Sebastian would no longer be known as Dirty Urkel, no longer the faceless boy; he was the translator, the death gardener, desperation's confessor. Sebastian stepped over Li'l Mike's wet skull, his dirty shoes sliding over the designer coat, and moved up the steps towards his sister. He entered the house, where Aurora sat in semi-conscious oblivion, her hair still sticky from the soda. He reached towards her. Grasping her arm, their unburned outlines locking together, he pulled her from the fire.

Opiate-eyed, she smiled as if they were both still children, and she was far from here, in a perfect world, and not this necropolis, this Hades. As he led Aurora outside, sirens splintering the night, he guided her over the bodies, and she gazed down at their faceless skull-fountains as if this was all a dream seen through a codeine veil. Sebastian held tightly to his sister's arm, pulling her down streets of fire, out of the darkness.

But Sebastian, unlike Orpheus, did not look back.

Spare Parts

John McFeteridge

The guy stepped up behind her as she was unlocking the back door, said, "I won't hurt you," and she was thinking, you're fucking right you won't, but she just said, "There's no money in here," and the guy said, "Yes there is, come on."

Jane pushed open the door and led them into the PayDayNow office.

The guy said, "The safe's on a timer, I know. It'll open at nine."

He closed the back door and Jane turned and saw him. He was smiling, looking calm and easy-going, waving the gun, motioning around the back room. Smile on his face.

Fuck, he looked like Billy.

"When it opens all you have to do is put the cash in here," he said, holding up a gym bag. "And I'm gone."

And Jane was thinking, yeah, sure you are, and then she couldn't help it and she smiled a little. Gone. Just like Billy.

Not right away. He said he'd marry her, said he'd be a father, be a man. She planned that summer wedding for months and then Billy was gone, just ran away. All the way to Texas, she heard, from Dave. Billy never said anything to her himself, left her standing there in her wedding dress in front of all her friends. She moved in with her mother. She was still living there. Noah was born that winter. Five years ago now. He was starting school in a couple of weeks.

Jane saw the guy look out the side window of the PayDayNow, saw a pick-up parked across the street, a guy behind the wheel, probably the getaway car, as if these bozos were John Dillinger.

"This place is such a rip-off," the Billy look-a-like said. "The interest rates this place charges . . ." He was shaking his head and smiling a little. "You know, annually." As if she didn't know what that meant.

Jane didn't say anything. She put her purse down on the manager's desk, her desk, and she was thinking, yeah, but who cares about the annual interest for a two-week loan? It's like telling me how much a hotel room costs for a whole year. Not like this guy would get it.

Then it looked like he just remembered something, and he said, "Hey, give me your purse."

"Why, you need a tampon?"

He grabbed the purse and tossed it into the corner, looking pissed off. "Maybe I should pat you down, too. You'd fucking like that."

So she'd never lost the baby weight, so what? She was doing good. This guy, like Billy, would never know how good because he'd never know how bad it had been. He'd just run away. He'd never be in his mother's house, walking a baby back and forth in that little room night after night, never going out, never seeing anybody, no parties, no fun, no life. Looking at his son sleeping in his crib. Crying and crying till he fell down on his knees and prayed.

He'd just run away.

"How much they pay you, be the manager here?"

Jane said, "Not enough," and the guy said, "You got that right, working in this dump all by yourself."

She didn't say anything but she was thinking it wasn't that bad. Not after what she'd been through, not after it got to be too much, so much more than she could take and all she could see was more and more of the same, more long days and longer nights, all alone with little Noah, not knowing what to do. She'd said to her mother, Ma, sometimes my whole life feels like one big mistake, and her mother looked at her and said, yeah, join the club.

And then she was standing waist deep in the Shawnee River, sun shining bright, mist on the water, holding her son and crying, telling herself it was for the best. For the best.

"Come on," the guy said, "it's fucking nine, open it up."

Jane said, "One more minute," thinking can't you wait one more minute before you run?

That day in the Shawnee she'd lifted Noah up in her arms and carried him back to her mother's house and when he fell asleep she put him in his crib and went to her bureau, got her engagement ring and her wedding dress, went straight to the pawn shop and walked out with some good, cold cash. Then she got the job at the collection agency, phoning people up and them calling her a fucking bitch all day, but she bought diapers and formula and baby clothes, and then she got the job at PayDayNow and got to see happy people once in a while, people getting money.

Jane remembered her first customer, Angela, worked at the salon in the same strip mall, came in needing three hundred bucks to get the brakes fixed on her car, saying how in order to get the apartment she'd had to give the landlord post-dated checks and if one of them bounced she'd get bounced out of there—along with her two little girls—and she needed the car to get to the salon and . . . and Jane'd said, Hey, it's what we're here for. Now Jane was the manager and Angela did her hair.

It turned nine and there was a click and the guy said, "Finally, fuck." Not as calm now as when he came in, but getting it back as Jane went to the safe where it was bolted to the floor. She entered the code and opened it up.

The guy, the Billy look-a-like, tossed her the gym bag and said, "Put it all in there, honey."

So she did. Then she stood up and held it out and the guy stepped up to her and took it and said, "See, nothing to it. And I'm a man of my word."

He turned and started walking out of the PayDayNow saying, "I'm gone," and Jane said, "Hey, wait," and he turned around with that shit-eating smile on his face and said, "What is it, honey?" And she shot him. Hit him right in the middle of the chest.

Knocked him off his feet and he grabbed at the doorframe on his way down.

Jane saw the pick-up take off.

The guy slid down the wall, blood pumping out of his chest and he said, "Shit, c-call an ambulance. Fuck."

Jane picked up her purse from the floor where the guy had tossed it and walked across the office and put the gun from the safe on the manager's desk, her desk, and got out her phone.

"C-come on, honey, h-hurry."

Jane held the phone to her ear and waited till it was answered and then said, "Hey, Ma, it's me . . . no, nothing special, just wanted to tell Noah I saw that backpack he wanted at Wal-Mart, I'll pick it up on the way home."

She'd call the cops in a minute. This guy wasn't going anywhere.

Does This Bus Stop at 82nd Street?

Ezra Letra

The train stations have been the stage for nobodies to die. I've always been a nobody, so I will find another way to get to Jackson Heights. It's been four days since I got out of jail and now I'm homeless. It's just the way my life has always been. Zephyr, my celly, would always say we had fallen as deep as we could, so the only way we could go was up.

He was young and still full of hope. There is no up for us. Slugs never fly.

Arturo, the friend I was crashing with before lockup, told me this morning I was no longer living with him. He spread word in the 'hood that I was a snitch. That's the thug's scarlet letter. A huge "S" on the chest makes you a villain around here. I didn't have time for the bullshit. I wanted to keep my nose clean. All I wanted was a warm shower, a meal I didn't have to guard from gluttons, and to listen to *Illmatic* straight through, without any interruptions. I was the outcast now. I ran those streets, now I run from them.

No cell phone, no money, no clothes, no friends, no family, no I.D. Only thing I have is a record.

Always wanted to be a musician.

♦♦♦

I spot Frankie, one of my custies that still owes me fifty. I was one of the few dealers that would front dope. This got me dependents and slaves more than customers.

Frankie, what's up with the half bill you owe me?

Oh come on, Tony, you know I ain't got it like that. Next time, I got you though, that's my word.

The problem is they never run out of excuses. I didn't even want to do Frankie like this, but I know he has something on him I can sell. These fiends always do. Like squirrels hoarding for the cold winter.

Listen Frankie, I'm not leaving 'til I get something that'll make up for what you owe me. Run your pockets, take the blanket off that shopping cart. You make a scene and I'll gut you right here like I did Omar.

♦♦♦

A PSP, a MetroCard that I pray works, one of those phones people on Medicaid get, and about three dollars in dimes. This was Frankie's payment. But I can get by a couple of days on this. I'm loaded like a custie, smell like one too. I'm not going to cry about it. I'm alive, a beast, a survivor of circumstance. I was always working the block, which they never let you leave.

I'm trying to get to Jackson Heights to see if I can meet up with Alex, an elementary school friend and the only person I know that wasn't associated with the block.

Alex grew up here but him and his mom left when he was twelve. His brother Brandon stuck around, got locked up for possession of narcotics with intent to distribute, served six years in Federal. Brandon was the kingpin of the 'hood in those days. There was a dry era after he went away. Soon as I could get my hands on the goods, I took over the throne.

The ghetto's hot heads didn't mix well with the cold hearts. The 'hood was like tornado valley. We knew at any moment we could be left with nothing, but fuck it, we had nothing else. I spent so many winters cooking product, I felt like that dude from *Jumanji* who got sucked into the jungle when he was a kid. The 'hood was my Jumanji.

◆◆◆

I'm waiting for the Q66 bus right in front of *Sports Authority*. Got my hoodie on, it's still too close to the block, and last thing I need is someone seeing me and spreading word where I'm at. I hate taking the bus. I'm used to walking anywhere I need to go but I'm exhausted and can use the time to rest up.

I'm not sure if this MetroCard works, and I don't want to spend the change on the bus. The best thing to do, to get a free ride is to look tired, ask a question. Always works.

Does this bus stop at 82nd Street?

No. It stops on 80th and 83rd.

The MetroCard didn't work. I acted like it was supposed to and didn't know why. Luckily there was a line of people behind me waiting to get on and the driver grew impatient. We were all ants trying to get back to the hole.

It's fine, head to the back, I'm already behind schedule.

◆◆◆

I get to Alex's house. I still remember it, even though it's been a good nine years since I was last here for Thanksgiving dinner. Made of the same brick that dressed our ghetto, but the white marble front porch made his home better, nicer.

I didn't exactly know what I was going to say after the door opened. I knew his mom must've heard about me going down.

Alex's mother, Silvia, is that 'hood mother, a mom to everyone and anyone. She'll always feed you but scold you if you're not doing well. Maybe I needed that. My mom is a drunk. She's given birth twelve times and hasn't kept one of them. Sometimes I'd wonder if my crew was actually blood brothers and sisters, sold off by our mother to feed her habit. I prefer thinking struggle made us siblings.

Hola, doña Sylvia, como has estado?

Tony! Que bueno verte mijo, entre.

She opened the door. It was going smoother than I thought. My smile has always gotten me in with parents. I was blessed with good teeth, even though I don't take care of them as much as I should. This smile was going to be my passport to leaving mischief. I'd at least get a free meal out of this.

Then I asked where Alex was.

♦♦♦

I couldn't believe Alex was dead. Finding out from his mother hurt even more. I didn't know. I was away.

So she told me how it went down. How some hopped-up crackhead had wanted his phone, but Alex being Alex had held his ground, tried to talk him down, help him out instead. Then the fiend shot him. Left him to die like a dog in the street.

What was I supposed to say to make her hurt go away? The pictures of Alex and all he accomplished tattooed the walls of her home. Him smiling at graduation. Standing with his girl at prom. Alex left the block to have a good life, not a short one. But you never really leave it behind, do you?

I left Silvia's house quickly after the tears became too much. I've never been the type to console others. The 'hood made me this way. If you're weak you become food. It was instinct.

The world seems different when you don't have a safety net to keep you from sinking too low. I now walk not knowing where I'll go.

Rudderless and full of doubt, prayer won't help, luck doesn't do foreign exchange, and money doesn't like to come around when you need it too much. Time to hitchhike to tomorrow.

It's Hard to Be a Saint in the City

Jen Conley

This isn't the city. It's Lakehurst, or Manchester Township, same difference, where the Hindenburg crashed, the cover of the Zeppelin albums. Those things pique your interest for about thirty seconds when you drive through the area. Springsteen's music still hums in the diner, in people's cars, but he never comes here. It's the middle of nowhere New Jersey, nothing but scrub pines, empty roads. You want a city? New York, sixty miles north. Philly, forty miles southwest.

But back in '91, Heather Sullivan is going to the city: London, England! And because Eddie and Phil are unsuccessful locating weed at an ex-girlfriend's house, because there's an altercation with the Webb brothers, leaving Ed with a nasty pain in his shoulder from smacking into the outside brick wall of a video store, Phil suggests they hit Wawa to brighten up the night. Then he smirks. Because two things are going to happen at Wawa: one, Phil will hook up with Carol in the back room; two, Eddie will get to talk to Heather.

Now these are the days when Wawa isn't the corporate giant it is now, when the convenience stores are small, when two women working alone deep into the night is no big deal. Back when Eddie

169

Callahan is on the skids. He's okay now. Runs the meetings. But every alcoholic has one of these. Not the shocking, sad, crazy tales—those are easy to reveal—no, this is more complicated. It's a moment, a possible turning point, a brief window when things could have gone another way. Maybe. Sometimes these things are bigger in our memory than they were at the time. You be the judge.

So here we are, one cool September night, and Eddie doesn't know why he's agreed to hang out with Phil. His head is mush and he looks like shit: eyes swollen, rims red, hungover from a three-day extravaganza of cocaine and alcohol, upsetting his father for sure. Eddie's dad is a good man, a parent who hasn't given up yet, although he has threatened to throw his son out when he turns twenty-four, just months away. It's sad the way he says it—calmly on Sunday afternoons, when Eddie sits in the backyard smoking a cigarette, staring at his stepmother's flower garden. "I have to, son. For your own good." His voice shakes when he speaks and it crushes Eddie's heart.

The convenience store is slightly tucked back off the main road, surrounded by woods. It's set in a strip mall with two banks, a travel agency, a bakery, a drug store, and a pizza parlor. At this time of night everything is shut but Wawa and the pizza joint. There are three senior citizen retirement neighborhoods nearby, filled with elderly people who lived through the Depression and World War II, but they don't come out at night. Only a ghostly quiet hovers over the parking lot.

Inside the store, a box radio sits behind the deli case and Jackson Browne murmurs softly. Phil and Eddie—jeans, jean jackets, grungy white sneakers—make their way to the back, finding Carol at the desk in a tiny, smoky office. She's on the phone and when she sees them she grins. Carol is Heather's aunt or something. She's a shift-manager, in her late-thirties, slim, cool, a former homecoming queen candidate, still hot, but she's got a head full of problems. You know the type.

Carol hangs up the phone, leans back in the desk chair, and stares at Phil. "Sweetie, where've you been all my life?"

Phil laughs. "Looking for you, baby."

Eddie turns and walks away, closing the door behind him.

He scans the store and notices Heather behind the deli case. Eddie doesn't know what to do, go outside or talk to her, but he loves talking to her, so he takes a breath and walks across the store, stopping when he reaches the deli case. She's hunched over, wiping tiny pieces of turkey and ham from the edges of the glass. After a moment, she straightens and faces him, tossing the dirty rag onto the back counter.

"You know . . ." he chokes out.

"What?"

Her angry tone shocks him but he soldiers on. "Two girls shouldn't be in this place alone at night. It's kind of dangerous."

She slams the deli case door shut.

He holds up his hands in surrender, then leans against the counter, near the sink, and winces from the pain in his shoulder. Jimmy Webb is such a dick. What was he so piss-angry about? Did Eddie owe him money? Eddie owed everyone money.

He takes out a pack of cigarettes. "Can I smoke?"

Heather walks past him, opens a bottom cabinet door and pulls out a box of sugar packets. "Sure," she snaps, dropping the box on the coffee station counter.

Eddie nods, lights up, and gazes across the dingy store. Remember in high school when he sat next to Heather at a party in the woods? She looked like she'd rather be in a thousand other places. He had his dad's car parked only feet away. "Come on," he'd said to her. "I'll take you to the Boardwalk."

"Ha!" she laughed, then smiled. "You think Jesse would let you get away with that?"

Jesse was her boyfriend at the time. Camo jacket. Chew in his mouth. Not a bad guy except he had what Eddie wanted. "Hell, I'll kick Jesse's ass," Eddie had said, throwing punches in the air.

Now she isn't smiling. "You don't have to hang around, Ed," she says, shoving sugar packets into black holders. "I don't need your protection. The knives are sharp here."

Eddie blows out cigarette smoke and chuckles. She cracks him up. But he doesn't want her mad at him and he doesn't want to bullshit. He wants to know details. He wants to ask her out. If he had a drink, maybe he'd have some balls. But he's an idiot when he drinks.

"Carol says you're going to London in a couple of months."

Heather nods.

"What are you going to do there?" He takes another drag on his smoke. His lungs ache.

She closes the sugar packet box, returns it to the bottom cabinet, and kicks the door shut. "Stay."

"Stay?"

She puts her hands on her hips and faces him. "Yeah. Get away from that shit." She flicks her head towards the closed office door. "And this place." She throws her hands up in the air, implying everything around them.

Eddie taps his cigarette ash in the sink, tries not to take it personal. Heather had been nice in school, although because she was a year below him, he never knew her super well. He just wanted to. Forever he'd wanted to.

The bell on the door chimes and a man walks in. Heather jogs to the register on the other side of the store and rings up a pack of cigarettes. When she returns, she picks up the rag again.

"Are you gonna marry someone in London and stay?" Eddie asks dryly. He puts his smoke out in a black ashtray on the counter.

Heather narrows her eyes. "Don't be so sexist. I don't need to marry to anyone." She starts to wipe down the counters at the coffee station. Then she sighs. "But marrying someone will make it easier to stay."

Eddie chuckles and shakes his head, trying hard not to look her up and down. She's slim but not skinny, fair-skinned, decent chest, cute in a Meg Ryan way. Surely she'd be hot as hell in a tight dress.

But that's not her style. Jeans, Converse, pissy attitude, that's her style. He adores it. "Well," he says. "Getting married shouldn't be a problem for you."

She ignores his compliment. "You know, they let Canadians and Australians stay in England for two years. But Americans get six months."

He's hopeful. "So you're coming back in six months?"

"I'm getting married. Remember?"

Eddie laughs.

"Why do we only get to stay for six months?" she asks again, but it's more a question to nobody. "Seems strange, don't you think?"

Eddie shrugs. "Must be all that Revolutionary War business."

"Ha!" Heather points at him. "You're probably right." She wipes the counters once more.

"How come you're not moving to New York?" he asks. "It's a lot closer."

"I don't want to get shot."

He grins.

"Everyone goes to New York. I wanna do something different."

"Can I come with you?" he asks.

She stops for a quick moment, frowns at him, and then continues wiping the counters.

"Yeah, I know." Eddie laughs but it suddenly turns into a cough. He leans over the sink to steady himself.

She quickly gets him a cup of water from the soda machine. "You should see a doctor."

"I should do a lot of things," he says grimly, coughing again, gripping the edge of the counter.

When he finishes, he turns to her, feeling flushed. "So I'm making an impression, huh?" He sniffs and wipes his nose.

"Are you sure you're okay?"

Eddie sniffs again. "It's nothing. So what are you gonna do in London? Do you have a job or something?"

Heather sighs and stares at him for a long moment. "I'm not working around food, that's for fucking sure. In fact, I'm going to find a real job, something that doesn't make me smell like ham and turkey."

Eddie smiles. "Like what?"

She shrugs, says she isn't sure, just that she wants to do something interesting and that she wants to wear something nice every day. "Maybe I'll work for a solicitor. That means lawyer in American." She winks.

Eddie nods. "I can see you dressed up in heels and a skirt. A city girl."

"Yeah?"

"Yeah."

She goes on to describe London, explaining that she'd been there for a semester in college, something Eddie already knew. "I just love it there. Tons of pubs and nightclubs. If you like music, it's an awesome place to be."

Eddie briefly closes his eyes, imagining himself walking along city streets, everyone looking like Boy George or Joe Strummer.

Then the cough returns. He hacks for an entire minute like an old man.

"Are you okay?" she says.

He shakes his head. "It's nothing. Too much partying, that's all." He wipes his mouth, turns away from the sink, and rubs his face.

A Bruce Springsteen song comes on the radio.

Heather swings around and spins the dial, changing the station.

"Don't like Springsteen?" Eddie asks.

She huffs. "I'm one wrong turn from being a character in his songs."

He chuckles and nods knowingly. "Yeah, I'm familiar with that."

Heather smiles gently.

Just then, the office door bangs open and Phil appears with a wicked smirk on his face. "Let's jet," he calls to Eddie.

Eddie doesn't move. It's too soon. He doesn't want to leave. He doesn't want to go anywhere. "Heather," he says.

She looks at him.

What if he goes home, sleeps off this hangover, gets up, has breakfast with his father, and calls her? He'll pick her up in his dad's car, take her somewhere nice, that new Italian place on Route 37, then to the Boardwalk for a bit. He can do this. He can straighten up for her, for himself. She likes him. He knows it. We all know it. But she's not going to waste her time on an alcoholic cokehead, so he has to get it together. She'd be good in his life. Maybe she wouldn't go to London. Maybe they'd get married. It's possible. It is. Take this road, Eddie. Take it.

But he can't. He wants a drink first.

"If I don't see you," Eddie says, touching that pained shoulder of his, "have a good time in old Londontown. And give me a ring when you get back."

"I'm not coming back."

The last words hurt terribly as if he's been knocked sideways against that brick wall again. He becomes depressed. He gets in the car with Phil, rests his head back, watching the dark roads sail by. Later, they're at Carol's house, and the three of them drink her booze and do her coke.

◆◆◆

Heather does return from London but Eddie is living in some hole in Asbury, drinking himself stupid. When she sees his father, she asks after him. Then, there's a car accident on Route 70, about a quarter mile from where the Hindenburg crashed. She and her little Honda are crushed by the tractor-trailer. Heather is twenty-seven. It takes a whole year for Eddie to hear about it.

Funny how people you peg for dying young come through. Eddie is in his mid-forties now, solidly on his way to old age. No cancer.

No aches. No nothing. He's got no wife, no kids, just tries to help young men like he once was, men missing all the good stuff that you get when you're twenty-three, twenty-four.

There's this too: he wishes Heather were alive. He doesn't dwell on it, it doesn't wreck his day, and he never has trouble with women, but it'd be cool if Heather were around. Maybe she'd be divorced, separated, something like that. He'd ask her out this time.

Atlantic City
Benoit Lelièvre

Princesses Café looked like the end of the world. The walls of the dining area were made of vertical wooden laths and the linoleum floor had missing patches, revealing even more wood underneath. Six flat screen televisions hung from the walls, each playing one hardcore porn flick. Girls taking it in the behind, oily girls getting tag-teamed by oily men, a couple, fucking the entire Kama Sutra, playing on an infinite loop. If Ted Bundy had a ski chalet, it would have looked like this. Places where two thrill-killers could grab a bite at 4 a.m., though, were few and far between, so Trey and Jane gave their order to the bare-chested waitress, Francine, and smiled at one another.

They didn't need a Gordon Ramsay five-course meal to be happy anyway. Trey took Jane's hand from across the table and gazed into her eyes. They played that game sometimes, at the restaurant. Their dining booth became a spaceship, leaving everything outside them behind. Alone in the universe, they enjoyed a moment of unadulterated bliss, because they only needed each other, after all. But this time Jane didn't return Trey's smile. At least, not completely. A lot had changed in their lives that night, and soon a lot would change everywhere in Philadelphia.

◆◆◆

Jane kicked Philip Testa in the face, *300*-style.

"We're taking back Philly, motherfucker," she said, like a child playing pretend. Trey noticed the panic, slowly dawning on Testa's face as he fell backwards into the basement stairs. Jane had bound his hands and his feet together, so Testa landed on the only contact point left, his face.

They set up a death chamber for him. Trey bought the hardware at the local store but it was Jane who designed the space. It was their project. Kill a man. Achieve complete symbiosis in blood. Jane's idea. Philip Testa became their guinea pig because they figured no one would miss him. Not the man who owned the neighborhood. The sad king who drove hard-working people and honest families to the edge. The man who owned so many abandoned houses where he dumped bodies and let the memories of good people rot. Jane kept the key to her uncle's house after he blew his brains out.

"You kids are fucked," howled Testa, as Trey dragged him to the execution chair. "You signed your death warrant the minute you jumped me like fuckin' cockroaches on a cheesesteak."

Jane shook her head and smiled. She had that hungry, wolfish look in her eyes. Trey knew better than to stop her when she was like that.

"Oh, Phil, Phil, Phil. Stop it, will you? You have about a thousand enemies in this town. Maybe more. Do you sincerely believe your dimwit friends will pin it on two random, star-crossed lovers? You're valuable, I get that, but not *that* valuable."

"Who are you workin' for, huh? You workin' for that stronzo, Angelotti? He's a jealous fuck. Is it the Russians? It's gotta be the fuckin' Russians. Fuckin' savages."

Trey observed Testa, away from the glow of the naked light bulb. There was a stark, fatherly anger in his voice but a child's fear in his eyes. He understood they were killers, maybe better than Trey did.

Jane walked to the workbench in that playful, mock-procession manner. There were two dozens tools to choose from—basic screwdrivers to a deWalt drill so big, she probably couldn't lift it by herself, let alone operate it.

"Every stupid, boring gangster movie ends, Phil," said Jane. "We don't work for nobody. We're the appropriate ending to the pompous *Scarface* tribute act you've been doing in the 'hood all these years."

"We're the disease you created," said Trey, from the dark corner, trying to psych himself up.

Jane picked up a massive screwdriver from the workbench and passed the orange handle to Trey, all smiles, humming a funeral march.

"Are you ready to do this, Sweet Pea?"

"Of course." Trey took a deep breath and gathered his courage. They'd discussed this moment several times before. Planned it. Dreamed it. This was going to be better than marriage. The unbreakable bond of unbreakable bonds.

Jane leaned over and kissed him on the mouth. A strong, vigorous kiss like a breath of life and renewed conviction. The knot in his stomach untied itself. This was the right thing to do. Jane was the one to do right by. The one he wanted to be with forever. Whatever the cost.

Trey smiled at Jane and, without looking, he took a large swing and jammed the screwdriver into Philip Testa's shoulder. The long, deafening scream changed everything.

◆◆◆

Philip Testa cried through the entire process. He sobbed like a terrified boy when Trey drilled through his nine hundred dollar Gucci shoes and into his feet. He called his wife's name in vain and said things like, "Christina. *Mi scusi*, Christina. I never deserved your patience," and "I don't deserve the peace. I don't. I just don't," over and over again. It was supposed to be a bonding experience, an exercise in symbiosis, but all Jane could focus on was Testa and his life leaking through every hole Trey punctured in his body.

"Cut it short, please," she said. "I've had enough of his bawling."

"What? You can't be serious?" said Trey. He was kneeling next to Testa's left leg and working the hacksaw through his calf. He said he wanted to pull a meat chunk out, just to see what would happen. "Isn't it the whole point?"

Spattered blood formed a constellation on his face, from which his big, brown eyes shone like two malevolent suns. This was not her Trey. Not her Sweet Pea. Not tonight.

"Just . . . get it over with, OK? We did it, Sweet Pea. We broke that barrier together. There's no turning back. Just seal the deal now, please."

"But . . ." said Trey. He pointed at Testa with the casualness of a butcher on the clock. The man who once reigned over Philadelphia's underworld was crying and drooling on his chest. His mouth formed expressions of pain that sound couldn't quite render, hacksaw still jammed in his left calf. "But he doesn't wanna die. It's not like it's my fault or something. I'm doing my best here, baby."

"Puh-leeee-eeease," muttered Testa. At this point, it seemed like the only word he could still articulate.

Trey walked back and forth between the workbench and his victim. His right hand browsed over several tools, only to return to his chin each time. He tapped his index finger against his jaw, something he often did when he was focused. Finally, he went back to the big orange screwdriver and launched himself at Testa. He stabbed him in the lungs so many times that Jane lost count.

"Fuck it," said Trey, out of breath. He threw the screwdriver in a corner of the basement and wiped his hands on his pants. Testa's supplications turned into a ragged wheeze. "Let's get out of here. He's done."

Jane followed Trey upstairs, silent and horrified. When Trey closed the basement door and sealed Philip Testa away forever, it didn't make her feel any better. She followed him to the kitchen, where he turned on the gas stove.

"I planned that part out," he said. "You'll see. Nobody gonna trace this back to us. I promise."

"Trey," said Jane.

He turned around. His eyes were not pulsing with this unexplainable, chaotic wrath anymore. They were not like before. Not like she loved. Something about them looked sealed, like Testa in the basement. Somewhere she didn't have access to anymore. Maybe he left a part of him downstairs.

"It's too late now. What's done is done, baby," he said.

They looked at each other while the room filled up with gas, trying to find that thing that bridged the gap between them. Later that night, when Trey launched the Molotov cocktail and the gambler's house went up in flames, Jane hoped it would bury that moment out of both their reach.

♦♦♦

The third time Trey went to the bathroom, there was only bile left to evacuate. The stale, putrid stench of trucker ass helped wrenching it out. Maybe they should have stopped at the Waffle House next exit.

Maybe the problem was Jane. Each time he sat across the booth from her, it was like it happened all over again: Jane's gleefulness, Testa, the blood, the cries, the whimpers, her doubts, the great ball of fire. The stench of death. Each time he left to go puke, it became a little more real to him. What seemed incongruous was that he was at the center of it all. He couldn't explain the overwhelming powerlessness.

Trey looked at himself in the mirror, his skin so white, it almost camouflaged into the cold glare of the neon lights. The few hairs sticking out of his chin seemed grotesque to him. This wasn't what was advertised. Trey walked back to the dining booth, resigned to make something happen. Jane leaned over her plate, picking away at her eggs.

"Baby, I gotta tell you something," he said.

"Yes, I understand," said Jane, reading his mind.

"There is some stuff I have to take care of, you know? Loose ends in Jersey. We gotta do this right, you know? Leave no trace behind. The sun is almost up."

He didn't make any sense, but it wasn't important. The only thing Trey wanted was to get out of there. Gather himself, get away from everything.

"Absolutely, it's fine," said Jane. "I mean, nothing's gonna happen right? Nobody will know it was us, right?"

"Of course not," said Trey.

"Right?"

"Yeah, baby. Don't worry. Don't worry about a thing."

"Right."

"It'll only take a couple of hours, OK? Then you can take the Greyhound and meet me later in Atlantic City."

"Sure."

Trey dropped five twenties on the table, leaned over the table and kissed Jane on the forehead. She smiled at him. An automatic twitch of the lips. Trey walked out Princesses Café, into the greater unknown.

Everything dies, he thought. The things he was most convinced of were set ablaze along with the anonymous house Philip Testa died in. But if Jane showed up tonight, all checked up, with her hair fixed pretty, who knew, right?

Anything could happen in this life.

Because the Night
Richard Thomas

She haunts my dreams.

I wake up coated in a sheen of sweat, a shadow passing in front of my apartment window. Cotton in my mouth, teeth marks on my chest, there is a stinging sensation up and down my back, my sheets dotted with blood.

Mine or hers?

I close my eyes and her laughter drifts to me, her lips at my ear, my neck, her bite an aching anticipation, her gentle embrace, enveloping.

At the window, the world is blanketed in a white blindness. I see her boot prints in the snow below me, the world outside gone dead.

Maybe it'll be tonight, when the darkness slips over me, and I descend into a bottle, wallowing in one subtle flinch after another, memories of her floating on my shaking fingertips. Or maybe she'll push off, disappear again, leaving in her wake another drifter, an echo of sweaty violence that happened in the night, between the car alarms, the door slams, a moment that falls away the harder I try to reclaim it.

There are no names here, no phone calls, technology failing, the rest of the mating dances that others do only false shadows, imitations, rituals created out of habit and reflection.

The weekend stretches out, and at the back of my head there is a tingling, a snake unfurling in my gut. Part of me hopes she'll keep on walking, never come back, a weight slipping off my shoulders, denting the hardwood floor, freeing me to go back to my life with my dignity intact.

But there is another part of me. It crouches and waits, arms wrapped tightly around a coiled anxiety, wanting more, regardless of the cost. It blinks almond-shaped eyes and aches for her scent, her touch, the back of her hand, the splitting of flesh, the taste of glossy copper swallowed with a grin. Her tiny fists are like pistons, her body a flurry of sharp angles and soft places to land. She gives me pleasure and takes it away. It's the only way I'll have it.

When the knock finally comes in the middle of the night, long after I've given up and gone to sleep, settled back into the day to come, the cubicles and concrete, the jostle of bodies and squinting eyes, muffled curses and surrender, her shadow slips under the door. A tremble runs across my flesh, parts of me gone rigid, nausea washing under and over, and her knuckles rap against the door, harder and harder, the urgency rifling the wood. I picture her white skin, the thin fingers, the way they must be pink now from her pounding, slowly bruising, and she keeps at it, insistent. And I know that those fingers will be in my mouth in moments, in my hair, pulling, slipped inside of her swollen flesh with a frantic urgency, wrapped around my neck. But they will also lie like sleeping birds, under her resting face, marbled peace donned like a mask.

I never ask her why.

Darkness on the Edge of Town
Lela Scott MacNeil

The sun never sets on Sun Burst! A desert paradise waits for you! Twenty-four hours of unbroken pleasure! Sunbathe to your heart's content along the white sandy beaches of the Sun Burst Sea! The future is now! Head on over to Sun Burst, where the Sun never sets on Fun! (Sun Burst Township is a presentation of Sun Burst Energy Corp., Incorporated.)

It was the kind of sun you couldn't escape, the kind that made any scrap of shade shrivel. A vampire sun, sucking your salty lifeblood, leaving you ready to discard yourself by the side of the road, a withered husk of whoever you used to be.

It was the kind of sun that hadn't gone down in four hundred and sixty-seven days. But who's counting? You know that song about the sun coming out tomorrow? What if it never fucking set? Where's your ditty for that, little orphan asshole?

That sun was the first thing that hit me when I came to that afternoon. It was always the first thing that hit me, though most days I wasn't waking up in the bottom of a giant pit at two in the afternoon. Or was it two in the morning? Did it matter?

Discovering your body spread out on cement that has been baking for hundreds of days in endless sunlight will give you a whole new sympathy for fried eggs. I twisted myself upward into something approximating a standing position. My brain sloshed around in whatever liquid I had left up there. The smell of rotting goldfish clawed at my face. They'd drained the artificial lake a few days ago, but they hadn't gotten around to the fish. The poor dead bastards were sprinkled all across the pale, gray wasteland, mouths still open because they died trying to live. I felt my stomach crawling up my throat.

I wondered if they'd say the same for me.

I stumbled downward. Ribs angry, forehead angry, my whole fucking body pissed. Sweat oozed out from under my armpits and breasts, sliding through my ass cheeks and down my thighs. Without asking for permission, my mouth retched out about a quarter cup of precious fluid. If I didn't get to water soon, the question of *now what* wouldn't matter.

I sat back. Lit a cigarette. Thought about it. I pulled the snack-size, crumpled Ziplock baggie from my shirt pocket and inhaled a fingernail of white powder. I kept one of my fingernails long for just this purpose, the rest short for the women I sometimes talked into bed.

I'd left New York City to get away from you. That's not quite right. I left New York to get away from the fact that you wanted nothing more to do with me. Something I could ignore when I was two thousand miles away and fighting the sun at the bottom of a concrete pit.

When I left New York, I told myself I was finished, not just with you but with women in general. I told myself I was going back to sleeping with men I didn't give a shit about, handing out my number and not caring about calls that never came. I told myself I was going back to being normal. Maybe I'd even find the man who could make an honest woman out of me. Or at least make my father happy.

The hotel where I'd been working as a receptionist had finally let me go. Soon there'd be no more funds for luxuries, but why not enjoy life while it lasted? The drug charged through me, turning my skin on like a light switch, spreading around a goosebumping sensation recalling refrigerated air.

They dubbed this pit the Sun Burst Sea, after the corporation that bought the naming rights a few years back. In exchange, the town was selected as the test site for a new energy technology that would do away with night, *once and for all*, they said, *think of the possibilities*, they said, *the productivity*. I got here twelve months ago, having read the travel section of the *Times* at the exact moment I needed an answer. The wording of the article made Sun Burst seem the kind of place that might not ask about a person's arrest record, and frankly, I needed a little sunshine.

I stood up, springy from the coke. That was the one thing I had to give this place. Its proximity to the border made for cheap access to some excellent blow. The metal ladder singed the insides of my hands as I climbed it, but the drug had given me a congenial relationship to pain. At the ladder's summit, the dried, cracking mud spread out before me like a spider-web empire, all that was left of the famed white, sandy beaches of the Sun Burst Sea. In the distance, dull, blue mountains ragged a gash across the neon sky.

When I left the City, I told myself I was done with women, but as it turned out, they weren't done with me. Sun Burst had a strange policy of hiring nothing but hot young things for their service positions. I guess I picked the wrong town to get over my bad habits.

The letters on the sign for the Pleasure Palace, where the few remaining citizens of Sun Burst bought our liquor, were falling off, so that now it just read "Pleas e Pal." I walked straight to the back, to the defunct coolers, and pounded two lukewarm Mike's Hard Cranberry Lemonades right there in the aisle, letting it dribble out the corners of my mouth and onto my T-Shirt. Bad form, even for me.

Sharon, the counter clerk, came over to my place about once a week, and in exchange she let me take whatever I wanted from the store. I knew I owed her some flirty conversation or at the very least a thank you, but I let the cans clatter to the graying linoleum and pushed myself back out into the sun, away from her protests that someday I was going to have to start paying for this shit.

◆◆◆

The night before, I'd made it all the way into the Sun Burst grid mainframe. You would've been proud. I'd made it all the way to where I could feel the buzz of the computers beneath my skin. As if the machines had recruited and absorbed me, enslaved me to the eternal illumination of this little slice of hell. I watched the barricade of red and green and yellow lights flash on and off. *Now what*, as you would have said. I hadn't expected to make it this far. When the blonde at the bar slipped me her swipe card and told me it'd be this easy, I hadn't believed her. Yet there I stood, feeling idiotic with nothing but a pair of pliers in my pocket. Which must have been when they came up behind me, silent as sin, knocking me into the next afternoon. Into that concrete pit surrounded by dead goldfish.

When I made it back to my apartment, I thanked whoever was left up there that the water was on. The shower wasn't cold, of course, I hadn't paid my cooling surcharge for more than a month, but there was a certain animal pleasure in the way the wetness pulled itself down my body. Like fingers or tongues. For a few seconds after the shower, as the evaporation coated my skin, I was bathed in a halo of miraculous cold. I shivered and tried, and failed, to avoid thinking about the exact sensation of your lips along my hipbones.

That was the night you held me down in the middle of the road, four in the morning and nothing was moving in the blackness except the whites of your eyes. You held me down because if you hadn't I would have floated away, so full of your helium was I. You held me down, but first, you had to catch me. We were playing a game, or you were. I was running, not from you exactly, but from what being caught would mean. You were that phone booth and I fell anyway, the only one who understood the loss.

♦♦♦

Armed with my tightest dress, my brightest lipstick, a few more lines, Ziplock baggie tucked underneath my breast, I walked over to the Paradise Lounge to spend the last of my money.

The bar was lukewarm and heavy with perspiration, but at least it was shade. A week ago, they started rationing the electricity. The air was sulking around the room like a petulant child. My plan was to thoroughly forget about yesterday. Buy a couple rounds of Jameson shots for me and Bartender Sue. See where the night took us. Where the night took us was a known entity, white lines and windowsill cigarettes, sweat slipping skin like zoo seals making a run for it.

My plan did not include the woman already at the bar. The only person in the whole damn town holding on to her water like it was worth something. A white silk dress, leaving just the right amount to the imagination. Skin so pale you could almost see right through it. Black hair, red lipstick, you get the picture. Like maybe she'd spent time with seven short men hiding out from her bitch stepmother. By the time the cigarette made it to her lips I was there with my Zippo, because how else do you respond to a woman like that?

The pale woman's apartment was cold as a slap. Outside the windows, blackness was swallowing the world, and though I knew what night was, I felt my heart grabbing at the wall of my chest. I pulled out my bag of treats and she laughed. The thing I liked best about this one was the way her lipstick was on just a little bit crooked. I wanted to smear it all over her mouth until it looked like she'd recently killed a small animal with her teeth.

I suppose you'll want to know why you wound up at the bottom of the pit, she said. I felt my stomach clench, and hoped it didn't show in my face.

Not particularly, I said. She looked at me with eyes that ripped out your guts, ate them, leaving you to bleed out on her white carpet.

I'm sorry we had to go to such extremes. Usually we try to be a little more civilized.

Aren't you supposed to call it the Sun Burst Sea?

Excuse me?

The pit.

When you paid for it, sweetheart, you can call it whatever the fuck you like.

I took the five steps that separated us and put my hand on her cheek. I let it rest there for a couple of seconds, then I spread the lipstick all around until it looked like she had recently killed a small animal with her teeth. I let my hand drop.

Which was when I felt them materialize from the shadows, grabbing my arms like vices, ready to break me at one word from that bloodied, lipstick mouth.

Radio Nowhere
Chuck Regan

Dolphins weave through the waves alongside the schooner. I feel like I'm speeding along with them as I watch from the deck. With the stars chiming overhead, and the moon crackling in the stripes of water slithering across their backs, the beauty of it all gets inside of me and my chest feels light.

A dolphin leaps out of the water shrieking. Then another shrieks the same tone. It isn't a playful sound. It isn't a pleasant sound. Their movements turn mechanical and brittle, synchronized and patterned, like broken toys on a rusty wheel.

Shriek. Shriek. Shriek. Shriek.

The moon above pulses in rhythm.

Pulse. Pulse. Pulse. Pulse.

◆◆◆

I snap my eyes open—alarms flashing in the sleep bay. Adrenaline tears apart my chest and I gasp, straining my shoulders as my lungs, still dreaming, can't take in enough air. I'm suffocating. I smack the lid off the sleeper and fall into the hallway, coughing.

My lungs wheeze out the last of the twilight gas and I take in a breath of oxygen as if it's my first. My chest stops burning and my shoulders stop heaving.

The alert says meteorites punched through my cargo bay. Contract says I have to fix the damage so I don't lose any more cargo. I hate spacewalks, but they break up the boredom at least. I open the locker and eye the exosuit like it's waiting for its chance to smother me.

I check the suit's datasync four times. Out in the Float with a stripped-down AI as the only cushion between you and oblivion, it's a survival measure to obsess over these details. I put on my helmet and open the airlock door from my suit control. I close the door, then open it again. Works fine. I lock it open, just to be safe, and climb outside.

♦♦♦

Out in the Float, spacers like telling stories to each other—makes the sucking void all around them seem less of a monster, I guess. One of their favorite stories is about ghost ships. The crew is either dead or comatose in long-sleepers, and the ship just keeps going on its rounds—landing, recharging, getting cargo, requesting maintenance, launching again. Ground crews never bother to check on the crew or their rations.

The story has a lot of variations. It's always someone's friend-of-a-friend who finds the crew, either dead or surprised at how long they'd been sleeping. One version I heard a couple of times has precious cargo discovered on board that's been missing for a hundred years, and all the crew has mysteriously vanished with weird clues left behind, pointing to some long-dead murderer.

Must be some kind of truth to these tales—the way we work every day out here, it could happen to any one of us at any time. Sleeper units aren't covered under contract, and maintenance isn't cheap. My schedule keeps me on the move—no time to get the sleeper checked even if I could afford it. If I was paranoid, I'd think the company wanted a fleet of ghosts flying out here.

The only reason I'm aboard is because of an agreement signed two hundred years ago. Always have a human crew. Even though the definition of what *human* is keeps changing, that rule doesn't.

I tap six, sometimes as many as ten commands, and sleep the rest of each trip. My ship does the rest. And every time I climb into that long-sleeper I wonder if I'm going to end up in one of those ghost ship stories. I keep telling myself to have them checked. Maybe as a birthday gift to myself after I dock.

On this trip, I'll turn sixty years old. All the time I spend in twilight sleep keeps me looking half that age. There are a lot of old youngsters out here. I met a guy once whose grandkids looked older than him.

♦♦♦

The rhythm of the respirator is soothing, and after crawling half the length of the hull, I settle down and let myself feel how peaceful it is out here. I can understand how the ancients thought the stars were gods. They wink as if letting me know they're still here.

My grip slips off the ladder and I get a feeling like liquid nitrogen pouring down my back. Even though the emergency impeller on my suit would carry me back to the ship if I did drift free, I hug the old rail like a kid clinging to his wire mesh mommy.

The gods don't look so friendly anymore. My breathing settles and, keeping my head down, focused on my grip, I keep moving.

Far below my feet I see that tiny gleaming pearl at the bottom of a black lake—the Sun, Sol. That delicate jewel chimes in my skull like a bell, calling me home. It's so tiny from out here. Our species should have never run away this far—my genetic memory tells me it's wrong for it to be that small. Something is wrong, my brain says.

We don't belong out here.

◆◆◆

Yeah, those meteorites did a good job. The corner of crate sixty-two is bashed wide open. I look inside and see the precious cargo I'm hauling. Face-of-Mars plushies. I laugh.

I key open a maintenance locker and find some tools. When I'm done patching up the hole, it looks like some neon green space fungus has gnawed off a corner of the crate.

I lost maybe four boxes of cargo in the impact, but my entry in the report will make what's left worth even more. The dirtnobs on Earth love that shit—the excitement and danger of life in space. Here's your plushie.

◆◆◆

I strap myself into the command chair and open my report. My words flitter across the screen as I speak them, and although I try to sound as official as I can about the "tragic loss of an unknown number of Face-of-Mars plushies to the unforgiving vastness of space," the absurdity of it all slams my mouth shut. The chronometer says I still have a month to go before I reach Luna 2. Plenty of time to finish the report. I switch on the entertainment.

Projected onto my retina, creepy grinning masks stare back at me as the three-meter-tall puppets dance and sing. They're the biggest draw back on Mars. The puppets tour all over the planet, singing nonsense. I suppose they are so popular because they are not trying to make sense of this world. People respect their honesty.

The videos I flip through are just as absurd as the puppet's songs. Some cater to the nanosecond-attention-span audience of the Transhumans—data streams and puzzle codes nested inside high-speed psychedelic fractals. It supposedly gives the brain-enhanced folks a magnificent high. All it gives me is a headache.

Something passes between me and the nearest relay station, and the pictures distort and seize.

I take it as a cue to switch to music, and am assaulted by Shatter rock. Each track of the noise music, generated by nanoreceptors in the "musician's" bloodstream, is named after the activity the artist is supposedly performing during the recording—Baby Rape, Titan Freefall, Acid Bath . . .

Eight hundred seventy channels are devoted to this crap, filtered by flavors of aggression. No rhythms—no patterns that my 1.0 brain can hold onto. I feel a wave of nausea creep into my skull and switch it all off.

The wailing horror of that aural assault bounces around in my head until I can finally hear my own breathing again. I run my palms along the top of the chair's armrests, feeling the slick-electric texture of the nanoweave and I think this the best the world has to offer me.

Up here, disconnected from the System and its loud, dumb information, senseless colors, and explosive noise, I can find peace. Cargo crate sixty-two reads all green—my patch is holding. I can go back to sleep any time I want. I can go back to dreaming about the ocean and dolphins and moonlight, and slip back into the cracks of this world.

I can sleep through my birthday and avoid the pathetic feeling I get when nobody but the System AI sends me a message. I can sleep and keep those ghosts of my past trapped up here with me. No apologies. No explanations, just me hiding from my demons.

I look at the tiny pearl sparkling up at me through the cockpit window. Sol, our good old sun, winks at me. The charts tell me it was Earth crossing my path. What were the chances that I was looking up at that very moment?

The Promised Land

Court Merrigan

Ruby Hix walked out of prison in Grants, New Mexico, just like the long-timers said to. Didn't look back the once. Two days later she was back down County Road 19 in Tate's End, Nebraska. The promised land.

The double-wide trailer she'd lived in there was gone. Shoulder-high rows of corn where it used to stand. A center pivot whirred water over the rows in precise streams.

Her third year locked up in Grants, Ruby got a letter from Mama. Postmarked Elko, Nevada. *Dad died,* Mama wrote. *Your older brother's doing ten-to-twenty in an Army stockade. Your little sister has a tongue tumor. We're moving on. Your dog's okay.*

Last Ruby Hix ever heard of them. Dog and everything, gone to dust.

Ruby looked back down County Road 19. The farmer she'd hitched a ride with long gone.

"You sure you want dropped off here?" he'd asked.

"I'm sure," Ruby said. "I been thinking about this place for seven years."

"Well," the farmer said, "you look like you can take care of yourself."

County Road 19 headed straight into town if you stayed on it. Ruby Hix veered off.

♦♦♦

She walked the backest of the back roads, where cheatgrass choked the shoulders and the curves narrowed down to one-ways. About sunset she found the field she was looking for. Pushed sunflowers aside to the old cement headgate. A squat ugly pillbox, unused for decades, it looked just like it had back in eighth grade.

Ruby Hix stuck her head in. Stale dirt smell. Blown tumble-weeds. Rat turds and cobwebs. Ran a thick finger over the old-timey cement, packed with pebbles. The pebbles her cheek pressed against. Back in eighth grade.

She crawled out. Cut across the bean field, tearing out vines with heedless steps, hopping ditches and fences. A couple miles later she came across a pickup converted into a service vehicle, lined with shelves of unlocked tools. She unshouldered her kit bag, loaded it up. Used her jacket and a shirt to muffle the clanking.

Kit bag heavy on her back, she searched out a road and thumbed a ride into town. Walked into the first pawn shop she saw, the Silver Chair.

♦♦♦

Cash pocketed, Ruby Hix went to Wal-Mart. Her monthlies had come on. Bought a pack of tampons. In the bathroom she tried to get comfortable on her first private privy in seven years but couldn't.

At the Play Center she stopped to watch a gaggle of kids picking on a little redheaded boy cowering on a Garfield teacup.

"Carrot-headed freak!" they shrieked. "Carrot-headed freak!"

At Tate's End School the kids never did stop tormenting Ruby Hix. White trash girl in patched-up dresses who didn't read too good and talked funny. She had full bouncy breasts and armpit hair. The boys chased her round the playground trying to lift up her skirt to see if she had hair down below, too, laughing at her stained second-hand panties. Girls followed her into the bathroom. Arced spit balls over the stall door.

All but Caleb McGee. He was a ninth grader who honeyed Ruby Hix up for days, saying it wasn't right what all them kids said. Don't you go listening to them.

"Am I supposed to listen to you, then?" Ruby Hix asked him.

Caleb grinned. "You bet," he said, leaning against his big green Dodge pickup, cow shit caked in the wheel wells. "Come on. Let's go for a ride, Roob. What do you say?"

Nobody had called her Roob before. She'd never had a nickname composed out of affection. Ruby Hix crawled up into the big green Dodge pickup.

"Carrot-headed freak! Carrot-headed freak!" the kids chanted to the little boy.

Ruby Hix shoved the bullies aside, sent them crying for their mommies.

"You all right?" she asked the little redheaded boy.

The boy looked up at her bulk. "Fuck off, freak," he said, then slipped off the Garfield teacup and ran away.

◆◆◆

Ruby Hix spent half her pawn shop grubstake on a cheap hotel room on the edge of town. Stood in the shower for a good hour, not quite believing she was alone, not quite believing the endless hot water.

Next morning she walked back to Tate's End.

◆◆◆

Halfway home that day Caleb McGee stopped the green Dodge pickup at the cement headgate. Said he had something to show her in there. No sooner was she on all fours than Caleb ripped away her stained panties.

"Big girl like you, this won't hurt a bit," Caleb said.

It hurt, bad, but Ruby Hix never said nothing. Cheek pressed against the pebbly cement. All the while Caleb saying, "Ah, shit, honey. Ah, honey."

He didn't say it for long. Yanked himself out and stroked her inner thigh.

"Would you just look at that," he said, wagging bloody fingertips in her face.

♦♦♦

Ruby crossed a hay field where a pickup towing a flatbed rolled along between rows of small bales. A limping old man climbed out of the cab and struggled to heave a bale onto the flatbed. Then he watched her come, leaning on the flatbed, seed corn cap soaked through with sweat.

"Afternoon," he said. "What can I do for you?"

"Looks like it's more what I can do for you," Ruby Hix said.

♦♦♦

After that, Ruby couldn't pull her panties down in the schoolhouse anymore, so she started holding it. But one day at recess she couldn't anymore. She snuck into the tall ragweed and sunflowers at the edge of the playground. The business well underway when Caleb McGee pushed through the weeds.

He grinned and reached to lift up her skirt. She swatted his hand hard. Caleb swore and pushed her right into a coil of her own shit. Then went down yelling into the schoolyard.

Ruby Hix stayed hidden in the weeds till Mrs. Custer came calling. Mrs. Custer tried to drag her down to the schoolhouse. But Ruby Hix was a big girl, after all, and at the edge of the weeds she belted Mrs. Custer so hard the teacher coughed blood.

That's how she and Mama ended up in front of the school board. Ruby Hix tried to lisp out her side of the story but weren't a one of them listening. The board expelled her and Ruby Hix never did much in the line of school after that. The family got evicted from the double-wide trailer later that fall and moved on. By the time Ruby Hix turned eighteen she'd done three stints in three different county lockups. An aggravated assault rap sent her down to Grants for six to ten. She did seven. Hard years every one.

♦♦♦

"You the cavalry, are you?" the old man asked.

"I can be. You got a extra pair of gloves?"

"You ever stacked bales before?"

"I'll learn."

He looked big Ruby Hix up and down. "All right, young lady. I could use the help."

♦♦♦

Ruby Hix and the old man finished the field and the old man handed her a warm Pepsi. Ruby Hix chugged the can and ran the back of her hand over her lips, stained green with hay dust.

"Bet you could eat," the old man said.

When they got to the old man's house, the missus never paused setting out a third place at the table. Rump roast with sauerkraut. Ruby Hix's stomach rumbled at the smell of real food.

"I never did introduce myself," the old man said. "Bernie Storn."

"I know," Ruby Hix said. "I remember you driving the school bus."

"I thought I recognized you. You didn't tell me your name."

Ruby told him. Mr. Storn nodded. "Thought so," he said. Leaned back in his chair while Mrs. Storn cleared the table. "I always have thought it was a damn shame the way they treated you. You and your whole family."

"Language, Bernie," Mrs. Storn said.

"Sorry, Mother," Mr. Storn said. "I do appreciate the help, Ruby." He laughed. "The way you come storming across that field, I figured you for a hay thief. I thought to myself, they sure have got brazen, haven't they. You believe it's come to that? Thieves lifting hay right out of your field?"

Mr. Storn made Ruby out a check. Ruby folded it up in her breast pocket.

"Well, Ruby, I got to level with you," Mr. Storn said. "I got no more work."

"The roast was good all the same."

"Mother's glad to hear that but I'm guessing you'd like more work."

Ruby nodded. Mr. Storn tottered to his feet for the phone.

"Dave Struble runs a big operation. Hay broker and all. He's always looking for help. Maybe you two went to school together?"

"I remember him," Ruby said.

◆◆◆

Mr. Storn drove Ruby Hix over, and Dave Struble came out of his big metal shed wiping oily hands clean on a rag. Spat out a black wad of chew.

"I'll be good and goddamned," Dave Struble said. "Ruby Hix. It really is you."

"It's me," Ruby Hix said.

"Well, come on. I got work for you."

Ruby Hix labored the next days alongside a couple broke-down old jokers hauling twelve-inch irrigation pipe off the fields. The pipes were heavy with dried mud and the jokers took a lot of breaks. Joking about Ruby's big tits rippling her T-shirt when they thought she was out of earshot.

Dave Struble let Ruby Hix stay in an old camper he had out by Lake Marie. Ruby Hix cooked beans on a hotplate and then lay down on the narrow bunk. Stared at the stains on the ceiling flickering in the unsteady gas lantern light. The camper like a cell. Oddly comforting for the fact.

Next morning Dave Struble pulled her aside.

"Ruby," he said, "I want you to know I always thought Caleb McGee was a son of a bitch."

"What?"

"For what he said about you."

Ruby leaned in so close to him Dave Struble could smell boiled eggs on her breath.

"What?" she said.

"Hell, Ruby. It was before a basketball game, in the locker room. Shawn Harkins had out a centerfold and Caleb started saying he didn't have to mess with no pictures. Said he'd had himself the real thing." He took a fat pinch of chew. "Always was a talky little shit. Didn't no one believe him. What was we, ninth graders? But then he showed us a pair of ripped panties. Kind of, you know. Stained up."

"Shit," Ruby Hix said.

"Look, I'm sorry. But, you know, all this time I wondered if that's why you done what you done. To Mrs. Custer and all."

"You could say that."

"I know it ain't none of my business. But you back for Caleb?"

"Why?"

"Because I know him," Dave said. "I know him real well."

◆◆◆

Caleb McGee's white brick house perched atop a rise overlooking Hiram Creek, green fields of Tate's End stretched out below. Cattle shifted in the fading evening light in the corrals below the home.

Dave Struble tapped out another pinch of chew. "I ever tell you your ol' pal Caleb down there's a hay thief?"

"No."

"He is. Don't seem fair, do it? That nice house and all. Compared to where you been living these last seven years."

Ruby Hix looked at him. "I don't know what you're talking about."

Dave Struble tapped the smartphone in his breast pocket. "It's public record, Ruby." He looked down at the house. "Your parole officer know you come this far outside of New Mexico?"

"No."

"We can sure keep it that way. Or not."

"There a reason you're telling me all this?"

"There a reason you walked into the Silver Chair Pawn Shop to sell off my neighbor's tools?"

Ruby Hix didn't say anything.

"Good. You do better with your mouth shut. You think a bunch of tools can go walking out of Tate's End without me knowing? The Silver Chair, the first person they call is me. Not the law. Me. Don't nobody take nothing in Tate's End without my say-so, Ruby. Nobody. You remember that."

Ruby Hix kept on staring at Caleb McGee's big house, butterscotch squares of light in the windows. "You go on ahead and call New Mexico if you got to."

"Nah," Dave Struble said. "I got a whole other proposal for you."

◆◆◆

Caleb McGee was working heifers in the mucky corral when a woman toting a branding iron came slogging at him.

"The hell?" Caleb McGee held up an arm to block the sun.

Ruby Hix swung the branding iron and smashed that arm in three places. Ruby Hix swung again and Caleb McGee tumbled into the mire. Ribs cracked. Lowing cattle swirled around the pair. Dave Struble leaned against the corral fence, watching.

"What do you want, for Christ's sake?" Caleb McGee said, sputtering blood.

Ruby Hix stepped between him and the sun so Caleb McGee could get a clear view. "Jesus Christ," he said. "Ruby Hix?"

"Fuck you, Caleb McGee." Ruby Hix raised the branding iron again.

After a time Dave Struble scaled the fence, smiling. Unhanded the branding iron from panting Ruby Hix.

He squatted by Caleb McGee curled fetal on his side. Spat out a tobacco wad, deliberately dipped another.

"Stealing hay, Caleb?" Dave Struble said. "Out of my valley? I thought better of you than that, son."

Caleb McGee's shattered jaw twitched.

"Shhhh," Dave Struble said. "Don't say nothing. Just make it up to me. Some flatbed trailers will be coming through here real soon. They're going to load up your hay and you're going to sign whatever they give you. Ain't that right?"

Caleb McGee nodded.

"Good. This ain't complicated, Caleb. Tate's End is mine. Don't make it so's Ruby here has got to explain that to you again."

Caleb McGee moaned through the blood burbling at his lips.

Dave Struble patted Caleb on the shoulder. "You'll heal. You just got the shit kicked out of you by one mean-ass heifer, that's all. Won't no one believe that story but that's the one you're going to tell." He stood to go. "Come on, Ruby."

"That's it?" said Ruby.

Struble chortled into his wad of chew. "Don't you worry," he said. "This is the promised land. I got plenty more work for you."

Open All Night
Eric Beetner

Elwood sat in the booth nearest the cash register. His fingers danced whenever the bell would ring and the girl stuffed another ten or twenty into the till. The skin on his fingertips burned, wanting to reach for the gun and get this thing started. To shout all the practiced commands for people to get down, shut up, empty their pockets—and watch them obey.

But patience meant a bigger take. He hated when one of these jerks paid with their goddamn ATM cards. Uncle Sam's genuine greenbacks too good for you, fuckers?

The crowd had thinned though. Almost time.

◆◆◆

Barb waited for the coffee pot to fill. Nightshift at a 24-hour diner had to be the slowest version of suicide she could measure. Twenty-six years and counting and still the sweet, quiet stillness of death hadn't claimed her yet.

Same couldn't be said for Newell, her husband. He was laid out back at home, growing colder. Probably starting to stink up the apartment by now. She'd left the windows open and fall had turned chilly, but not cold enough to keep a dead body in any kind of shape she'd want to see after her shift ended at six.

Barb looked at the clock. 2:16 a.m. The coffee pot stopped burbling, full to the brim. Ready to kick start more of these sad sacks into another night of fighting the loneliness or the guilt. Whatever it was that brought someone to a place like this at such an ungodly time of night.

♦♦♦

Martin wondered how long this guy could go without a piss. Sitting in the booth and making small talk was going to kill this fellow long before Martin had a chance to pull the trigger on the target seated across from him.

He hated business contracts. Martin much preferred a good old jealous husband or a vengeful wife. Having to fake a business meeting this late into the night made him question if he could ask for overtime in his fee. Not exactly a union for this line of work, though.

But the strip club had been too crowded, then this bastard invited those other jerks with them when they left. Martin had been waiting it out, watching the others slowly fall away until now it was finally only him and the target. All he needed was for the drunken, boorish bastard to get up and go take a leak and he could do it in the john, leave money for the check and get the fuck out of this place that stank of bacon grease and glowed with a neon buzz from the signs in every window hoping to lure truckers like moths to a neon pink flame. More like flies to shit.

And the fucker was *still* talking . . .

♦♦♦

Don, the owner of this fine establishment, sat on a stool behind the counter and glared at his customers wishing they would all choke on a cheeseburger and die.

Once his pride and joy, the EAT 'EM UP diner had become a chrome and Formica anchor around his neck. In debt up to his hair plugs, Don was getting the squeeze from the new plaza out on the Interstate. The one with a drive-thru Starbucks, a pizza/hamburger combo joint, smoothie shop and a frozen yogurt place.

His charburgers, weak coffee, and soft serve couldn't compete anymore. All he got were the losers, the cheapskates, the transients. Used to be he had regulars. Long haul truckers who would stop by as sure as Old Faithful for a tuna melt and a cup of joe to go. Guys who would come in just to flirt with Barb and order a piece of pie. Now Barb looked like forty miles of bad road and his pie supplier shut down so all he had was thawed out, preservative-packed hockey pucks with faux fruit filling.

Fuck it. Didn't make a shit worth of difference. Don was gonna burn the whole place down. If his mood didn't improve, he'd do it tonight with all these shitstains inside.

◆◆◆

Gene stayed in his seat a half hour after the guy left. His legs wouldn't work. Numb from the waist down. Had he really done that? Really bought a gun?

He pressed a hand to the paper sack on the bench beside him. Yep. He did.

Now, next question. Was he really going to go home and kill his wife with it?

◆◆◆

Elwood wanted to say no when the waitress swung around with a fresh pot of coffee, but his nerves wouldn't let him start the show quite yet. She looked even more disappointed than he did when he nodded yes for a top-off. She tilted her elbow and filled his cup. He'd rented the booth for another few minutes. Then he'd show them. He'd show all of them.

♦♦♦

Something about the sounds of the coffee splashing out made Barb remember the gush of blood that hit the floor after she stabbed Newell. She couldn't have planted the knife any better if she'd been working the knife-throwing gag at the circus for twenty-six years instead. A lucky shot between the ribs and her husband's heart did a spit take of blood all over her and the kitchen floor.

She barely had time to clean herself up before her shift. Barb hated to think how much cleanup awaited her at home.

♦♦♦

Martin flagged the waitress over, asked for more coffee for him and his new friend. The jerk tried to beg off with a quip about his back teeth swimming already. *So why not go to the toilet, you dumbass?* Martin thought.

♦♦♦

Don watched a fly land on the blade of his pancake and egg flipper. He didn't shoo it away, didn't swat at it. He let it nibble on the charred remains of late-night over-easy and hash browns. Let these useless wrecks get salmonella, dysentery, fucking Ebola for all he cared.

They deserved nothing less.

♦♦♦

Gene couldn't stop touching the sack. Like an itch. With his right hand he pushed around the remains of his burnt potatoes through the bright yellow crust of his burst egg yolks. His left hand probed the bag, feeling the outline of the gun through the paper.

When the waitress passed, he kept his hand still. Didn't want the crinkling sack to give him away. He shook his head at the coffee pot in her hand, a wordless transaction, and she went back to her post near the front.

At this hour, Marianne would be asleep. This would be the night she wouldn't wake up. If only he get could get his damn legs to work.

♦♦♦

Elwood felt the extra coffee in his joints. His fingers couldn't sit still, firing with tiny jolts of chemical electricity. Caffeine and adrenalin mixed in his blood and made a combo more potent than cocaine. Subconsciously, he sniffed.

The time is now.

Elwood shifted in his seat, but then went still. The two guys in the booth across the aisle were getting up.

♦♦♦

It wasn't until Martin complained about how bad he had to piss that the target took the hint. The power of suggestion came on strong and the guy rushed to get out of his seat as if he might piss his pants.

Martin, acting the gentleman, waved him by, then followed after, grateful the night's work was almost done.

◆◆◆

Don watched the two men rush to the men's room. What were they, five fuckin' years old? Can't tell when they have to go potty until it's too late?

He should've spit in their food. At least this meant they'd be paying up and getting out soon.

◆◆◆

Barb sighed and flipped through her pad to the check for table six. She totaled everything up in pencil, then tore off the check and dropped it on their table when they were gone. Better that way. She didn't have to humor them about more coffee or maybe some pie. They'd get the hint when they came back.

Both guys wore suits, so Barb crossed her fingers for a decent tip.

◆◆◆

Gene sat stone still as the two men passed. Did they know? Could they see it? What would they do if they found out he had a gun with him?

They'd be surprised. Shocked. Not as much as anyone who knew Gene well. They wouldn't be able to believe it at all. And that's how he'd get away with it. No one would think he was capable of such a thing. His name wouldn't even come up in the investigation.

Gene felt pins and needles in his right leg as it came back from the dead. His body had decided the time was right. He lifted a hand to the waitress at the end of the counter, made the check signing motion. She nodded and took out her pad.

◆◆◆

Elwood decided to wait until the two guys were out of the can. Two fewer people to mess things up. Two fewer witnesses. He'd miss out on the money in their wallets, but they'd make a deposit in the register for however much their check was, which would be his soon enough.

He set a hand on the gun inside his pocket.

♦♦♦

Barb dropped the check at the weird guy in the corner. That left only the jittery one up front. At least bussing their tables would give her something to do. Cleanup. More goddamn cleanup.

She made a mental note to stop off on her way home and buy some supplies. She knew damn well she didn't keep enough cleaning crap at home for a mess the size of Newell.

Barb wondered if he'd stopped bleeding yet. For a moment there, it seemed like it might go on forever.

♦♦♦

Don watched as one of the guys came out of the bathroom, moving as fast as he did when he went in. Maybe his buddy had the shits or something requiring a longer visit.

Good.

♦♦♦

Martin slowed his walk when it became apparent the waitress was in no hurry to move. He ran a hand across his forehead and pushed his hair back again, still wet from the sink where he splashed himself clean after a job well done.

◆◆◆

The bell over the door tinkled as one of Don's last remaining regulars stepped in. Officer Ronald McGiven of the State Highway Patrol showed up right on time. Barb already had the fresh pot of coffee made for him. Ronald unzipped his jacket and said, "Hi, Barb."

◆◆◆

Elwood's shot was the first to hit him. He thought so anyway. The air was so filled with gunshots he couldn't be sure of anything for a moment.

◆◆◆

Gene fired the gun through the paper sack. Any doubts if he would be able to pull the trigger flew out the window when he saw the uniform walk in. He fired four times and when he stopped, the bag around the barrel of his new gun had caught fire.

◆◆◆

Martin drew and fired before he knew he was doing it. Instinct and the high from the fix he'd just fired into his veins in the bathroom put him on autopilot.

When he stopped shooting and realized there were two other gunmen in the room, he froze.

◆◆◆

Barb almost screamed. She went from shocked to scared and then dumbfounded and dazed when she saw Ronald's body on the floor.

It reminded her so much of Newell that she couldn't move, and for the first time it truly hit her what she had done to her husband.

♦ ♦ ♦

Don sat very still. He watched the standoff in his joint. Three men with guns that came out of fucking nowhere. Three men all shooting a cop but not each other. It was like everyone in the place had been sleepwalking at the same time, and then with the tremendous sound of all those guns firing at once, they woke up and now stood around looking at a scene they'd been dropped into from the darkness.

Yep. This seemed about fucking right.

Don stood. "Okay. Everyone put 'em away. Y'all start walking toward the door. Go one at a time. I don't know you and you don't know me. You were never here. This never happened."

Martin was the first to move, then Elwood, then Gene. Barb stood still, gazing down at Ronald as each man passed by her in the aisle.

"You too, Barb," Don said.

Don brought his hand out of his pocket. He thumbed open the lid to his Zippo.

"I'll be right behind you."

Meeting Across the River

Steve Weddle

Tommy pulled at the bottom edge of his T-shirt, wiped his hand on his thigh.

Jesus, Tommy. Paul tossed him the dress shirt, white, pearl buttons, French cuffs.

This for?

Take off the goddamn shirt.

This is my lucky shirt, Tommy said.

It's a fucking eagle in a helmet.

He's a fighter pilot, man. Show some respect.

He's an eagle.

Whatever, man.

Tommy came back from behind the gas station, Paul flicking a spent cigarette into the weeds, the cans along the side fence, some honeysuckle that grew through the chain-link diamonds because no one gave a damn about the edge of the property, about the edge of anything.

Better?

Paul nodded, said yeah. Said they had to look like pros. You want to be big time, he said, you act big time. Only difference between us and them. Act like you been there before.

Tommy said yeah.

Only difference.

You patch things up with Sherri?

Paul said don't worry about, said it'll be fine.

Tommy scratched the back of his neck, asked was she still pissed.

Paul looked at Tommy until Tommy looked off somewhere else.

The lights from a Lexus cut across them, wheels crunching gravel like loosened teeth.

Paul stepped towards the passenger window. The car continued its curve, past the pumps and back into the street.

Tommy rolled the shirt cuffs up to his elbows, deep ink of two daggers, twisted wire along one forearm, a melted scar along the other.

Paul took a newspaper from next to him, folded it in half, half again, a misshapen brick never meant to build anything. Put it in your pants, he said. It'll look like you got something there.

He pulled the shirt over it, the little bump there that could have been anything.

How much I owe you for the shirt?

Fuck you.

No, man. Really.

Don't worry about it. Sherri's dad.

Her dad?

Yeah. Went through his stuff the other day, packing it up. Mostly smelled like a cat's ass. Church got a lot of that. Saved some shirts and shit. Nice chain for a pocket watch, too.

Fits good, I guess. Tommy pulled at the armpits of the dead man's shirt. So, what you gonna do with the money?

From this?

Yeah.

For fuck's sake, Tommy. Don't go getting your ass ahead of your dick, man.

I ain't. I'm just saying, two grand, you know? And then who knows, right? This goes good . . .

Well, yeah. It's gotta go good though. Then, well, shit, you know, then whatever.

Sherri?

Bunch of shit.

But her, yeah?

What are you so worried about with her?

Ain't worried, Tommy said. Just sounded like it was over between you and her.

Paul asked who told him that. Took a step, asked it again.

Nobody. Just, you know, I mean, from what you were saying. Just you. Saying stuff. You know?

Yeah, Paul said. I know. You know what else I know?

Tommy shook his head, waited for it. What Paul knew. So Tommy reached into his back pocket for the knife, felt the length of it inside his fist, across his palm, tried to visualize the movements, the block, the counter.

Paul said he knew someone was fucking Sherri behind his back.

Tommy thought "behind her back," but didn't say anything. Just waited for it, like he'd been waiting for the past three months of it. Knowing it was the wrong idea. Knowing someday. Just not knowing this was the day. Never knowing it would go down like this.

Paul said he bet it was that balding prick from outside Philly, said he bet it was that fucker.

Tommy took his hand from the knife, ran his hand through his hair, said, yeah, he never trusted that guy.

A truck pulled into the parking lot. Driver got out, left a couple teenage boys in the cab, was in and out of the store in under a minute.

Rolling papers, Paul figured, then said maybe this wasn't the best place to get a car.

Tommy said he knew another place, few blocks over.

Paul said they had to get a car in the next hour, get to the meeting across the river.

Tommy said, maybe this wasn't the job for them. Maybe they could just stop now. Work for his uncle again.

Paul said this was it. Their shot. You know that, Tommy. This is the one that gets us back in it. You get that chance, you take it, he said.

Tommy nodded.

You spend your whole life, you scrape by and you hope you get that shot. Hope you're in a spot to take it. This is it.

Tommy said he knew it was. Asked if Paul was taking Sherri someplace nice with the money they'd get.

Jesus, man. Give it a goddamn rest. Don't worry about her. I'll take care of her, he said, grinned a little.

As the next car pulled in, Tommy made his move.

Wrecking Ball

Chris Rhatigan

I need fire running through my veins for this.

Instead I've got a combo of caffeine, nicotine, and dexedrine.

I'm parked behind Parsons Government Center. Probably ten minutes left until the Economic Development Commission meeting starts, and I'm rattling like the muffler on a banger's Civic.

I pull the *Post-Herald* and the *Chronicle* from the back seat. The Rose Lensing murder is front page on both. The article I wrote for the *Chronicle* is above the fold, jumps inside. Greg McDuffy's in the *Post-Herald* is confined to the right column on A3, fourteen inches at most.

My bureau chief, Vickie Woodley, knows what sells newspapers, and fought for that placement. She gets it.

Not only is my writing superior—lean, clear, elegant—but I have more details than McDuffy. I could just picture him at his desk, slurping his vat of Starbucks, furrowing his brow. *She was strangled with a phone cord? Why didn't the cops give me that?*

What my article failed to mention was how spontaneously it happened. Or how her face fat turned the color of her eye shadow. Or how it was my sloppiest work—oily fingerprints everywhere and a half-smoked cigarette left at the scene.

I glance over the newspaper and spot a cop cruiser rolling through.

The cop's a young guy I've never seen before. He glares like he's surmised every detail of my life. But he circles around and leaves.

My heart beats steadily again. Steady and fast. The cops will arrest me. I've come to terms with this. I just need an hour or two.

Billy Macklowe and Harrison Willis arrive in a Mercedes SL Class with the top down. They're thirty-seven minutes late for the economic development meeting where they're supposed to be presenting. Also known as "on time" to hotshot, millionaire developers.

Billy wears sunglasses and has a pinstriped blazer draped over his shoulder. He says something and Harrison laughs, claps him on the back.

Here's how I assume that conversation went:

Billy: "Raping an Indian burial ground with a condo complex sure is fun."

Harrison: "Ha! We will profit from this venture."

I wonder if they'll even recognize me. I've talked to them on at least half a dozen occasions, but that doesn't mean anything.

A few minutes after they go inside I pull up to the fire lane and park on the grass. I pop the trunk, pull out the Mossberg 500, slip into the Parsons Center through the side door.

I've never gone after the real assholes before. I always aimed for the easy targets—the concerned citizens, all of those *local folks* who make a reporter's life insufferable.

Like Rose Lensing. For months she bugged me to write a feature about her cat, which had—fucking miraculously—survived a fall from the roof of her one-story house. Then she had the stones to complain when I misspelled the cat's name.

She wrote her last of many letters to the editor about how the *Post-Herald* hadn't hired anyone "worth their salt" since the Reagan administration. Vickie threw a coffee mug through a window when she read that line. That's the kind of editor I like; she stands behind her reporters no matter what.

I slide by the City Clerk's office, undetected, up the stairs, peek around the corner.

The hall is empty. A sterile tube of shiny floors with bland landscape paintings dotting the walls. The whole building reeks of "efficiencies" and "shovel-ready projects."

Room 237 is on the right. I'm revved up from the near-lethal combo of uppers racing through my blood. But I'm not as nervous as I usually am at this point. I no longer fear being caught. And I know my mission is sound.

My mission has been the same since I enrolled in journalism school twelve years ago: I want to make a difference. I want to have a positive impact on people's lives.

I press my ear against the door. Billy's yukking it up at the Economic Development Commission meeting:

"These are high-end, luxury condominiums that will attract the kind of young professionals your community is looking for."

That's developer speak for "no black people."

"It's a win-win proposition for all stakeholders—the neighborhood, downtown business, and the city's tax base."

How convenient, Billy—when *you* make millions, everybody wins!

Someone asks whether the site is an Indian burial ground.

"Look," Billy purrs, "I know some of our *friends* in the press are against this. They're out to paint us as a big, corrupt company, but are we really going to let them stand in the way of progress?"

Murmurs of agreement all around.

I open the door and swing the shotgun around.

Shrieks. Oh my Gods. Chairs rolling backwards.

Thirteen suits, as usual. Nauseating remnants of lunch—greasy, half-eaten sandwiches and potato chip crumbs—scattered across the board table.

Billy still has his laser-pointer aimed at a screen. And he's *still* smiling like he's trying to sell me something. "Hey, what's this all about?"

"Sit."

"What?"

"In the fucking chair. Sit."

Billy does as he's told, places the laser-pointer on the table. "Whatever you say, boss."

Harrison is swifter than his business partner and quickly grasps the gravity of the situation. He backs toward the window, tries to figure out if he can make the jump.

"How this is going to work is real simple, Billy. You just need to say my name. Do that, you save everyone in this room."

"You're . . ." He turns his palms up. "Gosh, it's right at the tip of my tongue. Why don't you put the gun down? I think that would help me remember."

Harrison can probably make that jump. Broken ankle at worst.

"Not good enough," I say. "We've talked many times—a smart guy like you should know by now."

"Okay—"

"But deep down, I'm a nice guy." I press the barrel into his Adam's apple. Feel his pulse radiating through the steel. "So I'm going to cut you a break, give you an easy one to start with. What profession am I in?"

He blinks. "Newspapers?"

I dial up Samuel L. "Check out the big brain on Billy! That's right, newspapers."

Harrison's back is against the window and he's nudging it open. For the first time, I have a sliver of respect for him. He's scrappy, a survivor. At least for now.

"You're used to high-pressure situations in your line of work, right, Billy?"

He nods. Loosens his tie.

"You can handle this. This is a whole lot easier than closing one of your multi-million-dollar deals. You know the ones I mean. Where everyone wants a cut and there's a mob protesting every zoning meeting." His eyes dart around like there's an eject button nearby. "So, tell me. What's my name?"

He presses fingers into gelled hair. I see the question running through his mind, a question he will never figure out how to answer: *Why me? What did I do to deserve this?*

"Take a guess, asshole."

"I—"

"Guess!"

His bloodshot eyes want to cry, but it's too human an action for him.

"Greg McDuffy?"

The window flies open. Harrison has a leg out when I shoot him in the chest. He falls, crashes into the juniper bushes below. Outside, a woman walking a dog can't wrap her mind around what's happened.

"No. It is *not* Greg McDuffy."

I pump the shotgun.

Billy wets his chinos. Trembles morph to shakes.

"I have a wife and a little girl. Please—"

Billy's big brains spray all over those screen shots of the high-end condominiums.

I drive to the office. I want to listen to Jimi Hendrix's *Live at Woodstock* one last time, but my ears are ringing like a tornado siren is going off inside my head.

I reload the shotgun and grab an envelope from the glove compartment. Go straight to Vickie's office and sit across from her. The gun is on my lap.

"Well, look what the goddamn cat dragged in," she says. "Should've known it was you."

"Cops are looking for me?"

She lights a Misty 120. Vickie was never much for company policy. That's why she never ascended past bureau chief. "All over the scanner."

I hand her the envelope.

"What's this?"

"My manifesto. I want it printed on the front page."

"You're screwing with me, right? Your *manifesto*? Who do you think you are, the Unabomber?"

"You should be grateful," I say. "Rose Lensing? Harrison Willis? Billy Macklowe? You despised these people. I've made everyone else's life—"

"You think you're a savior or something? Bullshit. You're satiating your own twisted desires."

A vein in my forehead throbs. "No, you don't understand. I used to think like you do. I thought I could change things by exposing corruption or shining a light on the work good people do. But that does nothing. The world needs action—direct action. Other people don't have the stomach for this calling, but I do. I'm like the garbage man, I—"

"Then make like the garbage man and can it, you crazy fuck." She drops the cigarette in a bottle of diet soda and it hisses. "You exact revenge against anyone who crosses you—not even that, anyone who irritates you. You're an ordinary psychopath, buddy, not some kind of altruist."

I brought the gun because I wanted to take out a couple of cops.

But I find myself raising it at Vickie.

"This your solution to everything?" Her blue eyes blaze. "You think I've got anything to lose? I've got at least another decade before the shitbirds in corporate let me retire. At which point I will be retiring to a coffin."

Sirens sound in the distance and keep getting closer.

She drops my manifesto into the shredder and presses a button. The grind of the machine mixes with her laugh, hoarse and mocking. "What you got up your sleeve now, Garbage Man?"

Three cruisers speed past the window and turn into the parking lot. Doors slam.

I run out into the awful, crackling, hot sunlight. Dry grass crunches under my feet and my whole body itches. My head vibrates with noise.

The cops are yelling at me the way cops do. But they're blurry and very far away, like I'm viewing them through the bottom of a glass.

I raise the Mossberg. But I never even get a shot off.

Born to Run

Lincoln Crisler

Jackson didn't often think of Wendy to keep his mind off the miles while he ran. He thought of the work he had to do once he reached the finish line. He'd never killed in cold blood before, but then again, up until last week, he'd never run ten miles a day, either. You just didn't know what you could do until you did it.

He had Wendy to thank for that, even more than the Army.

Two more miles to go, then he'd be done for the day. Jack popped out his headphones, taking away the constant stream of hard, driving rock he'd been listening to for the past hour and a half. Wendy would have wanted him to enjoy at least part of this, not focused constantly on his anger and loss. He took in the feel of the breeze on his skin, the people pushing carts through the shopping center on the other side of the guardrail, holding hands on the way to their cars from the movie theater on the corner, corralling their children to keep them safe, an opportunity Jack had been denied.

Jack had heard plenty of times about the despair soldiers felt while deployed in combat, the feeling of helplessness that sometimes came from being under fire, the whole reason for that saying about no atheists in foxholes. Jack hadn't felt helpless, though. Hadji had mortared his base every day, for weeks at a time, the entire year, but at least they were something that could be touched back, if not by him, then by someone else. If not hand-to-hand, by air strike. If not by that, then by the simple fact of living malnourished in a desert country. All the things the terrorists hated would still be standing long after they were gone.

As far as that line of thinking went toward keeping him together for the first six months of his deployment, Wendy anchored him for the following four. He'd found her blog while looking online for running tips to help one of his buddies. She'd spent the last few years of her life simply being part of the adult workforce, going out for drinks with friends on the weekends, paying her bills and trying not to screw up too bad, before discovering running. She'd since completed several marathons and had branched out into long-distance biking, and she blogged frequently about her various adventures, competitions and training events.

Jack wrote her to share how her posts had begun to help increase his friend's speed and stamina. Jack had already fallen for her through the pictures, the voice of her writing, the sound and look of her on the videos. A couple exchanges of mutual admiration turned into something more over the next few months. They traded pictures, emailed each other almost every day, instant-messaged each other when Jack wasn't out on patrol. Wendy, by some sheer stroke of beauty in the universe, lived in the same state as Jack's hometown, if on the other side. Both single, they quickly made plans to get together when his tour was done and he took leave to visit his parents. Most surprising, to anyone who knew Jack, he'd started running. *Seriously* running. It had never been his thing, beyond doing enough to pass the physical fitness test twice a year, but Wendy was so damn enthusiastic about it. Far more enthusiastic than Jack was about the military, for sure. There was no way he could work his way up to marathon distances under his harsh living condition, but four times around the base perimeter was still twelve miles, and that was a start.

He never told her, because he knew what it would sound like, but he had every intention of getting out of the Army when he came back from Afghanistan. He didn't care much for the work anymore. The biggest part of it was Wendy. He could have served twenty years and retired without any great strain, he'd watched his dad do it the whole time he was growing up, but it really wasn't for him. Nothing was. Until Wendy came along. He'd already bought her a heavy strand of pearls at an Afghani bazaar during a rare bit of free time, and had made plans on capping off a great weekend of running, good food, wine and lovemaking by draping them around her neck and asking her what she thought about the future.

He never had that chance.

Jack smashed the headphones back into his ears and cranked the music louder. He forced himself to sprint to the next intersection, sweat and tears mingling on his cheeks as he pounded the pavement, and himself by proxy. Poor technique, but he knew he'd finish the day's miles however badly he treated himself. He knew he'd get back on the road tomorrow, and the day after that, and the day after that. And he wouldn't be too tired to do what had to be done that last night, no matter how hard he pushed himself. At least he *could* push himself. Wendy no longer had that option.

He'd had to find out what happened from the news. One morning, he'd gotten in late from a convoy and taken his lukewarm field rations and coffee that would have killed a lesser man back to his billet, eager to get online and talk to Wendy after being off-base for a day and a half. She wasn't online, and her profile was full of comments from her friends, things like *gone too soon* and *there's another angel in Heaven* and *may you at last run with wind beneath your feet*. Even after months of communication, he didn't feel right inserting himself into her "real life" before they'd met, so he looked online. It truly didn't hit him until he saw the headlines.

Wendy was gone.

She'd been housesitting for a friend while they were on vacation, and someone had broken in. The reports said she'd been shot three times in the stomach and chest and hadn't been found until the next afternoon, when she didn't show up for work. Jack didn't even have the luxury of kidding himself that she hadn't felt any pain. Most likely she'd bled out slowly, writhing in agony as the man responsible for taking her beauty from the world loaded up his truck with the television, game systems, whatever assorted items the homeowners had reported missing upon their return. Jack couldn't go home for the funeral. He'd already taken his allotted leave a month before meeting Wendy, and the death of a friend didn't constitute an emergency for military purposes. For the first time, Jack had been hurt in a way he couldn't defend against or respond to.

That was unacceptable.

It hadn't taken the police long to find a suspect, Virgil Clawson. Clawson had gone to school with Wendy's friend and his prints were found at the scene. With less than two months left on his tour, Jack took advantage of his increasingly less demanding schedule to read and re-read everything associated with the case. There wasn't much. He wrote letters of condolence to Wendy's parents and an open email to the local runners' club she'd been a part of, expressing what Wendy had meant to him without getting too deep. The responses he'd received indicated how little she'd told those around her about him. It stood to reason. He'd told his friends about *her*, but she was the woman who'd been hailed by a complete stranger on the Internet. He couldn't blame her for wanting to see what he was really like before she trotted him out for those closest to her. It did make it harder for him to cope when Clawson was released on his own recognizance less than four weeks after being taken into custody. The reports he'd read weren't clear why, and Jack wasn't an expert on the law. All he knew was that Clawson was free to dance, drink, and fuck while Wendy lay in a box for eternity.

Jack slowed down to a jog and spared a glance at his GPS watch. He had less than a mile to go until reaching the cheap motel he'd set as an endpoint before setting out on his day's run. Three more runs just like today's would bring him to Clawson's neighborhood, barely twenty minutes from where he'd killed Wendy. Jack had sent the man a friend request on Facebook under an alias and, while they didn't talk much, Jack had gained access to Clawson's news feed and photos. It wasn't hard for him to determine that Clawson hadn't skipped town, or to figure out where his place of business was. With the confidence of a man who'd bested an unsuspecting woman in the dark of night, Clawson had no idea how fucked he'd be in a mere half-week's time. Jack lengthened his stride on the straight-away leading to the motel parking lot. He could just make out the name and logo in the distance.

He could have jumped in his car the day he got home on leave, but that was too easy. As much as he hungered for the sight of pain blazed across Clawson's face, as much as he could damn-near *taste* the screams of anguish he'd make the man produce, he'd seen too much easy killing overseas. Had *done* too much of it. This one deserved a bit of effort. The cross-state run, something he'd never gotten to do with Wendy, made him feel closer to her. And this way, there was no chance of a speeding ticket, a car accident, a stray bank machine receipt or gas station video screenshot to cause him trouble should the authorities pull out all the stops in their efforts to catch Clawson's killer. Jack liked to read about crime. So many did it so well, planned so thoroughly, just to be undone by a convenience store camera or the postmark on the back of an envelope they'd dropped in their wake.

Jack was still panting by the time he reached the motel. He dug into his backpack for his wallet, paid cash for the room under an assumed name and slipped the keycard into the lock. He hurled himself through the doorway and launched himself onto the crisply made, springy bed, his pack striking the mattress only a second later.

When his heart rate finally slowed, he stripped off his clothes, threw them into the sink, and began the ritual he'd started a week and a half ago. He dumped his pack on the bed, spread out its contents: the clothes he'd wear in the morning, his meager toiletries, his mp3 charger, the Ka-Bar knife he'd carried all year overseas, a sharpener.

He filled the sink with water and a few squirts of the motel shampoo, sat down naked on the comforter, picked up the knife and began to care for his equipment.

Straight Time

Gareth Spark

They always ask the same questions and I answer plain as I can: you get a routine and the days pass like lightning. No, I did not join a gang, and, no, I weren't messed with in no shower. You fight the thing inside yourself that put you behind those walls and say the right things and avoid company because, more often than not, even an act of kindness leads to trouble. I tell them how I swore never to go back. Eight years of a man's life is no mean sum.

Then after the boys from the waste plant go, leaving empty bottles and the stink of hydrogen sulfide and ammonia that nothing gets off your skin, I head out front, suck the cold desert air and wait for my heart to slow. The Interstate cuts through the dim land ahead, sign of a world that never stops here, a silver chain studded onto dark leather. I watch the lights go by and think about the next day, still passing time, still held apart from any kind of life. There was a prison yard and now there's a sewage plant, and what in the hell is the single-wide except another kind of cell, one I'm paying for with a broke back and knees that ache so bad at the night's end I can't even walk through to the bedroom. Nights like this I know I won't make it, and the old, wild voice shuttered deep inside raises itself to a yell.

My Uncle Jack runs stolen cars to El Paso. Mama's youngest brother, barely seven years older than I am. He rolls up on a Sunday evening. Ostrich skin boots and a black Hollywood Stetson, gold tooth and a laugh that comes all the time, as though everything in the world was fit to laugh at.

"C'mon Charlie," he says, "lighten up, son."

I don't see the humor of it. I open a beer and turn to the grill. The kids shout behind me. The trailer stands in a small park at the edge of town and the neighbors are Mexicans from the plant. Our boys know more Spanish than they do their own talk, which doesn't trouble me or Mary, but makes Jack crazy.

"They bring tons of shit all the way from New York City to dump on this goddamned county. To millions of people your home ain't much more'n a glorified crapper." He lights a Marlboro, breathes the smoke out slow. On the other side of the chain-link fence, a breeze pushes through short grass like a final breath.

I cook frozen burgers over gray cinders. Stars flicker in the wide blue and there is stillness in the air even the neighbor's radio, blasting some station out of Juarez, cannot slay. Fat sizzles in the ash, and I stare down at the meat. I wear work boots because I own nothing else, old jeans, a faded shirt. Mary watches from a rocker close to the trailer. She pushes her bleached hair back from red-rimmed eyes and shoots me a warning look. Something about Jack scares her, but she enjoys the whiskey he brings all the same. I say, "If there were a way . . ."

"There's always a way."

"I thought the same then they stuck me in a hole for eight years. That kinda changed my opinion."

"You'd rather live like this, buckaroo?" Jack's eyes are small, watery and mean, and he squints at me through the smoke. He leans in close enough I can feel his breath. "I'm in the hole, Charlie. They ain't currency in this for me no more. Kids used to bring me cars for meth money. I'd sell them to a gang worked out a garage in

Chihuahuita, trade VINs and slip them over the border to God-knows-where. Some new dog took it over, cut me loose, but I know that place is full of easy cash, son, enough to set you all up, get you off that shit ranch."

"I can't." I glance over at the boys, both dark like me, playing with toy cars in the dirt. Thin as stray dogs, dressed in whatever the thrift store in Van Horn has cheap.

"I done well by you ever since you came out the big house, son," he says, stubbing out the cigarette on his heel and then leaning closer. "Best you remember who your friends are. You're family, my only blood, and you used to be colder'n a whore's heart. All these years I never asked you for a damn thing. Well, now I need you."

I look up into the hard blue of the dying sky and then back to the trailer. The dark is falling fast.

Jack brings by an old hunting gun the next night and I saw off thirteen inches from the barrel while Mary works down at the bar. I take a hit from a pint of Balcone's corn whiskey. When the cut barrel falls from the vice and hits the floor, it sounds like a casket lid slamming shut.

The garage is a low, single story adobe building on a wide, dust-blown street surrounded by parked cars, some on blocks, some burned out, and a chain-link fence topped with barbed wire. Two boys stand outside, smoking in the early morning dark. Mexican Mafia. I recognize the dim ink and suddenly feel lost as a gnat in a hailstorm. Jack pulls on a wolfman Halloween mask, and cradles a handgun in his lap. "You all ready?"

"As I'll ever be."

"We get this done and you're walkin' tall, Charlie. Promise."

I start the car, a Chrysler. Wheels spin in dust like sugar and I aim for the two cholos. They stare as the vehicle jumps the sidewalk, dark eyes lit like burning oil in the headlights. They don't move, as if they can't see what's about to fall. The smaller guy disappears under the wheels. His buddy pulls a pistol, suddenly awake and dangerous. Jack leans out the window, shoots him down before he can fire. I pull the pantyhose over my face, hop out the car and aim the scattergun at the door. Jack, crouched by the side, pushes it open and I fire at a figure running towards the street, a young woman. The shot takes her hand away. She screams as I push past her into the dark.

In the office, a kid shovels currency into a bag, rushing before whatever ugly outside ruins his night; money always comes first with these boys. He's big enough to hunt bear with a stick and stares up at me with black eyes crackling with hate. Jack charges past me but struggles with the mask, and it's clear to me and the kid Jack can't see for shit. I aim and the gun misfires.

"Piece o' shit!" I yell.

The kid lifts a hand cannon as Jack pulls the stupid mask off of his head. They stare at one another, the hot room deep with the stink of blood and dope. The Mexican snarls. "Dumb motherfucker, Jack," he says. His pistol bucks like a crazy steer, a flash of light fills the room and my uncle falls ass-backwards over a chair, dead as ever he will be. I'm out the door, quick as a hiccup, before the kid can pull the trigger on me.

There are shots behind as I crash through the place, slipping in blood running out the chola whose hand I shot off. She moans at me as I scramble into the car. Gun the engine, screaming tires in dirt, cursing all the time, rubbing smoke-sore eyes with dirty palms as I tear down and out of the neighborhood. I don't feel a thing, no sorrow, fear, anger, pain; there ain't nothing but the cold.

Home is eighty miles of bleak desert highway. Home is four dead men away. I was always dumb, falling too quick and too easy. The Mexicans will be on me tighter than bark on a tree after this. I know that for damn sure, after that kid made Jack. One day they'll catch me up, and I don't know what in the hell to do about it.

I pull Jack's car up close outside town. Lights are on over at the Plant, burning white and gold against the first glow of morning. I light a cigarette. My hand shakes and the dry leaves rustle with flame. The tank's near enough empty and I leave the Chrysler by the roadside and walk through dust and scrub grass to the park. Mary's sleeping. She wakes when the screen door slams behind me in a breeze that stinks of shit and chemicals.

She smiles up at me, rubs her face, and reaches for a plastic tumbler of water. "How was the game, darlin'?"

I smile at her. "It was fine, baby."

"I know how them ol' boys cheat you last time. Did you get all was comin' to you?" She drinks some of the water and waits for my answer.

I watch her a while. Then I tell her, "We'll see."

This Little Light of Mine

Jamez Chang

Dirty Elbow is sitting on a tall black stool, with a notebook on his lap. I can barely make out his figure in the dimly lit vocal booth, some forty feet away; that is, until he flicks on his lighter—and I see him, sunglasses shimmering above an orange flame. I wonder how much sinsemilla I can scrape off his rhyme journal, once the session's over. In a few minutes, he'll be ready to record.

I'm standing directly behind the mixing board, in a different room called Control, where our studio engineer slides the monitor faders down and mutes the intercom mic.

"Yeah, I'd get wasted too if I wrote that crap. Fezzie, more Sharpies!" Andy says.

I dig inside my pockets for a three-marker stash. Place the pens along the console's armrest for Andy. Lined up like needles.

He nods his head. "Now get your ass back there and babysit doors!"

One of the main duties of a general assistant at Hit Corner Studios is babysitting doors, making sure no one gets in or out once the light turns red: Live Recording. Through an 8½-by-11 sheet of glass, I'm supposed to tell a Biggie Smalls from an angry fat man, a Kid Capri from a kid with a demo tape; and while my dad would say I'm just a glorified bouncer, in Studio B, discrimination matters.

Andy rolls his swivel chair to the right. "Artist my ass. This one, they should call Dirty Crisco. One sick bastard."

My eyes dart past Andy's head into the live room, one of those quick glances I take when I'm screening the doors, surveying: board, patch bay, pop filters, processors—just keeping invisible. No one notices how I can steal a stare, or how Dirty keeps shaking his head inside the sound booth.

A blonde groupie in a doo-rag peers in from the opposite end, back door of the control room. The girl wants in.

"Well?" says Andy, tapping his Sharpie.

Stocking pen caddies. Run to Starbucks. Detailing rooms. Go fetch a snake wire. For the past two weeks, it's been "proper positioning of pens"—plain hell with Andy Trachsell.

I walk to the back of the room and notice she's slapped her phone number on a scrap of paper, palm to glass.

Right up close to the windowpane and her puppy-dog smile, I mouth the word "no."

◆◆◆

The side door opens and Taro, the session assistant, bounds in from the tape-machine room. "Nothing puts the fear of God in an engineer like a shot of cooking oil!" says Taro. He's been in that side room for the past twenty minutes, loading Dirty E's master reels onto 48-track. Though I know he's been on the phone for nineteen of them.

Taro slides to the center of the room and sits on a stool in front of the producer's table. He taps at the drum machine on the counter: kick-kick-snare, kick-kick-snare—and Dirty looks up from the sound booth with a grimace, adjusting his headphones. The heavy bass from the 808-drum ripples out of our speakers and rattles a clipboard.

"And they call that music," says Andy, giving Hit Corner's prize assistant his due respect. "What ever happened to live drummers, Taro, actual musicians who aren't named after body parts?"

Ba-dum-bum-CHING—Taro taps on the pads to acknowledge the punchline. Then he lifts a Heineken bottle from the counter and takes a sip. "Never forget, a session's all about vibe."

And he winks back.

So I take Taro's cue. "Vibe?"

He'd know better than anyone—Taro the Tonka Truck—working his way up from general to second to assistant engineer in less than six months. Practically lived in Studio B half those months, just chillin' with clients.

Andy twirls a sharpie, looking bored.

"Vibe?" I ask, louder this time.

Taro puts down his beer. "It's when the session seems like you're just . . . hanging out. I mean, look at Dirty E. When I'm setting up his mic, I'm always like, 'How are the kids?'"

"I guess it depends on which state you're talking," Andy jokes. But there's no rim shot this time. "Don't listen to Taro-*san*, man. Those animals will take a shit on your sheepskin rug if you don't show 'em some muscle—same thing with Dirt."

Another orange light ignites in the live room. Smoke leaving nostrils.

"And so what do you recommend?" asks Taro, who walks back to the front of the room, taking his place next to Andy.

"Whatever it takes. Pack a little piece if you have to." Andy reaches under the console and lifts up a black duffel bag. "Let those hoodrats know, Fezzie, you know how to roar."

I'm looking in Andy's general direction. He's saying something about Darius Jones now, how he got the name Dirty, tabloid stuff: the white groupies, the shooting at Popeye's, the cooking oil he injects inside the faces of foes—though at some point, the hum of electrons has masked Andy's words. I've tuned him out. My attention trains on the live room beyond him, which is now empty.

"Do you really think Dirty got to where he is today on talent? On vibe?" says Andy, rummaging for something in his bag.

I shift my focus to the center of the board where the light on the room-to-room intercom is gasping at dim—our microphone left on the whole time.

"Well, Fezzie?" says Andy.

I look over at Taro, who's gripping the console's armrest— wheeling his chair ever so slightly away from Andy.

"Well?"

As Andy squints into the distance behind me, I can almost see through the clumps of his skin.

"Are you getting the door?"

Last to Die

Richard Brewer

The blue neon sign read Martelli's. It was one of those new upscale "eateries" that had been springing up in the now-gentrified neighborhood. Seventeen-dollar burgers, twenty-dollar house drinks.

"Okay kids," said Billy. "We up for this?"

"Yeah," said Eddie from the backseat of the car. He took another quick sniff of the powder. "Let's get this thing goin'. Curtain up, man. Light the lights."

"Michael?"

Michael Donahue shook himself. He'd been staring out the window of the car, his mind far, far away.

"Yeah," he said. "I'm ready."

"Look, man," said Billy. "This is all good. Pricks will never know what hit 'em. We're in, we're out, and then we all have a merry fuckin' Christmas. Think about that."

Michael did think about that. He'd been thinking about Christmas for weeks. Last December he'd been laid off from his factory job. Budget cuts. Last hired, first fired. And as hard as that had been, he hadn't been overly worried. He and Bobby Jean had some savings and the unemployment would help. It would be tight but there were other jobs out there.

Then came the baby.

When Bobby Jean first told him they were expecting, he was elated. They named her Rose after Bobby Jean's mother. And she was the most beautiful thing he'd ever seen. But still, he couldn't find a job. Bobby Jean did what she could to help financially, but she had only ever worked part time, and she had to take time off after the baby. It wasn't long before their small savings were gone. And soon after that when the arguments began.

It was a few months after his layoff that Michael had run into Billy Crow. The two had gone to high school together, and though they were never close friends, they had been friendly enough to sit and share an occasional beer. It was good to get out once in a while and have someone from the old neighborhood to shoot the shit with, grumble over the fate of the American workingman and remember the glory days. It was during one of those beery afternoons that Billy brought up Martelli's, the new restaurant that had taken the place of Mickey's, a long-standing local bar in their old stomping grounds.

"That was a great place," Billy said to Michael. "Good food. Good beer on tap. Decent prices."

"I remember," said Michael.

"Now, you can't even afford to walk in the door."

"Plenty do," said Michael. "They aren't missing our money."

Billy took a long, thoughtful swill of his beer.

"How much you think they take in on a Saturday night?"

And that's how it all began. That's what found these three men sitting in a car outside Martelli's late on a Saturday night, guns in their hands, loaded and ready.

"Okay," said Billy. "Remember the plan. Eddie, you watch the door. Michael, you keep any customers under control. I'll get the money. We keep it simple, keep it quick."

"We keep talkin'," said Eddie, "we ain't getting shit. Let's go."

"You want to calm down," Michael said. He hadn't expected Eddie to be a part of this deal. The cokehead would occasionally join Billy and him for a drink, but Michael never liked being around Eddie and would usually leave early whenever he came around. But Billy felt they needed a third man, "for insurance."

"What did you say to me, man?" said Eddie. "You don't tell me what to do."

"Stop it," said Billy.

"But—" Eddie started.

"I said stop it. Michael, you got a problem?"

"No. I don't have a problem. But this snow sniffer does."

"I can handle myself, asshole. Don't you think I can't."

"Eddie, cool it." Billy turned to Michael. "You don't worry about him. You worry about your end and think of the payday here. Think about the good Christmas you're gonna give your wife and kid. Now, you ready or not?"

"Yeah," said Michael. "I'm with you."

"Then let's go." Billy opened the car door and stepped out into the night air.

The three of them walked quickly across the road to the front door of the restaurant. Billy took the lead, entering first, with Michael and Eddie behind him. A quick look around showed them the place was nearly empty. The bartender was already starting to count the money from his cash drawer, a cloth bank deposit bag next to him. He looked up from his work, like he was about to tell whoever was coming in that they had stopped serving for the night. But instead of hungry yuppies, he saw three rough-looking men with guns, one of which was pointing at his face.

"Hey, Sunshine," said Billy "We'd like to place an order to go."

The bartender stood frozen, eyes locked on the gun in Billy's hand.

"Yo, dude," said Eddie. "Just put the money in the bag."

Before the bartender could comply, two men came in through the kitchen door. Both wore dark suits, crisp white shirts and silk ties. The first one through was the bigger of the two, the suit tight over his well-muscled physique. The second one wasn't in as good shape as the first, but he carried himself in a way that exuded more than physical strength. In his right hand he carried a solid-looking briefcase.

"What the fuck?" said Briefcase.

Billy shifted his gun to cover the two new arrivals. Michael noticed that neither of the men so much as flinched at having the gun pointed at them. He began to get a get a bad feeling in the pit of his stomach.

"Nothing you need to worry about," said Billy. "We're just here for the money. We get that and then we're out of here."

"I know you," said Briefcase.

"You don't know shit, man." Billy kept the gun trained on the two men, but it wasn't as steady as it had been before.

"You're that punk, Billy . . . Billy something," said Briefcase. "You used to live around here."

Billy brought the gun back around to the bartender.

"Fill the bag," he said.

"Do you know who owns this place?" said Briefcase. "Vincent Cole. You do not want to be messing with something that's his. He will not be forgiving."

The bartender finished loading the cash into the bag and Billy took it and started backing toward the front door.

"Crow," said Briefcase. "Billy Crow." His eyes moved to Michael. "And you're . . . Mitchell? No, Michael. Yeah, that's it, I knew . . ."

That was as far as he got before the bullet took him square in the chest.

Everything stopped. Michael and Billy looked dumbly at their unfired guns, then turned back to look at Eddie, who was practically vibrating as he shifted from one foot to another in a mixture of adrenaline and coke-fueled energy.

"He knew your names," said Eddie. "He knew who you were. We had to—"

That's when the bullet hit Eddie, knocking him backward in a stumbling fall to the floor. Michael and Billy dove to different sides of the restaurant as a spray of bullets tried to find them. On the way to the ground Michael caught a glimpse of Muscles, holding a huge gun, flame coming from the barrel.

Without looking, Michael raised his piece and fired back. Billy did the same, letting off a quick series of shots. Michael locked eyes with Billy, who nodded toward the front door. On a silent count of three, the two leapt to their feet, guns blazing, blindly sending bullets around the restaurant as they ran out the door, across the street and to the waiting car.

With a screech of tires, Michael peeled away from the curb and down the dark road.

"What the fuck was that?! Christ, Billy, what the fuck?"

"Vincent Cole. Of all the . . ."

A cough cut Billy off.

It was then that Michael saw Billy was slumped in his seat, head lolling against the passenger side window, a red, wet stain spreading across his shirt. He pulled the car over and leaned into his friend.

"Billy," he said.

Billy's head turned slowly to Michael.

"I'll get you to a hospital."

"Don't be stupid. You gotta dump me and get out of town."

"What?"

"Listen to me," said Billy. "Vincent Cole, dude. Vincent fucking Cole . . . he's . . ."

"What?"

"He's big, man. Connected. Connected all the way. I didn't know. Swear I didn't know."

"But . . . we got away."

"You don't understand," said Billy. "That guy with the briefcase that Eddie just whacked? That was Peter Cole. Vincent's son. He was a couple years ahead of us. That's how he knew us."

The weight of what Billy was saying settled into Michael's head.

"You got to get out of town, man. You gotta move. I don't know if the bodyguard's dead, but that bartender ain't. Someone will talk. Word's probably already out on the street. He'll come for you, man. He'll come for you and yours. You gotta . . . gotta . . ." Billy's eyes took on a vaguely quizzical look, like he was seeing something in the distance he couldn't quite make out. He started to speak again, but not to Michael, and then he was gone.

Michael left the body in an alleyway, the Christmas lights of a downtown window display casting shadows on the plastic garbage bag that acted as Billy's shroud.

The baby's car seat in back jostled as Michael jerked onto the highway, praying that the late hour would keep the traffic light and afford a few minutes' head start home. Once there he'd grab Bobby Jean and Rose and make for Bobby Jean's sister's place. Then they'd figure out the next move. But first, he had to get home.

He took the exit at seventy-five miles an hour, tires hitting the curb and sending a hubcap flying into the distance. Turning onto his street, he screeched to a stop in front of his apartment building, leapt from the car, and raced inside.

Running up the stairs, the pounding of his boots echoed the pounding of his heart. Reaching the door, he fumbled with his keys, Billy's blood still sticky on his hands. He found the right one, pushed it into the lock, and rushed into the room.

Everything looked normal. Small apartment with simple furniture, a baby monitor sitting on a side table, Bobby Jean asleep on the couch. But that wasn't right. He'd made a hell of a noise crashing into the room. Bobby Jean hadn't stirred. Hadn't even looked up. Then he saw the blood. Michael took a hesitant step toward his too-still wife. Then he saw the baby monitor. He started for the bedroom just as two men walked out.

They were the same size and shape as Muscles from Martelli's. One held a gun, the other held Rose. He was actually cooing at her.

Michael stopped mid-step and sank to his knees.

"No," said Michael. "How?"

"Words of wisdom dipshit," said the gunman. "You pull a job? Wear masks. Don't rob a place in the same 'hood where you used to live, and most importantly, if you leave one of your own behind? You better make sure they can't talk."

"Please" said Michael, "please, don't hurt her."

The man with the gun motioned for his associate to take the baby out of the apartment. Michael started to rise, but the barrel of the gun placed against his forehead convinced him to stay down. His eyes followed Rose as she was taken away.

Tears ran down Michael's cheeks. He turned his face up to the gunman, his eyes pleading. "My mistake. It was me. My mistake. Please." The gunman put a finger to his lips, and Michael stopped talking.

"I think," said the gunman, "that Mr. Cole would have preferred it if you'd had a son, but a daughter will do just as well." With that he lowered his gun and walked past Michael.

Michael took in a ragged breath, his mind desperately trying to think of what to do next. That's when he heard the click of a gun hammer being pulled back. His last thought was in the form of a prayer, a plea to the God he barely believed in, begging him, it, her, that this would be the end. That he would be the last to die that night.

Down on the street, Rose slept peacefully in the crook of an elbow and never heard the gunshot.

About the Authors

Lynne Barrett's latest book is *Magpies*. Her fiction has appeared in *Ellery Queen's Mystery Magazine, Miami Noir, Delta Blues, A Hell of a Woman,* and *Simply the Best Mysteries,* and she's received the Edgar Award for best mystery story. Originally from NJ, she now lives in Miami. More at: www.lynnebarret.com

Eric Beetner is author of several novels including *The Devil Doesn't Want Me, Dig Two Graves, The Year I Died Seven Times* and *One Too Many Blows to the Head* (co-authored with JB Kohl) His award winning short fiction has appeared in over two dozen anthologies. For more info visit www.ericbeetner.blogspot.com

Richard J. Brewer, a native Californian, has always been a lover of stories and storytelling, leading him to work as a writer, actor, bookseller, story editor, book reviewer, audiobook narrator, and just about anything else connected with the stringing together of words. He is currently working on his first novel.

Jamez Chang is a hip-hop artist, poet, and editor, whose work has appeared or is forthcoming in *PANK, Underground Voices, Metazen, FRiGG,* and *Thrush Poetry Journal.* He is currently the flash fiction editor at *Counterexample Poetics.* Visit http://jamezchang.word-press.com

Joe Clifford is acquisitions editor for Gutter Books, managing editor of *The Flash Fiction Offensive,* and producer of Lip Service West, a "gritty, real, raw" reading series in Oakland, CA. He is the author of four books: *Choice Cuts*, *Junkie Love*, *Wake the Undertaker*, and *Lamentation*. Joe's writing can be found at www.joeclifford.com

Jen Conley's stories have appeared in *Thuglit*, *Needle*, *Beat to a Pulp*, *Out of the Gutter*, *Grand Central Noir*, *Big Pulp*, *Literary Orphans*, *Protectors*, *Plots with Guns*, *Yellow Mama*, *All Due Respect* and others. An editor at *Shotgun Honey*, she's been nominated for a *Best of the Web Spinetingler Award* and shortlisted for *Best American Mystery Stories*. She lives in Brick, New Jersey, where she writes in her spare time. Follow her on twitter, @jenconley45

Mike Creeden grew up in Fall River, Massachusetts. His stories and non-fiction have appeared in *Miami Living*, *Everything Is Broken*, *The Florida Book Review*, and *Tigertail*. He lives in Miami, Florida.

Lincoln Crisler is a horror and science fiction author and US Army noncommissioned officer. He lives and works in Augusta, Georgia. Visit him online at www.lincolncrisler.info

Hilary Davidson won the 2011 Anthony Award for Best First Novel for *The Damage Done*. That book launched a series that continues with *The Next One to Fall*—set in Peru—and *Evil in All Its Disguises*, about a missing journalist in Acapulco. Hilary's first standalone novel, *Blood Always Tells*, is out now from Tor/Forge.

CS DeWildt is the author of books *Candy and Cigarettes* (Vagabondage Press) and *Dead Animals* (Martian Lit). He lives in Arizona.

Les Edgerton is an ex-con, matriculating at Pendleton Reformatory in the sixties for burglary, armed robbery, strong-armed robbery, and possession with intent. He's since taken a vow of poverty (became a writer) with 18 books in print. His latest books are *The Rapist* and *The Bitch* from New Pulp Press, and forthcoming is a black comedy crime novel titled *The Genuine, Imitation, Plastic Kidnapping* from Down & Out Books.

Peter Farris is the author of the novels *Last Call for the Living* and *Ghost in the Fields*, which will be published in France by Éditions Gallmeister. He lives in Cherokee County, Georgia.

Paul J. Garth has had stories published in *Shotgun Honey*, the *Flash Fiction Offensive*, *Thrills Kill 'n' Chaos*, and has other works forthcoming, both online and in print. Perpetually in transit between Nebraska and Texas, he can be found on Twitter by following @pauljgarth

James Grady's first novel *Six Days of the Condor* became the Robert Redford movie. Grady has received Italy's Raymond Chandler Medal, France's *Grand Prix Du Roman Noir*, and has been an Edgar finalist. In 2008, London's *Daily Telegraph* named Grady one of *"50 Crime Writers to Read Before You Die."*

Jordan Harper has worked as an ad man, a music journalist, and a TV writer. His stories have appeared in *Thuglit*, *Out of the Gutter*, and *Crime Factory*. Someday, a novel. Follow him @jordan_harper

Chris F. Holm's work has appeared in a number of magazines and anthologies, including *Ellery Queen's Mystery Magazine*, *Needle: A Magazine of Noir*, and *The Best American Mystery Stories 2011*. His critically acclaimed *Collector* trilogy blends fantasy with old-fashioned crime pulp. He lives in Portland, Maine.

Christopher Irvin has traded all hope of a good night's sleep for the chance to spend his mornings writing noir fiction. He is the author of *Federales*, as well as short stories featured in several publications, including *Thuglit*, *Beat to a Pulp*, and *Shotgun Honey*. He lives with his wife and son in Boston, Massachusetts. For more, visit www.christopherirvin.net

David James Keaton's fiction has appeared in over 50 publications. His book *Fish Bites Cop* was named *This Is Horror*'s Short Story Collection of the Year 2014, and his first novel, *The Last Projector*, is due out soon from Broken River Books. He also invented chocolate harmonicas.

Mystic, Servant of the Most High, founding member of the Low Writers Collective, one-fifth of Zelmer Pulp and The Last Ancients, **Isaac Kirkman** was born in Greenville, South Carolina, and currently resides in Arizona. He was trained at the Tucson branch of the Philip Schultz-founded Writers Studio. www.IsaacKirkman.com Twitter: @79797x

Photographer **Mark Krajnak** hails from Allentown, New Jersey. His work has appeared on book and album covers, in *New Jersey Life* magazine and the off-Broadway play *Two Detectives*, and on numerous corporate and entertainment websites. He's traveled to 19 different countries but considers New Jersey the place to be.

Chris Leek is the author of *Gospel of the Bullet*, *Nevada Thunder*, and *Smoke 'Em If You Got 'Em*. He is a contributing editor at western fiction magazine *The Big Adios* and part of the team behind the Zelmer Pulp imprint. He can be contacted at his blog: www.nevadaroadkill.blogspot.co.uk

Dennis Lehane grew up in the Dorchester section of Boston. He's published 10 novels, three of which (*Mystic River*, *Gone Baby Gone*, and *Shutter Island)* have been made into award-winning films.

Lehane adapted his short story "Animal Rescue" into a feature film called *The Drop* for Fox Searchlight, scheduled for release in September 2014. He and his wife and children divide their time between Boston and Los Angeles.

Benoît Lelièvre is an author, blogger, sports nerd and social media professional living in Montreal, Canada, with his better half, Josie, and his dog, Scarlett. You can read him 5 times a week at www.deadendfollies.com

Ezra Letra is a man with many muses: rapper, photographer, writer, director, graphic designer, producer. His work has appeared or is forthcoming in *University of Arizona Press*, *Literary Orphans*, *Out of the Gutter*, *Sugar Mule Press*, and *Gutter Books LLC*. Born in Queens, NY, and residing in Phoenix, AZ, Ezra holds a BA in English and Creative Writing from the University of Arizona. His debut poetry chapbook, *When La Migra Stopped Coming*, is published by Nostrovia Poetry. He is currently touring the U.S. Southwest to promote his latest musical venture: *The Nobody EP*.

Matthew Louis is the founding editor of Gutter Books and *Out of the Gutter*. His novel *The Wrong Man* is currently being produced as a major motion picture by Acclaimed Cinema Entertainment and Throughline Films. Learn more at www.matthewlouis.com.

John McFetridge is the author of four novels in the *Toronto* series. His latest novel, *Black Rock*, is set against true events in his home-town of Montreal in 1970. He currently lives in Toronto with his wife and two sons.

Lela Scott MacNeil was born in Los Alamos, same as the atomic bomb. She received her BFA in Screenwriting from New York University. She works for the University of Arizona Press and teaches creative writing at The Writers Studio. She is pursuing her MFA in Creative Writing at the University of Arizona. Her work is forthcoming from *Gertrude*.

Court Merrigan lives in Wyoming. He is the author of *Moondog over the Mekong* (Snubnose Press) and has short stories in *Needle*, *Weird Tales*, *Thuglit*, *Plots with Guns*, and *Noir Nation*, among others. A novel is forthcoming.

Brian Panowich is a Spinetingler Award-nominated author from East Georgia. His short fiction can be found in various print and online collections. He is also a founding member of Zelmer Pulp, and his first novel, Bull Mountain, will be published by Penguin/Putnam Fall 2015.

Rob Pierce is the editor of *Swill Magazine*, co-host of Nikki Palomino's Dazed radio show, and has been nominated for a Derringer Award for short crime fiction. His fiction has appeared numerous places, including *Flash Fiction Offensive*, *Pulp Modern*, *Plots with Guns*, *Revolt Daily*, and *Shotgun Honey*.

Tom Pitts received his education on the streets of San Francisco. He remains there, working, writing, and trying to survive. His new novel, *Hustle*, is out now (Snubnose Press), as is his novella, *Piggyback*. Find links to more of his work at: www.TomPittsAuthor.com

Keith Rawson is the author of over 200 short stories, essays, reviews, and interviews. He is a regular contributor to *Spinetingler Magazine*, *LitReactor*, and the *Los Angeles Review of Books*. He lives in Southern Arizona with his wife and daughter.

Chuck Regan is a part-time writer, full-time designer/illustrator working in advertising. His short fiction has appeared in *Shotgun*

Honey, *The Big Adios*, and two Zelmer Pulp publications. He is revising his fourth manuscript, Little Agony, a science fiction novel about a veteran returning home to Mars. See more at www.cdregan.com

Chris Rhatigan is the editor of *All Due Respect*. More than fifty of his short stories have been published in venues such as *Needle*, *Shotgun Honey*, *Pulp Modern*, and *Beat to a Pulp*.

Todd Robinson writes sometimes.

Ryan Sayles is the author of *Subtle Art of Brutality* and *That Escalated Quickly!* He won *Dead End Follies'* 2013 award for best newly discovered talent. *Subtle Art of Brutality* was nominated for best crime novel at *Dead End Follies* and top Indie novel at *The House of Crime & Mystery's* 2013 Readers' Choice Awards. Ryan is 1/5th of Zelmer Pulp and on the masthead at *The Big Adios*. He may be contacted at www.VitriolAndBarbies.wordpress.com

Gareth Spark is a writer from the Northeast of England. He is author of the novel *The Devil's Waiting* and *Rain in a Dry Land* (Mudfog Press). You can read his work online at *Shotgun Honey*, *The Big Adios*, *Near to the Knuckle*, and *Out of the Gutter*, among others.

Richard Thomas is the author of five books—*Disintegration*, *Transubstantiate*, *Herniated Roots*, *Staring into the Abyss* and *Four Corners*. His over 100 stories in print have appeared in *Cemetery Dance*, *PANK*, *Gargoyle*, *Weird Fiction Review*, *Midwestern Gothic*, *Arcadia*, *Pear Noir*, *Chiral Mad 2*, and *Shivers VI*, among others. Visit www.whatdoesnotkillme.com for more information.

James R. Tuck is a multi-published author, professional tattoo artist, and photographer in Atlanta. Best known for his Deacon

Chalk series, Tuck has more crime fiction in the collection *Hired Gun*.

Steve Weddle's debut novel, *Country Hardball*, was called "downright dazzling" by the *New York Times*. He lives with his family in Virginia.

Chuck Wendig is the author of the published novels *Blackbirds, Mockingbird, The Cormorant, Under the Empyrean Sky, Blue Blazes, Double Dead, Bait Dog, Dinocalypse Now, Beyond Dinocalypse* and *Gods & Monsters: Unclean Spirits*. He is co-writer of the short film *Pandemic*, the feature film *HiM*, and the Emmy-nominated digital narrative *Collapsus*. Wendig has contributed over two million words to the game industry. He is also well known for his profane-yet-practical advice to writers, which he dispenses at his blog, www.terribleminds.com and through several popular e-books, including *The Kick-Ass Writer*, published by Writers Digest.

Dyer Wilk lives and writes in Northern California. He is currently at work on a novel.

CPSIA information can be obtained at www.ICGtesting.com
Printed in the USA
LVOW12s0304101214

418103LV00001B/46/P